WASH
P9-AFK-568
3 1235 01787 2503

Ordinary Horror

Ordinary Horror

DAVID SEARCY

VIKING

VIKING
Published by the Penguin Group
Penguin Putnam Inc., 375 Hudson Street,
New York, New York 10014, U.S.A.
Penguin Books Ltd, 27 Wrights Lane, London W8 5TZ, England
Penguin Books Australia Ltd, Ringwood, Victoria, Australia
Penguin Books Canada Ltd, 10 Alcorn Avenue,
Toronto, Ontario, Canada M4V 3B2
Penguin Books (N.Z.) Ltd, 182–190 Wairau Road,
Auckland 10, New Zealand

Penguin Books Ltd, Registered Offices:
Harmondsworth, Middlesex, England

First published in 2001 by Viking Penguin,
a member of Penguin Putnam Inc.

1 3 5 7 9 10 8 6 4 2

A portion of this work first appeared in *Grand Street.*

Grateful acknowledgment is made for permission to reprint "Primitive" by Gerald Burns. By permission of the Estate of Gerald Burns.

PUBLISHER'S NOTE

This is a work of fiction. Names, characters, places, and incidents either are the product of the author's imagination or are used fictitiously, and any resemblance to actual persons, living or dead, business establishments, events, or locales is entirely coincidental.

LIBRARY OF CONGRESS CATALOGING IN PUBLICATION DATA
Searcy, David, 1946–
Ordinary horror / David Searcy.
p. cm.
ISBN 0-670-89476-1 (hc: alk. paper)
I. Title.
PS3569.E176 O73 2001
813'.54–dc21 00-043355

This book is printed on acid-free paper. ♾

Printed in the United States of America
Set in Caslon
Designed by Lorelle Graffeo

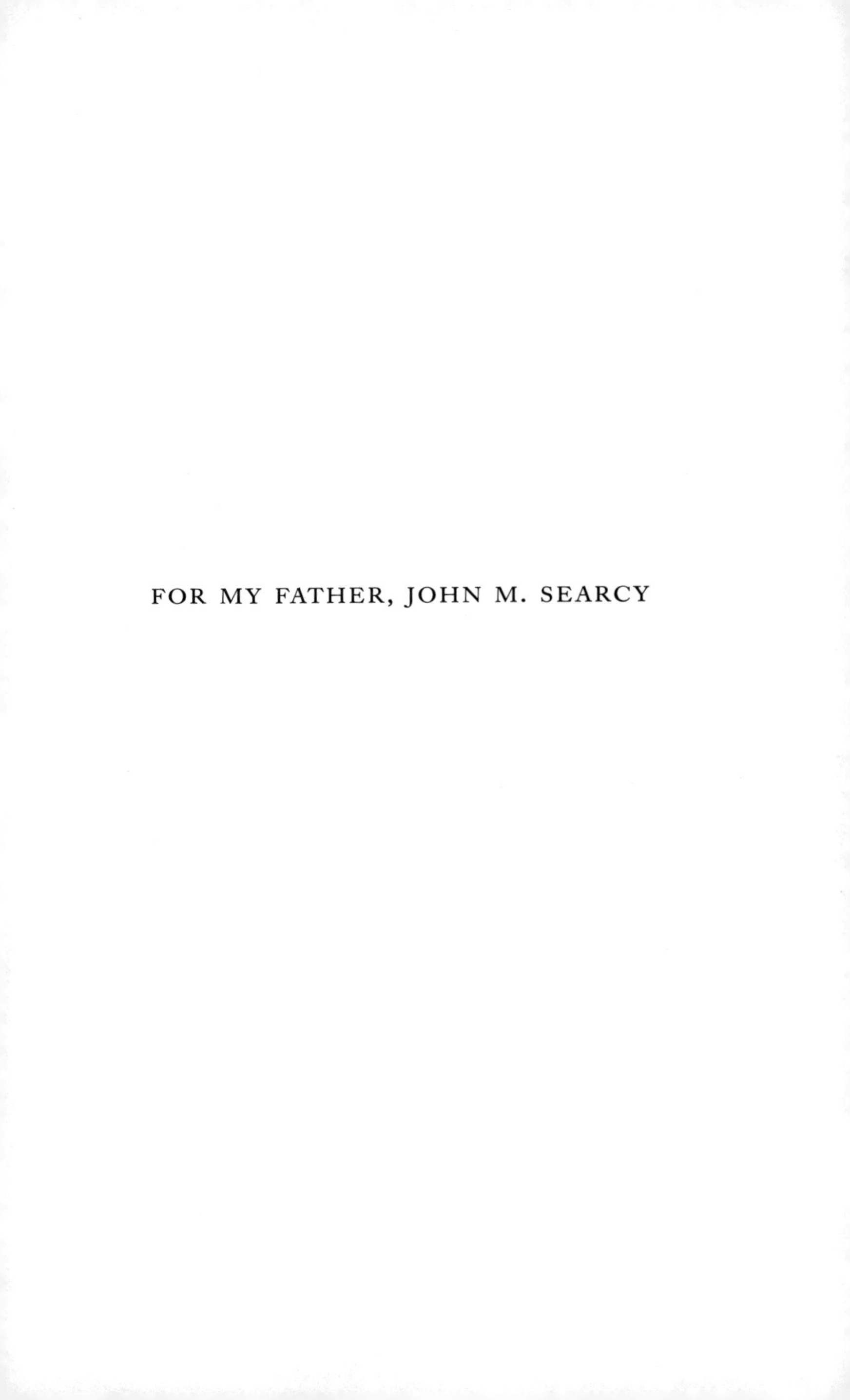

FOR MY FATHER, JOHN M. SEARCY

PRIMITIVE

Let us affirm the real world at the expense of everybody
Bushes, with their dry particularity
Earth (thank heaven mother was a gardener
so "dirt" has wholly pleasant connotations)
Sand I do not understand
Mud
"Pets"—the animals it is so astonishing are living with one
like fire in a pipe-bowl
This is a picture of a dog—*Jubilate Cano*
Tigers
Elephants
Boa-constrictors
The pictures of Rousseau

—Gerald Burns

ACKNOWLEDGMENTS

Thanks to Anna, Lizzy, John, and Jean for their examples, suggestions, corrections; to Tim Coursey for his dreadful sympathies, Doug MacWithey for letting me jabber; to Steve Anderson, Paul Black, Sarah Brownlee, Melanie Coursey, Charlie Drum, Mike Edgmon, Barbara Epler, Amy Gelber, Jim Haining, John Lunsford, George Nicholas, Sudie Thompson, Bob Trammell, Adrienne Cox-Trammell, Karan Verma, and Alison Victoria for reading and encouraging.

I'm grateful to Drs. Richard Fullington and James Lloyd for advice on firefly behavior, and to Professor Richard Evans Schultes for his kind and meticulous response to my ethnobotanical inquiries. All departures from reality are my own.

To my agent, Becky Kurson, to Michael Millman of Viking, and Esther Allen and Erik Rieselbach I owe more than I can say.

I am indebted, as well, from way back, to Margaret Hartley, Charlotte Whaley, and most of all and always to Gerald Burns.

I

Here's a horror story for you. An old fellow, a widower about seventy years old, lives alone in an aging tract house in one of those extended tract house neighborhoods that, given twenty or thirty years to mellow, lose none of their bleakness but gain some comfort from the fact of survival–the fact of such ordinariness being able to survive, coming to seem more or less permanent, which gives the people who live there a kind of necessity or inevitability whether they know it or not.

This old man loves to grow roses in his backyard. And, whether he knows it or not, he loves their springing from such ordinariness. He even has them blocked off, gridded into organized beds like a neighborhood of roses so when they bloom, when he looks out the sliding glass door of his little den at them blooming, they're even more miraculous as if no amount of constraint or definition can keep them back and the arrangement of his garden, designed to emphasize this of course, has symbolic implications as well.

He likes a cup of coffee in the morning on the patio among the rose beds probably better than anything–better than gardening, in fact, because his inactivity is proof the roses are stable for the moment, protected and receptive to the notion, however faint, that protection is reciprocal in some sense. Nevertheless there's a little anxiety most of the time and he probably understands he's set himself up for it having invested so much so visibly. It's the character of the neighborhood for things to be visible in any case; so many similar houses that close together make anything not belonging to the architecture stand out. Especially, one imagines, viewed from above. There's a feeling of overexposure to sky or space which has to derive from the uniformly limited elevation of everything–low-pitched and flat-roofed single-story houses and not enough nor the right sort of trees to provide a canopy. Domestic space stops about twenty feet up, which makes afternoon light seem too abrupt striking everything at once and dawn and nightfall more sudden and even alarming in a way on cloudless days in the summer when there's hardly any transition.

Lately the old man, whose name is Mr. Delabano, is concerned about his garden more than usual because of the appearance of little piles of sandy soil here and there in the yard and on the grass paths between the beds. He thinks at first it might be squirrels but it's too early in the year for that and this is too destructive anyway. Nor does it really look like excavation. The piles of earth seem to have been pushed up from below. So he decides it must be moles or gophers and does his best to control the damage, hoping that whatever it is might just be passing through and he won't have to confront the problem directly with poisons or the terrifying spear-traps he recalls having seen advertised somewhere for this sort of infestation. He's determined, as long as it doesn't get out of hand, to wait before seeking advice. He's like someone with a suspicious physical symptom afraid to find anything out but he dwells on it anyway, especially at night when he imagines the damage to occur.

Every night he thinks in the morning there'll be fewer new mounds than before; he'll pack them down, replace the grass and maybe that will be that; he won't have to consult anybody or speak to his neighbors about it or buy chemicals or dispose of dead creatures or anything at all. Just let nature take its course. The last thing he wants is to hire someone. Who knows what they might do, like firemen in the house destroying more than they save. Just have the patience to let things alone for a bit. These things are bound to come and go.

But naturally it gets worse. He begins taking his coffee in the kitchen now, looking out the little window above the sink and wondering if his yard is really more heavily infested than his neighbors' or if it's only his repairs that are more conspicuous. He wonders if maybe a cat or a dog might help. Weren't terriers supposed to chase rodents? Then, leafing through the Sunday newspaper supplement, he experiences one of those moments of perfect coincidence or grace. A big display ad on the inside back page in very large print reads, "How to Chase Gophers from Your Yard and Garden: Get Rid of Burrowing Rodents without Traps or Poisons," beneath which is a strange heraldic-looking cartoon of three gophers or whatever in the process of being cast out, suspended in mid-trajectory, each emitting a cartoon drizzle of anxiety droplets and flanked by four spiky plants (one on each side of each rodent) that look like schematized bromelaids of some kind. Below that are several paragraphs of fine print and an order form. It's the plants that do it–exotic, South American, never-before-available and now only briefly in limited supplies. Nonflowering and more effective than spurges. Root systems antithetical to garden varmints but harmless to pets and everything else. Thirty-nine dollars and ninety-five cents. How wonderful, he thinks; just a post office box. Gopherbane; Grand Rapids, Michigan. Nothing to do but send in the form.

In a corner of Mr. Delabano's garden right next to the patio in its own raised bed with a white wooden trellis where the light strikes first in the morning is an "antique" rose that he and his wife discovered clinging to the remains of an old fence rail on a trip through Virginia a couple of years before she died. He's certain it's not wild but beyond that determination has no interest in research, preferring to keep to himself the thought it might be unique–the only example of some unspectacular nineteenth-century cultivar not far removed from the wild but improved nonetheless, an artifact of sorts like a little flame about to wink out when they found it. It's here his attention turns in the weeks that follow. Waiting for the UPS or the postman to ring he thinks about that rose. Listening to the winds that come up at nightfall so violently at times in the summer, sweeping across the plateau of rooftops and mimosa trees and buzzing the weather stripping like a bassoon reed, he thinks about that simple thing.

In the mornings he attends to it more carefully than the others and when little piles of dirt erupt within the rose beds themselves, he drives lengths of concrete reinforcing rod at two-inch intervals entirely into the ground around it. This takes him the better part of a week and, although it exhausts and calms him for a while, it's obviously an escalation of the disruptive sort he'd hoped to avoid when he responded to the newspaper ad at the first of the summer. Now he feels compromised, tries to think of this as a temporary measure although he can't really see himself ever pulling up the spikes. Certainly it's better than poisons. He doesn't even like to use sprays. Most of his roses were chosen for their hardiness and resistance to disease and, even though this required rejecting some of the showier varieties, he feels compensated by a kind of vitality that permits him to imagine his roses outliving him–at least in theory–carrying something of his affections along like the antique rose which he imagines somehow still retains, in a way not clear but powerful to him, the possibility of the people in whose garden it grew.

To whatever degree such thoughts are driven by particular longings or regrets, these are absorbed in his regard for the roses. It's the sentimental absorbency of roses that's most valuable to him, in fact–relieves him of any lingering sorrows, draws them off and releases them to the air. This is an image that actually occurs to him sometimes in a dreamy sort of way: an almost mechanical, even industrial, relation between himself and the roses–little chimneys of the spirit concentrating and releasing something essential to him and (by vague and mysterious extension) to the whole neighborhood which he feels is such a superficial imposition on the prairie, the great flatness above which his roses bloom like a signal and whose ancient surface he suspects is still detectable as a subtle topographical inflection of the network of little streets and alleys. On the whole this seems to be a satisfactory cosmology. It invigorates the bleakness–gives a glow to the pale brick, the white-trimmed green asbestos siding and thin white curtains in the late afternoon. But it's delicate. It can't support serious turbulence. It has to be maintained and balanced against ordinary necessities; so he thinks of the spikes as a kind of prosthesis, rusting away as balance is restored, pinning things in place until then.

Cleaning up after supper, standing by the kitchen sink and looking out the window he can't detect any damage to the roses really. One or two might have fewer blooms than he'd like but that's so variable. He looks around for the newspaper ad to study it again. He's had nearly two months to memorize it but he likes to keep it and look at it now and then for reassurance. He looks under the phone book where it's been; he looks in the drawers of the telephone table and everywhere else it could possibly be but he can't find it. He looks in the back of yesterday's Sunday supplement but now there's a different ad. In fact he can't recall it having appeared in the paper at all since placing his order. Maybe it only ran once or maybe he just never noticed it before and now it's stopped–supplies used up or the company out of business. What was the name? He's lost it. He should have express-mailed his order. What if he missed the tail end of the offer and that's why the package hasn't come? What if all this time depending on it, putting off any sort of aggressive treatment in favor of the perfect solution were wasted, completely lost and now some truly radical operation were required: everything to come out. At this point he's really horrified at what he's done, how stupid he feels he's been. In the sudden twilight he rushes outside, unreels the hose, strikes open the faucet and begins stamping with his heel as hard as he can on the grass between the most recent repairs where he thinks the tunnels must be. Wherever the ground caves in he jams in the hose but the mud collapses ahead of his efforts clogging whatever tunnel there was as he plunges the nozzle into the mess again and again anyway, soaking himself and splashing mud everywhere hoping to break cleanly through into some main artery or chamber and flood the things out. By now it's totally dark, the wind has picked up and he's cold and his shoulder hurts and he's aware of the barbecue going on next door audible and visible through the chain-link fence–the sounds of plastic plates and silverware, a couple of kids making noise. He sits up holding his shoulder and looking up at the dark sky barely blue around the edges. A clinking like bells as the people next door bring out the drinks. In one direction, he notices, he can see nearly down to the horizon–clear through the chain-link fences, between the houses and right out to the horizon.

That night the winds are worse than usual, keeping him awake past midnight listening to the weather stripping and worrying about his shoulder and thinking he should have put a trash bag over the antique rose to keep it from getting whipped against the trellis. For a while he lies there trying to remember exactly what the cartoon plants looked like in the ad–how many spikes each had and whether these emerged symmetrically or alternated along the stem.

The next morning he decides to try the local branch library but he's too early and has to drive around a while until it opens. Then, unwilling to deal with the computerized card catalogue and disappointed with the depth of the old newspaper file, he wanders more or less at random among the stacks taking much longer than he would like gathering, at last, a not very satisfactory general gardening book with a chapter on pests and something from the medical section called *Amazonian Biotoxins: Their Perils and Promise* that attracts him because the pharmacological society emblem on its cover features a stylized plant that looks a little like what he remembers from the lost advertisement.

By now it's past eleven and he's afraid he's missed the mail. He's afraid he might get home and find a yellow note on his door telling where to claim his package the following day after eight or tens hours of miserable uncertainty. But there isn't a note; there's a package. Right by the front door. About a two-foot cube, plain brown paper and no return address. What else could it be? He places it in the center of the kitchen table, then puts on his yard clothes and goes out to repair the damage from the night before; it's not quite as bad as he feared and it only takes about an hour to fill in the trenches and replace the sod where he can. Then he's back in the kitchen, washed up and ready for the package. Could it have been in the mail all this time misrouted or something? How long can plants survive wrapped up like that in the summer? He tries to make out the postmark but it's smeared. It looks like July maybe–that's only last month; but it might be June.

Holding a paring knife just back of the tip he scores through the paper and then through the masking tape along the top seam of the cardboard box, folds it back and is struck by the smell. It can't be spoiled. He can't believe it. He pulls out the wads of foreign-language newspaper and withdraws a little foil-wrapped, wire-reinforced wooden crate inside which, nestled in a bed of what looks like moist rubber bands, are the plants, four of them, much smaller than he expected but alive as far as he can tell. The smell seems to come from the rubber bands. They're sticky like old newspaper rubber bands that have begun to decompose and they smell terrible but he can't say like what. They must be a sort of mulch or peat moss, he thinks. There are no instructions anywhere, absolutely nothing except the little crate and its contents. He eases one of the plants out of its nest, picking off the rubber bands. It's only about four inches long with a root system nearly the same size and it doesn't really look much like the pictures in the ad. It's not really spiky; the leaves are more spoon-shaped, each with a fringe of short nettlelike spines and covered with fuzz like an African violet. A flickering of the light like a power surge brings his attention back to the room which seems gradually to have become quite dark for midday. Through the glass door he can see heavy clouds moving in; a flicker of lightning again and a long roll of thunder. He'll have to hurry to get them in the ground but there's root stimulator already mixed and an open bag of peat. He'll throw in some of the rubber band stuff as well–make them feel at home perhaps and it can't hurt.

The rain starts almost immediately, however, and by the time he's finished he's soaked once more and his shoulder is worse but he's in a better frame of mind. He stands by the sink looking at the garden in the rain. There's one by the antique rose just outside the defenses and the others like traffic lights at intersections of the paths between the beds. Tomorrow he'll place rings of aluminum edging around all four.

He sleeps late the following morning, awakened about ten by cicadas chattering so loud he thinks there must be a new crop. Light seems to rush in through the curtains as if the air had thinned–the glare and the noise sort of combining to make him feel (not unpleasantly) precarious, barely contained, his house paper-thin as he imagines Japanese houses to be. He lies there for a long time listening and admiring the light. He remembers finding cicada husks–nymphs, whatever they're called–translucent like wax paper, attached to trees and the sides of the house, empty and open along the top where the new forms had emerged. Maybe these loud ones were the seven-year kind. Or was it seventeen? He'd heard of seventeen-year "locusts" he thought, and maybe some that stayed in the ground even longer. What possible use could that be. He can hear cars go by every now and then but other than that there's no neighborhood noise, everyone's left for work or day camp, everything's fallen silent but the cicadas chattering in waves like breathing. It's hard to think of the last time he stayed in bed so late. He can remember being sick as a child and the strangeness of the vacuum of the weekday midmorning when all the day's business had left him behind. How everything glows now, how the room almost blooms with light.

Outside there's some sweeping up to do after the rainstorm but things are in pretty good shape. The new plants look all right and there aren't any fresh molehills, if that's what they are, although the rain or even his activities the night before could have something to do with that. He can tell it's going to be hot and, though it's nearly eleven, he takes his coffee out on the patio, faintly aware that as a celebratory move it might be premature. Still the day seems promising and there are two buds on the old rose about to open.

He makes the rounds shaking the rain off the rosebushes and returns to the old rose, shakes it gently then teases open the small apricot-colored buds with his fingertips, blowing into the blossoms to help them unfold. There's nothing like it, he thinks. None he knows of smells quite like it; all that's left to carry the scent of someone's garden, some household, a family–who knows, a hundred years ago–as if they still existed; still pumping out the smell like baking bread.

The cicadas are overwhelming. Ordinarily he likes their gentle buzzing in the summer coming and going more or less with the blooming season. He plucks an empty one from the antique rose and, looking around, notices quite a few others. Just about every available vertical surface in fact seems to have acquired at least one or two cicada husks–the trellis, the rubber wheels of his garden cart, and there's a very good collection along the brick of the house just above the foundation. Surely, one can't actually have a plague of cicadas. They weren't really locusts. He didn't think they fed after emerging or even had mouths for that matter. All they do is buzz. He leans back in the recliner. It's hypnotic after a while–the oscillating buzz, the heat and the clear sky like the ocean or the TV after sign-off. He can hear the summer-school carpoolers, the first wave of the day, the youngest ones returning–barely audible above the cicada noise, away down the street doors slamming, little yelps and squeals. It's amazing, he thinks, how sound travels through the neighborhood. With everything so flat and open it seems it should reflect off the concrete and diffuse straight up but especially in the summer it's as if there were a heavier layer, a high-pressure zone or something hovering just above, keeping sound from escaping and sending it along like whispering through a pipe.

He rouses himself after a while and gathers his tin-snips and a roll of corrugated aluminum edging for the borders around the plants–mostly just to mark them, distinguish them from weeds. He leaves about an inch and a half showing above the ground; so much the better if it catches a little water.

It's uncomfortably hot now and the cicadas have become oppressive. He returns to the kitchen where the noise is muted and he can still see the little plants–maybe already a shade greener than yesterday–protected and waving slightly in the breeze.

Mr. Delabano is used to the sounds of the blackbirds and starlings that have lately begun passing above his house at about the same time every morning. Now and then, if they come by directly overhead, he goes outside to watch as they stream across in a fairly continuous ribbon for maybe a minute or so crackling and whistling like radio static. So it's only after this same noise continues the next morning for quite a while longer, and with much greater volume than usual that he puts down his electric shaver and listen to it. His bathroom has one of those frosted glass privacy windows so he can't actually see what's going on outside but something peculiar is. Some sort of commotion, most of it birds but something else as well–a chattering and batting against the house like hail or the first big drops of heavy rain. Something hits the frosted window, then another–he can't make it out. But there's a great flurry of wings–furious, darting shadows projected onto the translucent glass. The racket is pretty alarming by now. He ties his robe, retrieves his glasses from the top of the TV, slides open the glass door to the patio and immediately is struck sharply in the forehead by a small flying object and involved in such a terrific flapping and buzzing swirl of conflict that he loses his balance and falls back against the door frame banging his ear and losing his glasses in the monkey grass. Now it's like trying to see through frosted glass again. Blackbirds are everywhere jeering and whistling and cicadas rattling wildly about. It's some sort of feeding frenzy. He recovers his glasses and edges around toward the fence keeping close to the house. He's startled by someone yelling practically right behind him, "You must have something they like."

Mr. Delabano jerks around; it's his neighbor, the one who likes to barbecue outdoors.

"You've got something they like over there." He's standing just the other side of the fence with his hands in his pockets, smiling and watching the terrible goings-on with evident delight.

"It's the cicadas," says Mr. Delabano aware now of the extent to which the invasion appears restricted to his own backyard.

"You must be raising them, I guess."

"Oh no," says Mr. Delabano turning away, unsure but sensing one of those teasing jokes that always make him uneasy and uncertain how to respond.

"That's the Grackle Express."

"What?" says Mr. Delabano feeling trapped against the fence.

"The Grackle Express. Just kind of folded back and swooped right down. Amazing. You alright?"

Mr. Delabano takes his hand from the side of his head and looks at the blood.

"They get you? Boy, that's Alfred Hitchcock." To Mr. Delabano's horror, the younger man jumps the fence to examine the injury. The sudden movement and the clatter of the cyclone fence seem to disturb the birds and a general departure begins; like unfurling a flag, they lift up in a single great undulation then, swirling around, roll out toward the northwest leaving behind a few stragglers and a scattering of damaged cicadas intermittently buzzing and flopping around.

"Now that's kind of spooky isn't it," says the neighbor after a moment, watching them go. And it does seem strange–such concentrated mayhem just to stop, reverse like that; like an event run backwards. His ear is bleeding all over his shirt. He stares at his hand, the blood, allows himself to be accompanied into the house.

"Did you ever make buzz bombs or whatever they were called when you were in school?" asks Mr. Delabano's neighbor putting away the medical supplies.

"I don't know," says Mr. Delabano with a towel around

his neck and a complicated-looking bandage covering the lower part of his right ear.

"Oh, it was sort of a practical joke," he continues, gathering up the Band-Aid wrappers. "Kids used to make these things–addressed to someone like a regular note all folded up, the kind kids passed around all the time in class but these were sort of like letter bombs. Somebody would get one passed to him and right in the middle of class he'd open it up and the thing would just rattle and buzz as loud as anything; sounded just like those cicadas out there but even louder so the guy who gets it gets in trouble. They had a wound-up rubber band inside with a little paper spinner so when you opened it it rattled like hell and you never could find out who sent it."

"No, I never got one of those," says Mr. Delabano who has no idea what to make of this but urgently wants to inspect his garden and would prefer to do it alone. But his neighbor just stands there, his hands back in his pockets, silent now and gazing into the backyard through the open glass door. A light breeze carries a faint spicy, musky scent into the room.

"Boy," says the neighbor softly after a minute, "my wife sure loves your roses."

It's mostly the old rose–more detectable at this range than the others. A powerful fragrance, Mr. Delabano assumed, was one of its primitive characteristics.

"Hey, I'm going to be late, his neighbor turns suddenly, Listen, if you need anything, if you think you want a ride to the doctor or anything, let me know. I'm Mike Getz. This is crazy, you know, we've lived next door for a year and now I'm introducing myself."

Mr. Delabano takes his hand. "Frank Delabano," he says.

"Yeah," says Mike Getz, "we've admired your mailbox; my wife wants one of those too. So maybe I can get you to come over for a hamburger some weekend–tell my wife how to grow roses. You aren't dizzy are you?"

"Oh no, I'm fine," says Mr. Delabano trying to look recovered.

"Well I'm really sorry about your ear. Anyway, let me know, okay, if there's anything." And then he's gone. Out the back door and over the fence.

Mr. Delabano doesn't move for a while. He sits at the kitchen table waiting for events to die away a little, feeling the breeze through the open door. In a minute he'll get up and go look at his ear in the bathroom mirror; then he'll check the roses.

2

The last days of August settle into a pattern of storms and drizzle which gives Mr. Delabano a kind of cover, keeps him indoors most of the time and makes it easy to avoid social contact. It's not the best weather for roses but it's comforting to him, filling the outside world with predictable phenomena and washing away signs of disruption.

For a day or so following the grackle invasion he's startled by an occasional death rattle in the house–once in the middle of the night, a furious buzzing and thrashing about right under his bed that unnerves him strangely, sets his heart racing all night as if something were concentrated in the incident, even in the silliness of it. A thorough sweep of the house turns up quite a number of cicadas, a few of which reactivate when disturbed. They seem to be off or on, nothing in between; like an old wind-up toy that having apparently run down, pops loose another coil in the spring and whirls into action again. He tries to imagine the sort of noise the paper grocery sack containing them would make if they all switched on late at night in a chain reaction. This thought is so unpleasant he takes the sack out to the alley in the rain, pausing on the way back to check on the roses. But it's the new plants that interest him. Kneeling under the umbrella he decides they've definitely grown. Maybe an inch; it's not just the soil settling at the roots. And really a deeper green as well. There's no doubt. He realizes he hasn't any idea how large they're supposed to get. He had thought perhaps a foot or so but what if they really took off? Huge, exotic, waving fronds overwhelming the roses. Surely not. How could they sell something like that? In any case there hadn't been any new mounds. Not a one. There would be some patching up to do when things dried out–places where soggy ground had slumped above the tunnels. But no new activity at all.

He scoops up a little dirt and packs it around the base of a plant to replace what's washed away and encounters something that feels a bit like insulated electrical wiring. "My goodness," he says to himself, excavating and uncovering a substantial tangle of the stuff. "Goodness," he whispers again. It's the root system. They're growing more down than up. Like a carrot. Of course it's the roots that do the trick–"antithetical to garden varmints," he remembers that phrase. Still, it's phenomenal. They must love the rain. He packs the soil back down around the roots then stands up to survey the garden. Roses and roses with names like racehorses. Maybe something huge and primitive wouldn't be so bad. No gophers for a hundred miles.

He gazes down the line of backyard fences. It's still pretty early–nothing going on in the neighborhood. Just steady rain. All the kids would be inside watching Sunday morning cartoons. He's glad there's no one to see him standing among the roses with his black umbrella; he probably looks silly, somewhat funereal. How sad Mike Getz's red barbecue grill looks in the rain. How sad all the yards look. All the swing sets and wet grass. The whole neighborhood seems like a camp. An old campsite. As if no one had really expected to stay so long but simply got used to it. Forgot to move on or forgot the reason for doing so and the houses, never built to withstand so much time and weather, finally resemble those World's Fair pavilions preserved for civic or sentimental reasons beyond their intended life, settled into a condition of continuous rejuvenation and repair. He remembers a very old inn in Virginia where he and his wife stayed for a night one summer–the summer they collected the rose. Parts of it were supposed to be seventeenth century and in the dining room there was about a two-foot-square hole in the wall that had been glassed-in and framed with a little plaque next to it explaining how they had dug into the wall looking for a water line or something but what they found–and what made them decide to leave it alone–was a stratified sequence, a foot and a half thick, of older and older construction and reinforcement going all the way back to what seemed to be mud and wattle at the very center. It had to be the earliest structure on which the hotel was based–maybe not much more than a hut or a barn and everything had just been built on top of it year after year getting bigger and shinier like a pearl.

Off to the north he can see a stream of blackbirds–the Grackle Express, Mike Getz had called it. Maybe they've altered their route, which would be all right with him. He touches his ear. He needs a fresh bandage if he can figure how to undo this one. Purely out of habit he gives the old rose a gentle shake as he walks back in the house.

It's difficult to see in the mirror exactly what his neighbor has done. It's an elaborate construction of gauze and Band-Aid ends for tape; probably quite expert but it's hard to know where to start. So he starts at the top with his right hand, holding his ear with his left. Then he stops, concerned about the odor. It can't have gotten infected so quickly. It's not that sore and it wasn't a bird anyway, just the door frame. He pulls the bandage off quickly and sure enough the wound's not too bad–the bruise is impressive but the cut is beginning to heal. The odor, however, is puzzling and disturbing–not decay exactly but as if it carried some very unpleasant association like that or like the smell of alcohol which as a child he hated more than anything because it reminded him so vividly of the doctor's office that all it took was a whiff and he could feel the needle or the lance. Alcohol smelled, he felt certain as a child, like needles. But what does this smell like? And where is it coming from? Is it him? He sniffs around the bathroom. It's in there someplace. It reminds him of something. The plants. Or the mulch, the rubber band stuff. Something like that, definitely. He looks at his hands. His left is soiled from scraping around in the garden. He brings it to his nose and it's really unpleasant, as bad as the doctor's office. Just the left hand though. He remembers digging around the roots of the plant. For a second he just stands still, trying to isolate the association; it's not just the smell of the rubber band mulch; there's a component of that but the main thing–what is it–something else altogether, actually uncomfortable like when the cicada went off under his bed. He turns on the hot water and washes his hands, then washes again and a third time with Comet cleanser which seems to do the job pretty well. Powerful stuff, though, whatever it is; he looks at the pale reddish stains that won't wash off the fingers of his left hand.

He finds it hard to get into his daily routine, somehow. He tends to pause in the middle of things, forget what he's doing, finding himself at one point with a lapful of dirty clothes, sitting on the edge of his unmade bed and gazing at the curtains, lost in the gray light and letting his thoughts dissolve, go nearly blank as if waiting for something to appear. Something should, it seems to him. Any minute. The unpleasantness, or at least the sharpness of it, has evaporated. He's left with mostly a sense of depth or distance, something descended toward, approached but withheld and the odd suspension that follows. It's not unlike the sort of evocative but mysterious odor anyone may encounter from time to time in the way it sets one's thoughts rummaging, working down through the possibilities toward something as faint as an old girlfriend, a whiff of elementary school. Disinfectant and manila paper. Except for the feeling of inaccessible depth it's like that, except for an inability to reach the right level. Something before grade school. Even before the tastes and smells of things that don't belong in one's mouth like pennies or bitter dark brown furniture varnish. Even more primitive than that, and even stranger.

The rain continues all day and into the evening–white noise like that of the cicadas making a sort of blank screen against which random musings seem illuminated that might otherwise pass, nearly unnoticed, into the background. He's gradually lost all sense of the disturbing odor, having reflected on it too long and too closely he's desensitized, unable to summon even a reliable report of his own reactions; it's a rumor. And, as such, dismissable. Nevertheless he seems captured by a pattern of idle reminiscence. Locked into it, his eyes defocusing toward any old memory, paused above the running tap with an empty glass in his hand; the running water and the sound of the rain.

3

The start of the regular school year marks a favorite time for Mr. Delabano. The approach of fall, the strollers and cyclists who appear as the evenings get cooler, a sudden rise in the overall bustle, the to and fro of the neighborhood activity breaking around him, coming and going like a tide. At no other time does he feel so embraced and isolated–the best of both; so invisible in the garden, less likely to be greeted or noticed, yet necessary somehow, a consequence of what surrounds him. For some reason this year it seems more subdued, however; reluctant to quicken. Maybe the population is aging or maybe everything's just waiting for the first cold snap–the first call to autumn that, in the best years when it's sudden and clear, can really stop one for a moment, spin one's mood around like a weather vane and hold it in an odd direction, an oblique combination of exuberance and longing. So far, though, it's a bit flat. Summer tailing off to nothing in particular; a general deflation detectable especially in the gaps, the spaces between movements.

By now he's fairly confident of having escaped Mike

Getz's threatened invitation. Sunny weather brings him outside with increasing certainty that the critical period has passed, an exchange of waves across the fence having provoked no further approach. The trouble is he'd have no way to refuse. He'd have to go, stand around in the kitchen and the backyard, speak to the wife and meet the children. That would be difficult. It's not that he doesn't like children. In fact he really loves them in a way, at a distance–distant voices, bright, loud little blips up and down the street marking the centers of people's lives, so alarmingly scattered as it seems to him at times. At some level he's suspicious of children–not as personalities but as potential inconsistencies were he to admit them completely into his world model. Children, he suspects, at close range are incompatible with roses. And today the roses need weeding. The ground has had time to dry out and it's a nice day. Following the rains a pretty good selection of grassy and leafy odds and ends has begun to poke up through the pine bark and, although it's tedious, he finds it soothing working from bed to bed; his shoulder feels fine and his ear no longer bothers him. Best of all no molehills, hardly even a trace–the pits are filled and he's patched in some sod. How quiet it is this time of morning, the ebb of daily events. The cicadas have largely vanished–just a ghost of their former presence barely audible from somewhere, part of the background. No traffic to speak of, no wind. Not a cloud in the sky. He works his way over toward one of the new plants. He thinks he'll tidy up their little beds too, but reconsiders. They're okay, he decides; it's best not to fiddle with them if they look okay. And they do. Healthy as they can be–a very deep green now, almost blue-green, and somehow plumped up as if storing moisture. They're about a foot tall and, until recently, seemed to have stabilized at that height, somewhat to his relief. However, each plant has produced a little spike or tendril at the top and he's been anticipating another growth spurt, expecting it to unfold into a new leaf or leaf-bearing segment. Looking at it today, though, it's obviously a different sort of structure. The tiny knob at the end appears to have doubled in size since yesterday and deepened in color as well. It looks like a little bud now at the tip of the spike, definitely blue and convoluted like a complex knot–what's it called, a Turk's head.

Something intrudes into his peripheral field of vision and he has to stop himself from turning around. Someone's standing at the fence. It must be Mike Getz, but he doesn't want to look. Maybe he'll go away; just stay busy, pull some more weeds and he'll wander off. Why isn't he at work? Maybe it's possible to reach the tool shed; it's in the right direction if he can just get up quickly and head for it with sufficient purpose and urgency he can escape among the pots and peat bags.

"Hey, Frank."

Or just pretend not to hear; old men are hard of hearing–just scoot over to the next bed and keep weeding.

"Mr. Delabano," his neighbor calls again and there's no help for it. Mr. Delabano rises, wipes his hands on his trousers and approaches the fence. Mike Getz looks dressed for work–blue blazer with some kind of ID card affixed to the lapel–and he's holding a dog leash.

"How's your ear?"

"Oh, fine," says Mr. Delabano, "completely healed I think."

"That's great. Say, I've got a problem. This is silly I know but my youngest one is having a fit; we can't find the dog–Mitzi, she's real important to Janie and she just took off last night I guess, dug under the fence, and we both have to be gone all day so we thought since you'd be here maybe you could sort of keep an eye out."

"Sure."

"In case she comes back–you know what she looks like, little curly black mutt."

"Oh, yes."

"We sure would appreciate it. That side gate's open; if she turns up you could just put her back in. I've got the hole plugged."

It occurs to Mr. Delabano later that morning, sipping his coffee and contemplating the dog leash on the kitchen table, that he's acquired a moral dilemma. Recovering the dog would probably get him invited to a cookout. Failure, on the other hand, might leave everyone too distracted to think of such things. Maybe the dog got run over.

He moves to the living room and opens the curtains to the picture window. No dog. That's that. It remains only to return the leash with minimum engagement. But he continues to look. Up and down the street nothing's moving. No people. No cars. Even the trees are perfectly still. He can remember seeing the little girl and the dog playing together. Much yapping and dashing about. He turns to get the leash, pausing to survey the room for a moment, unaccustomed to this light. It's kept as his wife kept it. The sort of formal little front room no one's really intended to occupy unless there's an occasion. Floral print upholstered furniture set at precise angles, porcelain knickknacks here and there and a real oil painting above the couch: Texas hill country, a dirt road receding through rolling bluebonnets. Bluebonnets as far as you can see on both sides of the road and not much else all the way to the horizon.

Outside, standing on the front walk with the leash in his hand he feels ridiculous and exposed. He's got about an hour before the preschoolers begin to repopulate the neighborhood. So many children, he thinks. It's hard to make a case for an aging population; the neighborhood's like a playground sometimes–several swing sets in several backyards going at once, squeaking in sequence, sound like echoes, like a flight of geese or loons. Why, he suddenly wonders, should Mike Getz's wife want a mailbox like his–tulip silhouettes and the name and address in stamped aluminum. It's like an historical marker out there by the street. You'd have to live here for twenty years to need a mailbox like that. Perhaps longer. Have watched the last houses go up, the last open field divide into lots. There must have been wildflowers then, even bluebonnets. Maybe a few. He can't recall.

He looks up and down the street again. It's so flat and open and quiet it's hard to imagine anything hiding, anything really out of place. There's no little dog out there, he's sure. If it had really been run over Mike Getz would have found it. He's not going to find anything. There's not even a squirrel. He hangs the leash on his neighbor's front door and hopes it's enough. Then he stops on the walk again for a minute taking a last official look around, listening for something–dogs barking he supposes, just a chance. It really is abnormally quiet. Quieter than summer, these vacancies in the daily traffic. More quiet than he can remember; in the country at least there are insects and birds. Maybe he's actually getting hard of hearing. He can hear his footsteps, though. He can hear himself breathe. But don't people sometimes become deaf to certain frequencies? He listens for the cicadas, the survivors out there somewhere, tries to distinguish them once more from the subliminal hush of the general background but there's nothing, no insects, no birds. This must be like what they mean when they talk about earthquakes, how quiet it can get. He's heard stories about how animals, even insects, respond to a big earthquake–to something–before it happens, before people can feel it. Some kind of tension they're supposed to smell or sense in some way. And just for a second he feels slightly chilled, uneasy for no reason he can think of. He hopes he's not getting sick, a touch of fever. Maybe he ought to lie down for a while. He's certain the dog is gone for good. Somehow there isn't any doubt. He can imagine it still running, miles away by now, hightailing it down the middle of the street.

Every day for a while he expects to hear from Mike Getz. But there's no phone call, no greeting across the fence. In fact there's hardly a sign of anyone next door. It was probably impolite just to leave the leash hanging on the knocker like that. He thinks how sad and abrupt it might have been for the little girl to come home and find it there and he hopes things hadn't worked out that way.

But he doesn't dwell on it. He's become preoccupied with developments in the garden. The little tendrils issuing from the tops of the new plants have thickened considerably and extend now another foot above the leafy portions. What's really interesting, though, are the knobs or buds–whatever they are–at the tips. They're the size of golf balls, deep blue and still growing. The entire arrangement is quite remarkable–more like exotic garden ornaments than real plants. The leaves, once spoon-shaped, have inflated and the fuzzy covering is more pronounced so that in a certain light there's a kind of halo around them. The fringe of spines, on the other hand, has disappeared entirely.

He wonders what sort of season they have and how it's going to look after the roses drop their leaves and these are left on display. What neighborly enquiries that would invite. Most of all he wonders about the big knot-shaped structures on top. If they really might contain flowers. Every day they're a little larger and, he's fairly certain, bluer. It's likely to be impressive whatever it is and, although he's enchanted by the possibilities, there's some concern, as well, about the effects–how much attention it will attract, if there will be a fragrance.

By the weekend he thinks he can detect some separation among the ridges and convolutions of the buds. A slight pulling apart–all four plants on exactly the same schedule apparently. They're going to be flowers, he's sure, and he's hardly able to concentrate on anything else, tending to wander back and forth between the kitchen and the garden all day. Gazing out the window.

When the wind picks up at night, he worries about the possibility of the stalks snapping–he has no idea how resilient they are, what kind of conditions prevail where they come from. But he hesitates to interfere, install supporting stakes or anything, for fear of disrupting something. He feels he should keep his distance, let things happen.

In his bed he thinks about them, what they must be like in the wild–fields of them perhaps, quiet fields receding to the horizon. And in the morning he awakes with a disturbing conviction that there's something wrong: they're not supposed to bloom. They're nonflowering. He remembers that from the ad. He's certain it was one of the main points, as if it were a desirable quality. Nonflowering is what it said. "More effective than spurges," whatever those were, "and non-flowering." As if to suggest one wouldn't want them to. So what are they doing? If not flowering then what? He lies very still; there's something else. "Gopherbane," he says aloud after a minute, sitting up suddenly, "Grand Rapids, Michigan." He'd forgotten that completely. Entirely forgotten. What time is it in Michigan? It doesn't matter, it's Sunday. Just get a number, find out if there is one.

Standing barefoot in the kitchen, thumbing through the front then the back of the phone book he can't seem to find what he wants. He tries Information who refers him to the regular operator who gives him the area code and a long-distance Information number and then he's got Directory Assistance in Michigan looking for a listing, unable to come up with anything and asking for the spelling again but by this time Mr. Delabano isn't paying attention. He's looking out the window into the garden, holding the phone but unaware of it until it starts buzzing at him. He hangs it up slowly, still looking out the window. "Oh, Lord," he says softly, "Oh my goodness." He steps out onto the patio and pulls his robe around him. It must have been a front last night. He can't stop shivering, the concrete's so cold. It's like a dream. They've bloomed. Huge blue roses. Completely open and so much like roses, the nearest one, the one by the old rose, already in bright sunlight and glowing blue–not powdery blue but deep like the kind of glass some medicines come in and almost transparent like that. He moves a little closer. The musky scent of the antique rose–the last blossoms of the season probably–and that's all. Still he keeps that distance, looking at all of them. It's like a moment from childhood–a seminal encounter with some intense and basic thing, memorable forever afterward; fascination so deep and simple it doesn't even communicate with the higher faculties, maybe only a stage removed from the impulse toward the mouth. He can almost taste the blue. They're not really like roses so much as rose schematics. Like Tudor roses. Stiff and symmetrical. Monumental. Representing roses or something essential to them. For a second he remembers the smell–the chilly, unfathomable discomfort–then it's gone. His feet are so cold he's really starting to shake but he stands there for just a moment longer listening, wanting reassurance, reconciliation with the ordinary facts. Down the block there's a honk and a door slamming and much farther off someone calling a dog, it sounds like, whistling for it now, over and over until Mr. Delabano's feet are too cold and he retreats into the kitchen.

Monday is Mr. Delabano's day to get groceries. He doesn't really need to stock up every week but he imagines it's good for him to get out at least that often and probably good for the old station wagon as well. Lately he favors a new shopping center at the edge of town–it looks like the edge of the world and that's one reason he likes it. It has anticipated development and preceded it into the uncharted regions to the north, the flat prairie remnants otherwise penetrated in that direction only by highways and a few farm roads and which, in a couple of years, will be apartments and expensive-looking prefabricated neighborhoods no doubt. But now it's still possible to feel as if one has come to the verge of something. An outpost of sorts. It interests him the way a roadcut or maybe even a subduction zone might interest a geologist to be able to see the laminations of which the everyday world is composed. Sense the process.

Visible from the parking lot in front of the Tom Thumb is a farmhouse right out there in the hard scrabble on the other side of the highway, maybe half a mile beyond. It's obviously unoccupied–sold or abandoned some time ago probably; there's no hint of cultivation around it, no fences or outbuildings, just a windmill that still spins occasionally if the wind is in the right direction. Once he thought to drive by it on the chance there might be an old rosebush or two but he couldn't get to it. Somehow no road seemed to go the right way and after a while he gave up having become frustrated and self-conscious driving back and forth raising all that dust.

More than groceries what he wants to get is film and a neck strap for his camera which, to avoid mistakes, he's brought along even though he's afraid its antiquity might excite some comment. It's the camera he carried on trips with his wife and he wants to use it now to take pictures of the blue flowers.

"Do you know why news photographers used to love this camera?" asks the clerk, a very young man with a ponytail and round steel-rimmed glasses who seems to regard the old Leica range finder with a sort of reverence.

"No," says Mr. Delabano, his heart sinking, wishing he'd gone to a different store.

"You never lose the subject," he says looking straight at Mr. Delabano and smiling as if this were an obscure point. Then, to illustrate, he holds the camera to his eye, scans the store, dry-snapping winding and snapping again and, still peering through the camera, continues: "You've got wonderful optics just like the best reflex, but you never lose the subject, there's no mirror flopping around cutting off the view; you never lose the moment. It's a continuum."

He places the camera on the plastic pad on the countertop and opens the back. "Worth more now than when you bought it."

"It was a gift," says Mr. Delabano.

"Really nice. It's worth a lot more now, I bet."

Out on the parking lot Mr. Delabano loads his two sacks of groceries onto the front seat then hangs the camera around his neck and walks about fifty yards to the edge of the pavement. It's an unambiguous transition. There's the pavement and there's the prairie. It's as if shopping centers were laid down somehow without disrupting anything beyond the site itself. Men working on stilts. Or maybe only that prairie is so fundamental and undistinguished that anything not exactly shopping center tends to become prairie again by default. He pops open the front of the case, removes the lens cap, advances the film a couple of times and looks through the viewer, scanning around like the young man had done, trying to imagine a discontinuous panorama. How can it be possible to lose the moment? Through the camera the old farmhouse looks much smaller. It will be tiny in the picture, he knows, but he doesn't want to walk any closer; he'd have to go across the highway to make any difference and he already feels self-conscience standing out here at the edge of the parking lot. Anyway he rather likes it that size–hardly distinguishable at all, inaccessible. He clicks once, just one picture, and the farmhouse is still there, the moment is intact. A continuum, the young man had said. He looks through the camera again at the farmhouse and the windmill which has begun to turn slowly with the shifting wind.

Driving home he takes a meandering route down small streets, his window open, enjoying the cool air–almost cool enough to constitute the first snap of fall, almost suggesting the smell of smoke but not quite. He tries to imagine these houses growing old and abandoned and strange like the farmhouse but it's impossible. They're part of the collective, the streets and walks and other houses. They're intended to face each other, not emptiness. At least not directly. If everyone simply left one day, how long would it be before you noticed something wrong? If it were late fall and the grass weren't growing it might be a while. All those colorful toys would still be in the yards–brilliant plastic tricycles and such. And even deteriorated it wouldn't look right; it could never look quaint or interesting like a ghost town or one of those mysteriously abandoned Incan or Mayan cities in South America or wherever any more than an old tent could look quaint or interesting or even strange. These houses are so plain. They don't aspire to much so there's not much possibility of failure. Anything quaint has to have failed in some way, he suspects. Maybe, after all, the shopping center isn't so far removed from the prairie. Think of Rome. Goodness, the possibilities. Like living on a fault line. Here, though, collapse seems hardly possible–perhaps a gradual subsidence but that's all. That's the serenity of it. The flatness; the ordinariness and even the safety in a way. Not to be threatened with quaintness, to have no intermediate stages between the present and whatever the final one is–dissolution, the prairie. Younger people seem always to be moving in and out of this condition which is fine with him; it keeps the neighborhood young and, as long as one avoids attachments, stable in a peculiar way, continuously rejuvenated. They move in, produce children, or having produced them, stay awhile and leave. Presumably for something grander, a more complicated situation–and, perhaps, away from the sense of exposure that comes with ordinariness, the flatness of it. The emptiness overhead which, he can understand, might become oppressive to younger people whose gaze is less constrained and habitual, who are more likely to crane their necks to follow footballs or tossed children or, just hanging around outside at night, pay attention to the suddenness of the vertical transition between home and space.

He's approaching his own neighborhood now, the intersection where, he has always felt, a stop sign is needed and where he always stops on principle, sometimes irritating people in cars behind him. There's no one behind him now though, so he waits there long enough to scan the lawn service and lost pet notices stapled to the telephone pole. He's never seen so many. Fall cleanup, general yard work. Lost boxer dog, reward (with ornamental dollar signs). Lost white male cat, "Rocky." Firewood. Lost schnauzer. Lost dog. Lost dog. There's a honk behind him and he has to move on, slowing down again and pulling over a little as the other car zooms around. "Rocky," he says to himself, wondering about a cat that would really answer to that. Probably it wouldn't. It was such a carefully printed sign though; there must be others around. The "Rocky," in quotes was a kind of desperation it seemed. It had always been hard for him to understand that sort of devotion to a creature that seemed so ephemeral. Weren't house cats supposed to be accidents in a sense? Hadn't he read that? Not your ordinary natural selection exactly, nor, at first, intentionally bred but a prehistoric accident–some wild ancestor having taken to following human (or semi-human) camps around and then catching a virus which altered the genetic makeup toward something adoptable and that's why house cats and people share vulnerability to certain diseases. And that's why the bear has a short tail, he thinks. Oh, dear what's that? He twists around to look behind him, then in the rearview mirror as he slows down and stops in the middle of the street. It looks like an animal, a dog maybe. What if it's that dog, the little girl's dog. Mitzi, he remembers its name. What if it is. Got run over after all. He backs up slowly, easing over to the side, watching in the mirror. He still can't tell what it is. Maybe it is just trash. It's been a week since the dog ran off. He parks by the curb and turns off the engine and sits there for a minute surprised by the silence. It wasn't like this in the parking lot. Maybe it's having the window rolled down–the wind and the engine noise and then the contrast suddenly stopping like this. He gets out and looks around, feeling self-conscious again, but everything's quiet. No one outside. He walks back toward the object. It's not a piece of tire or clothing, although he keeps trying to resolve it into something like that even as he comes quite close. It is an animal. But it's not a dog or a cat. It's more like a raccoon or something. Lord, what is it? It's dead but not badly damaged. What could it be? It's not a raccoon–no little mask and the snout's too broad. He feels he ought to know what it is–just lying there like any commonplace dead animal, nothing really extraordinary about it; but unidentifiable in a way that's frustrating like not being able to name something simple like a color. Everything's so quiet. He looks around again then walks back to the car and returns with the camera. He realizes this is probably going too far, that right here he's passed into the realm of the truly eccentric but he wants a picture nonetheless. He glances around once more then frames the animal in the viewfinder and snaps a picture. He moves back a bit, looking at it more from the front. He should be embarrassed, right out in the street taking pictures of a dead animal. He kneels to get a better shot. From this angle he can see the animal's black nose and its mouth barely open, a thin line of teeth and, behind this, the bulk of it–a little hill of fur, dark brown, almost black over the head, its feet pulled under except for one front paw, the claws very long and blunt. It's one of those cool, sunny but very hazy days–

no clouds really, but uniform haze, enough to scatter the light, make everything bright and almost shadowless. Ideal for taking pictures. He snaps one more. He can't seem to withdraw from this. What would he say if someone approached? Road Victim Inspection; what would he really say though? Old man in street taking pictures of dead animal. He stands up, replacing the lens cap. He looks around again. But the quiet seems to isolate him. All the houses look unoccupied, dormant–Monday morning, everyone at work or school. There's no one to notice him. It occurs to him that he lives mostly in these little spaces, comes out like a mouse sniffing the quiet, testing the absence. Goodness, he thinks, it's not that bad. Look at all those houses. All so straight and simple with a street down the middle. Why would any wild animal want to come here? It's not as if there were no place else to go. What would such a neighborhood even look like to an animal like that–it must look uninhabitable, a place designed to leave wild animals dead by the curb, channel them into the street like a chute and leave them by the curb. He wonders if it were coming or going. Surely it wasn't going. One would have noticed such things living in one's neighborhood. It can't be a badger can it? Badgers have stripes. And wolverines live up north don't they? Mostly Canada and Alaska. A generic dead animal then. Proto-animal. Ex post facto animal. He thinks of all the lost pet notices. A mysterious exchange program. He looks down the street. There's a car approaching and he'd better go.

4

Next door to Mr. Delabano on the side opposite Mike Getz live two sisters in their mid- to late sixties–widows or spinsters, he has no idea–who tend to keep to themselves, seldom venturing farther into their backyard than the big screened porch where, in the best light on warm days, he can sometimes make them out as shadowy figures sitting together and watching TV, occasionally on into the evening looking more and more ghostly through the screen in the glow. In his opinion they look a bit ghostly even in broad daylight under the best conditions although such glimpses are fairly rare. Mr. Delabano judges them to be a different species from himself–not truly reclusive which, he imagines, requires reflection and intent. Rather he suspects they are loonies. Fluttering about each other, adrift in some dim fantasy which entirely insulates them. So it's a little surprising while making his morning coffee to look out the kitchen window and spot one of them standing at the fence, glancing back and forth between the blue flowers and his patio door as if hoping for him to emerge like a curator or a sales clerk. He assumes it's the blue flowers. They've never shown any interest in the roses which, this late, are not at their best anyway. It's the blue flowers. He pours a cup of coffee and moves away from the window slightly, watching her–a thin, yellow housecoat, both hands on the fence rail and gazing across his driveway at the huge blossoms, the housecoat and her loose gray hair lifting a little in the breeze. Except when she pauses to glance toward his back door, her mouth moves constantly. She's talking to herself, he thinks. There's no sign of anyone else. What in the world could she be saying? The breeze is toward the west, bending the tall stalks in her direction so that it looks as if a very strange sort of communication is taking place. Loony to beat the band, he decides, leaning against the stove and sipping his coffee. He's almost tempted to go outside just to see what it's all about. Now she's stopped talking; she's stepped back from the fence, standing there with her hands clasped in front of her, still looking at the blue flowers. What an expression. She's beaming–the sort of smile one might bestow on a virtuous child.

His clothes dryer is dinging at him. It won't stop until he attends it which only takes a couple of minutes but when he gets back she's gone. He waits a little while to be sure, then he goes outside to look at the blue flowers.

They look a little bigger than when they first bloomed but he thinks that's mostly because they've stiffened, solidified somehow, the petals straighter, less delicate and less like a rose. The color and the glassiness, though, are more pronounced and, especially at the centers, the blue has darkened or actually reddened–a very deep red where it funnels in toward the central structures, the stamens or pistils, whatever they are. It's curious how it grades to red without passing through purple; the eye tends to follow it as blue, denser and denser, into the center without immediately realizing the color shift as if a cue were missing. He remembers some plant book's contradictory description of the foliage of a certain tree (a type of Japanese maple, maybe, at a certain time of year) as greenish red. He had wondered about that at the time but later saw a tree of the sort described and, perhaps, fooled himself into believing he understood what was meant although, reflecting on this, he doubted it–it was probably just gray or brown invested with the suggestion; with the memory and/or expectation of green and/or red.

There's a slight fragrance now. Nothing disturbing but not very floral either. It reminds him of cherry laurel or photinia–the clusters of tiny white flowers that appear in the spring with such a dry, penetrating smell that carries no sense at all of flowers or finished product but rather something less refined and more essential escaping through little blossoms inadequate to transform it. A smell that seems to give more direct access to the forces involved–a little like the smell of an overloaded electric motor; suggesting heat, insulation about to burn and for some reason the bees love it. A whiff of it tends to make you look around for bees and maybe that's why it seems so penetrating that you sense it at the back of your neck.

There are no bees here though. No insects at all as far as he can tell. He bends down close to the flower–very faint but there it is like that dry springtime smell of tiny white flowers, inappropriate for something so heavy and coherent, especially this time of year. Maybe it will improve. He looks across to the sisters' yard, toward the screened porch trying to detect them. But it's too early; the porch is all shadows and he doesn't think they've rolled out the TV yet. It's fairly loud when they do that, usually in the mornings–wheel the TV on its little trolley out on the screened porch, noisy plastic wheels, it sounds like, rattling across the threshhold and onto the concrete. He wonders why things are so quiet on the other side. He hasn't heard anything from Mike Getz lately. No cookouts or weekend gatherings in the backyard. No yappy little dog either, of course. Maybe they're out of town. He can hear the Thursday morning garbage truck banging and whining its way up the alley. Now he can see it. Bright orange like a rescue vehicle. He returns to the kitchen to wait for it to pass. Sometimes the men like to talk and he can't imagine what he'd be able to say if they made some remark about the flowers. It's uncharitable he knows, but he's a little mistrustful of the good-natured garbage men. Like a merry undertaker, it doesn't seem quite right. Undignified maybe. Disrespectful. He wonders why they want such brightly colored garbage trucks. It seems to him they'd prefer inconspicuous ones. He thinks of an old Andy Griffith movie in which Andy played a bumpkin buck private who, for some hilarious transgression, is given latrine duty which he mistakes for an honorable and challenging assignment, rigging all the toilet lids with a system of cables connected to a foot pedal whereby he can pop open a whole row of them at once for inspection like a presentation of arms. The humor seemed to reside in the effortlessness with which notions of honor and worth can be appropriated, how malleable they are. He remembers it was a funny scene–the inspecting sergeant saluted by ranks of Prussian toilet seats–but it made him uncomfortable. Not the suggestion of the arbitrariness of military behavior which is fair game, but the apparent depth of the buck private's gratification, the idiotic assumption of glory. It's really uncharitable though. Probably un-American as well, to feel that way. In any case it's not exactly the same as with the jovial garbage men who make him uncomfortable, he suspects, because their manner suggests they know something he doesn't, although it's possible the other might reduce to that also. The truck is at Mike Getz's house. It looks like the cans are full so, presumably, he's home. Here it comes slowly past his house now. Mr. Delabano's cans are still upside down so it continues on with the crusher whining, one man driving and two on the back. Not a glance toward his backyard. It must be a new truck. It's a brilliant orange. Passing behind the blue flowers it looks radiant and he's quite struck by it. It's like the huge whale shark he saw once on a television documentary swimming past the submersible's viewport so slowly and so close it seemed to take several minutes dragging one's thoughts with it down toward unimaginable depths and leaving the little submarine feeling precious and accidental. The blue flowers seem like that at this moment. Inexpressibly compressed and precious as the garbage truck moves past. He can hear it for what seems like a very long time, whining on down the alley to wherever it goes. Then he hears the clatter of the TV trolley next door rolling out onto the porch–a sign that it's going to be a nice day.

Mr. Delabano doesn't watch much TV. His wife used to watch it and liked to go to the movies as well but without her he hasn't any interest. Tonight, though, he wants distraction. All day he's felt a little uneasy–nothing he can put his finger on, just sort of anxious for no particular reason and what he'd love to find on TV, he's decided, is one of those nature documentaries like the one with the huge whale shark. He's got cable (his wife insisted) so there are quite a number of possibilities. Surely one of them will have some kind of nature program; he used to flip past them all the time. Something far away. Really exotic.

He puts a frozen dinner in the microwave and turns on the TV. The remote control stopped working long ago so he kneels in front of the screen flipping channel by channel down from the top: first the weather, news and public service channels, then into the lower thirties and twenties (tending to old movies and children's programming) followed by a couple of Spanish-language channels and the mysterious Channels 20 through 17 (usually jammed or blanked out) and on down to the single digits and the networks. He backs up. There was something. A patch of desert with foreign-sounding music. Where is it. He can't seem to get back to it. Then he has it again but only for a couple of seconds before it goes blank. It's Channel 17. Something restricted. He checks the TV section in the newspaper but there's nothing worthwhile. Channel 17 isn't even listed. So he eats his TV dinner in silence, standing at the kitchen counter and looking out into the darkness. He wonders what that was on Channel 17. Desert and foreign music sound like just the ticket. He finishes up and returns to the television, flipping channels down from the top again till he gets to 17. How strange. There's a voice-over now in a foreign language and a shot of a group of large animals of some kind on a ridge very far away beyond which rises an incredible mountain range, snow-covered and rosy orange with the most wonderful light–all this in about two seconds and then it goes blank; not staticky, noisy blank but dark and quiet like his kitchen window. He turns off the TV. Maybe that will do. Maybe just that glimpse can carry him to sleep. He puts his dishes in the sink and gazes out the window for a moment then turns out the light.

Something bothers him in the night. It's like mosquitos, something nagging at him, pulling him out of shallow dreams to listen for it but there's nothing at first. Then later he hears it. He wakes up and it's still there; he thinks it's a cat. It's coming from Mike Getz's house–Mr. Delabano's bedroom is probably not twenty feet away. Cats can sound like anything. There it is again, breathless and thin, a sort of oscillating wail; a pause and then again. Oh dear it's a child–surely not; that's what cats always sound like, a child or a woman, and it's so startling when one does that–invests, by mistake, a human being with the weird passion of even such a small animal. Then you realize it's a cat and it's okay. Perfectly all right for that sort of thing to continue as long as it's a cat. But he's still listening and when it begins again it's a little louder, really desperate. It isn't a cat. There's what sounds like a door slamming inside the house next door and then the other sound fades and then it's gone. It has to be the little girl, he thinks. Such a sound; what could be the matter? Maybe it's only because it's the middle of the night but he doesn't think he's ever heard a sound like that. He stays awake for quite a while, sitting up in bed unable to stop listening, receiving every little noise as information. Toward morning he drifts off for maybe two or three hours but that's about it and he's up at the usual time peering through the curtains at the overcast sky, feeling the chill of the glass against his cheek. Another front, it looks like; maybe fall is really here.

Outside, standing in the driveway and holding the paper in its plastic wrap, he wonders if this could, in fact, be fall. Probably he should watch the weather report at night. It's actually rather cold and there's a hint of smoke. The first smell of smoke really counts as far as he's concerned. And it's always instantaneous, somehow; as soon as the temperature drops below a certain threshhold there's smoke as if someone were always ready, logs in the fireplace and set to go. Now let there be briskness, he incants to himself; let there be cyclists and noisy children. He waits for the mood to communicate itself, waits to be melancholy and invigorated at once but it won't come. Maybe he's finally too old. His thoughts keep returning to the sounds last night and the little girl. It's just cold air and that's all–no content.

Walking back in he has an urge to open up the front of the house. He withdraws all the double drapes in the tiny formal dining room–the heavy damask outer curtains (with some difficulty) and the gauzy inner ones. He does the same in the living room, uncovering the full width of the picture window then he sits down facing it, sinking a little into the floral print couch, still in his robe and holding the newspaper. Let's go, he thinks. He wants something accidental, exuberant perhaps or disruptive–not much. There's a carload of kids on the way to school but that's not it. He wants the world passing by the viewport with some energy. Things should be happening all the time out there–little, noisy, random things; the excess one expects and gets used to. But it's not there or it hasn't been or maybe he's really too old. Not detecting it; lost his ability to sense it or to respond. It's become too subtle for him. Like losing one's ability to taste–he's heard of that; old people to whom everything tastes like pabulum. That's what he feels like, looking out the picture window sensing only the most requisite and general things. The fact of houses and the fact of street. It might as well be prairie. Maybe this is the way it happens when one gets old without an illness to provide a format. Sooner or later the particulars go away. You're left with generalities. Everything gets more and more generalized eventually including yourself and then that's it. Look how big that picture window is. That was something when he and his wife installed it. It was something new. Very fashionable and expansive. They spent a lot of time in the living room then, admiring the view, passing by the window on the way to some other room, standing by the picture window–it really let in a little too much in a way and so after a while there were curtains. Now it seems to let in very little. Like an ear trumpet, hardly any use at all. He has an image suddenly of the animals in silhouette in the distance against the radiant pink range of mountains. Where could that have been? The Himalayas? Afghanistan, Nepal; someplace like that. It's hard to imagine it. Someplace that far away. Somehow it's not comforting. Not restful. He gets up and looks at the bluebonnet picture above the couch. He decides he doesn't like it either, the empty horizon, everything going over the edge.

He starts the coffeemaker then goes into the bedroom, opens the curtains and looks out the window facing the side of Mike Getz's house–a plain wall of red brick with a single window and a low boxwood hedge. It looks so dark in there. It must be the younger girl's room or maybe both girls use it but he's sure it was the younger one he heard last night. Such a small, simple house. What could go wrong in there? There shouldn't be room enough for anything to go seriously wrong it seems. It shouldn't be large enough to contain the sort of threatening darkness he imagines as he looks at the window and thinks of last night. He strips the bed and carries the sheets to the little alcove behind the kitchen where the washer and dryer are. Then he pours some coffee and takes the paper over to the recliner that faces the glass door to the patio. It really is official now, he thinks. It has to be fall; the vinyl of the recliner is so cold on the backs of his legs he has to force himself not to move for a minute until it warms up. He pulls his robe under him a little more and settles back. He can see the garden quite well from here–a few roses, but mostly the blue flowers. He can see all four. On such a gray day they seem unnaturally brilliant and concentrated. He takes off his glasses and he can still see them–dense blurs like blue lights.

He reads without his glasses which are only for distance. He has to hold the paper pretty close but it's better than bifocals which give him headaches and he refuses to deal with a separate pair. Above the newspaper he can see the blue blurs. It's an interesting effect. Everything tends to wash toward gray except the flowers. He flips through the paper and folds it back. Every now and then he glances up again at the blur of the garden. All gray except the flowers and a streak of pale yellow–the four blurred circles and the yellow off to one side. He puts on his glasses and for a minute he's still not sure what the yellow is. And then it resolves and for some reason he's startled. She's standing a little away from the fence, perfectly still this time, none of the quirky behavior she displayed before, just standing there in the same thin housecoat looking at the blue flowers apparently. She must be freezing. Where's the other one, he wonders–the one he thinks of as the older one? He lays the paper in his lap and rests his coffee mug on it. If this one were a child, he'd expect someone to call her in or bring her a coat. What in the world is it? Such attention. There's something it reminds him of–the wire fence and the motionless figure. Transfixed. At the zoo he's seen that. He remembers noticing once or twice when a child seemed to have fastened on some caged animal–a very young child almost in a trance, ecstatic it seemed to him, engaging some creature, entering in some deep childish way the real possibility of it, ice cream dripping, until jerked along by an older member of the family. He remembers a screaming baboon, a male mandrill. Whether the screaming was a response to the child's attention or the other way around, he had no idea; but the little boy seemed altogether beyond fear, completely captured by the moment, the big baboon right up at the front of its cage, its terrible blue and red face wide open with inch-long canine teeth, barking and screaming impelled by who knows what. It was early spring but cold. Even a few snow flurries. He had come from the hospital still dazzled by the whiteness of that place–his wife's room, whatever color it was, probably not white but it seemed like white, functioned as white, blankness to signify that anything might happen, anything good or bad was possible, the quiet and the whiteness meaning a kind of reluctance or maybe, at last, an inability to interfere. So he had gone to the zoo. Not thinking about what he was doing, it was like walking into it straight out of the elevator. So surprising that the plainest, most clinical sort of experience could grade directly into Africa, shift suddenly and naturally, the light snow and the local sparrows drifting about among the spectacular caged birds; the barks of the mandrill. The distinctions were softened. He's dozing off now; the edge of a dream. He places his coffee mug and his glasses on the side table and drops the paper on the floor. He should turn up the thermostat a little but he'd rather be motionless, drift off in the slight chill. The pale yellow has gone and now there are just the blue flowers. How long do they last, he wonders. What would they be like in the snow.

Mosquitos again or cicadas. He doesn't want to wake up. It's chilly all around him but if he doesn't move he'll stay warm, a boundary of warmth right next to him if he can stay asleep. A dream of animals, dogs and cats–a menagerie in his house, his backyard. Dogs and cats and cicadas and something else rattling, making too much noise; a fearful racket like rattling and barking, then the awful baboon face suddenly close up, shrieking him awake with a jerk. He's in the recliner. It takes a second to remember. He can't focus yet, doesn't have his glasses. The noise continues, intermittent rattling and squeaking not as loud as he dreamt. Straight ahead at the glass door. He doesn't move at first; he's paralyzed by the imminence of it–all pale yellow, a field of pale yellow or a curtain, overwhelming and impossible to reconcile immediately. A rattling and squeaking and something spoken–inaudible. He begins to see it; he was trying to focus past it but it's right there; she's standing at the door knocking at it, causing it to rattle and squeak on its tracks; more like pushing, it looks like, with her open palm every few seconds. He reaches for his glasses slowly, without turning his head, like reaching for binoculars or a gun. She seems so large against the glass door, backlit, a yellow glow around her edge where the light comes through the housecoat. Like some animal one is accustomed to seeing only faintly at a distance suddenly confronted, enormous, reared up on its hind legs. She's looking down at him, right into his eyes and saying something–it seems to be the same thing over and over and every now and then jostling the glass door with the palm of her hand. He's unable to move. Why does she keep doing that? She can see he's awake. Somehow it's actually difficult to move; he has trouble getting a grip on the wooden lever to raise the recliner. He's got it all the way back, his feet toward the glass door. He's terribly exposed. He wonders how long she's been there. He tucks his robe around him then with one hand gives the lever a tug while jerking his body forward and bending his legs against the elevated footrest. This practically launches him into a standing position no more than a couple of feet from the woman on the other side of the glass who immediately shifts to a conversational mode unconcerned with the barrier. "Oh, Mr. Delabano," she says, flattening the second *a* then something about her sister and the flowers–this close he can hear her pretty well through the glass as long as she's facing him but when she turns and gestures she fades out so he catches it in waves; he thinks of the birds that used to fly into the glass occasionally until his wife put up a large decal of a cat's face, the ghostly adhesive residue of which is still visible and still working as far as he can tell except in the present instance. "Century plants," she says, fixed on him now, "my sister says they are," she must have come in the gate on the other side, walked around the front of the house to find a way in. "They're not very tall but they're blooming and it's wonderful; they almost never do–every hundred years or sometimes not at all; not at all sometimes," and here she turns to look back at the flowers and he loses it again except for "wonderful" a couple of times. She's perfectly happy for him not to open the door. She needs him to stand up but that's it, nothing else–this, he senses, is just what's required, exactly right. If he were to open the door it might get out of control; she might panic and start flapping around the house or something. He should wait. Presently it will conclude, he suspects, as long as he does nothing exciting, avoids kicking it into some higher gear. ". . . the little book about the Century plant," she's facing him again; he's getting a sort of book report. Her hands are clasped in front of her–through gesturing apparently–like the hands of a schoolgirl making a presentation, her eyes so large and far apart as if gazing over an audience, past the light: toward something in general, really into it now and sure of the situation, his passiveness beyond the glass. "Such pictures," she's saying, "and so many very good ones, pastel and gouache; we think some were gouache but so delicate the way they emerged from the gray pages, highlighted, whitened like those wonderful Renaissance drawings and just one page a night; just one every night till he finished–so exciting, we wanted to peek but he'd hold the book so we couldn't and we really didn't want to, it was so exciting every night to see how it looked, how the little boy grew up and older and older but the Century plant never bloomed; he could only imagine it one way or another, every page with a different one, every night a different flower in his imagination until he's simply too old and it was so sad; it was too much for us and we couldn't bear to look at it again . . ." At this point she drifts off into a whisper; she's lowered her eyes, running down now perhaps, still talking although he can no longer hear what she says. He can hear the refrigerator humming and every now and then a gust of wind and the buzzing of the weather stripping at the front door. If he closed his eyes there would be no way to tell she was there. He imagines, for some reason, she is heavily perfumed–that she's whispering through clouds of scent and if he opened the door he'd be enveloped in it. The pale, thin skin of her face is like waxed or oiled paper as if, for many years, having had applied to it on a regular basis, away from the sun which would cause evaporation, some fragrance or scented lotion whose aromatic volatiles have combined with the tissue, rendered it translucent–her eyelids so thin she must see light through them like oiled paper windows in houses long ago, frosted glass, white curtains. And densely perfumed he imagines. Some strange trade-off having been accomplished. Opacity for scent. She's stopped talking now, but holding that position–eyes lowered, hands clasped in front. Has she closed her eyes. He can't tell looking down at her. Is she really standing there now silent facing his glass door with her eyes closed? Maybe he can back away. He glances behind him; he doesn't want to trip or make a noise but when he turns back she's looking at him without speaking. She gives him one of those competent, automatic smiles that self-assured people know how to produce for strangers on the street whose glance they have engaged for just a moment too long; and automatically he returns it as she turns and disappears around the east side of the house. He waits until he thinks he hears the clink of the gate latch then slides open the glass door and steps outside. He's quite surprised. The air is still for the moment but there's nothing. Not even the slightest fragrance. Nothing at all except the faint smell of smoke.

"Century plants," says the nurseryman on the other end of the line, "there's nobody that stocks them as far as I know; I had to chunk the last ones I had."

"Why is that?" asks Mr. Delabano.

"Just no market anymore; outdoor cactus and stuff like that went out of fashion. You can probably find one someplace but I couldn't tell you where."

"Are there problems with gophers?"

"Where? You mean here?"

"No, with Century plants. Do gophers like them?"

"You'd have to ask the gophers I guess; I sure don't know. I never heard anybody say anything–can you hold on just a minute." Mr. Delabano can hear the cash register, loading instructions for a birdbath. Maybe he should get a birdbath except what if the birds wouldn't come? He's on the kitchen phone and he can see the four plants from here. They're not Century plants. He thinks he knows what Century plants are and they're not like these. The flowers seem to be spreading open even more. They're stiffer and their centers more intensely red. He can see the red from the window now.

"Yeah, is there anything else?"

"Can you tell me what a Century plant looks like?"

"What, the whole thing?"

"Yes, the plant and the flower," says Mr. Delabano thinking he should have waited a couple of days for his rose man to get back from vacation.

"Well the flowers aren't much but you know what a yucca plant looks like?"

"Yes," says Mr. Delabano, not entirely sure.

"It looks like that but bigger and when it's ready to bloom a real long spike with side branches like a big coatrack or a TV antenna stuck in the ground. Think that'll do it?"

"Yes, thanks very much," says Mr. Delabano still looking out the window at the blue flowers swaying in the wind on their springy stalks, winking red occasionally when they bob in his direction.

He turns off the coffeemaker and rinses his mug in the sink. Then he gets a lemon from the refrigerator and plops the entire thing into the disposal. It makes an awful noise at first but grinds down to a hum in a few seconds. It's a trick his wife used when the smell got too bad. Now the sink smells like lemons.

But the rest of the house seems to have acquired an odor, he decides, walking in with the mail, most of which gets tossed into the unexamined pile accumulating on the wing chair by the front door. He suspects it's time for a general housecleaning although he hates to do it; it saddens him inexplicably. Especially the sound of the vacuum cleaner. He opens the front door and then the one to the patio letting the breeze flow through to the back. Maybe just an airing out, he thinks. And a few cut roses. He gets his jacket and his pruners but back in the kitchen he finds himself immobile, his garden gloves in his hand, sitting at the table and looking out the open door at the flowers, feeling the breeze pour through the house and listening to the clothes dryer dinging away like a radiation leak.

Around midday the wind really starts to pick up–the front's still arriving apparently. Straight out of the north. He's holding a rose catalogue and standing by the picture window. Somebody has lost a load of trash it looks like, bits of paper floating over the houses across the street, swirling around and shooting up into the air. Some of the pieces look like they're not coming down at all; somebody's canceled checks or something just sailing away like dandelion seeds, propagated essence of living in a small house, paying bills, receiving goods and services. He thinks of the strange sisters next door. He wonders what goods and services they receive; what gouache might be.

His front door is humming a low note, softer and louder with the wind; and the mimosa outside the unused front bedroom is batting against the window. It's like someone waiting for something–fingers tapping. For a second he worries about the antique rose but it's all right; it's nearly finished blooming and the wind won't hurt it. There's something else. He can't think what it is. Something to worry about. Maybe the smell. It could be him, of course. Isn't that supposed to be a kind of pathological symptom–unpleasant odors that aren't really there? Some sort of metabolic problem. It's not very strong though. It could even be imaginary at this point–

thinking about it too much like hearing mosquitos at night after you've swatted one. Even if there aren't any you keep hearing them.

From the back of the garden late in the afternoon the wind blowing through the front door weather stripping seems even louder, resonating through the house and out the open patio door into the quiet. It sounds like a huge saxophone or a conch. With the back door open there's a suction created sometimes when the wind is blowing and if everything is just right it makes a very peculiar sound–really amplifies the reed-like effect. He wonders if the neighbors can hear it. If the little girl next door can hear it humming, rising and falling to that same low note, softer and louder until a sudden gust breaks it to a higher frequency, some harmonic above the next octave. It really does sound like someone blowing a conch when it does that, what he supposes conch-blowing ought to sound like anyway, or maybe one of those weird vibrating instruments the aboriginal Australians play. He glances toward the sisters' house. They'll be watching TV inside; deaf to everything else. He wonders what they watch. Perhaps they get Channel 17. He zips his windbreaker the rest of the way up and steps back a little more to see his TV antenna where it's broken away from the chimney, the ends of the three main horizontal members resting on the white composition shingles as the whole assembly rocks a little in the wind. He's not really concerned about the antenna, which isn't useful anymore unless the cable goes out. But the roof is pretty old and the sharp edges of the antenna rods will dig a hole before too long. From inside he can hear the scraping.

He drags the wooden ladder out from behind the garage. It's no longer safe but unless he does something there's going to be a hole in his roof by morning. He's got a roll of duct tape–the only thing he can find but it should hold for a while if there's enough.

Just outside the back door he leans the ladder into a corner of the eaves, nudging it toward vertical as far as he dares to avoid damaging the gutter. A few nails have crept out but if he keeps his feet to the side it seems okay. And if he holds onto the rails instead of the steps. The duct tape goes over his arm like a bracelet.

Halfway up he's really struck by the wind sweeping across the roof, swirling down around him, inflating his jacket and making him feel buoyant as if he were approaching the summit of something important, a significant transition here a few feet above the patio. There's a problem shifting from the ladder to the roof–it's been so long he can't summon the right move; he has no instinct for it and he's afraid the ladder might fall, it's so nearly straight up. He runs through the possibilities–what he'd do if he were stuck up here; how to fall (how he used to know how to fall and roll as a young man, how to balance these sorts of risks). He's off balance right now though. No confidence. It's shocking to him how something so fundamental can evaporate like that practically unnoticed. But he seems to be committed, one knee on the roof and both hands on the top of the ladder. He wants to bring his other leg around but he can feel his knee about to slip which would probably be enough to tip everything over. He looks behind him. It's so shadowy down there it's hard to judge but he figures he'd land on the old rose. The patio really is so dark and the moaning of the weather stripping suggests great depths–it makes him feel more precarious than he probably is. As if he were on a rock face above a chasm, the white roof like snow. How ridiculous, he thinks.

But his left leg is starting to shake and he's got to make a move. Instead of swinging his left leg around, he brings that knee over the top and onto the roof, hooking his foot over the top step to keep the ladder against the eaves while he leans out onto the shingles pulling himself forward with his hands and forearms like someone trying to reach safety across thin ice. He rolls over into a sitting position. The roof seems so bright. It's still daylight up here and there's a kind of glow. The overcast is breaking up and off to the west he can see the sun about to touch the horizon. He scoots slowly backwards up the roof, facing the sunset. It's a very low pitch but his leather shoes tend to slide on the grit and the wind is pretty strong. At the top he finds a spot where he can get his back against the chimney. He wishes he had the camera. It's as if he'd ascended to an altogether different realm–a radical shift of reference at this moment on top of his house like having emerged from forest onto a continental ridge, a great divide. Like one of those grand, romantic nineteenth-century landscape paintings–one or two human figures in the distance just for scale, perched above some incredible vastness incredibly illuminated, brought to the very edge of it. Here the whole neighborhood at ground level is in shadow while the rooftops are radiant, especially to the southwest, most of them old white roofs like his, glowing in the sunset like the reflective paint on highway signs, like patches of snow, the scattered clouds violet to orange to red at the horizon and the rooftops like a mirror, a progression of pink toward rose nearly merging with the sunset, the angles of those distant roofs exactly right, apparently, to catch the color and transmit it. He can feel it on his face like standing by a bright window in a cold house. He feels suspended as if having found neutral buoyancy at this level, the top of the roof, the edge of comfort and the ordinary world. That's why the light is so strange, he thinks; why there's such a glow. It's a limit. Right up here at the peak of the roof there's an interface, reflective, like that between water and air or even air and space, he imagines; detectable when the light is right, when light gathers and streams along the boundary for a moment.

He pulls himself up and edges along the chimney to the opposite side where the antenna is anchored. The mast isn't broken; it's just the top strap, loosened over the years and finally sawn through by the corner of the brick. He gives the mast a couple of wraps with the tape then a couple of twists around an odd masonry bolt to hold it up while he works his way around the chimney. One circuit is all he gets, so he ties it off at the bolt. The sun is down and the glow is following it. Going over the edge, still radiant. Still worth a picture. It must be out over the prairie. He thinks of the old farmhouse bathed in light. Maybe at the very edge of the western horizon, the intense light, the brilliance there is the reflection of the prairie–sand and dry grass at just the right angle like the white roofs a moment ago. A continuum. He thinks of that word–how sophisticated to insert it into the camera, into ordinary experience as if otherwise something had been missed. Or maybe the radiance is coming from farther away, beaming over the thin edge of the world like light through the edge of a glass, like a mirage, exotic, orange, pink light from other lands, snowy peaks. He's standing by the chimney holding onto the antenna. There's a soft whistling now that it's up. He thinks he can feel it slightly. A vibration. The wind through the tubing, blowing along the open ends like reed pipes. The sound of television waves. Electromagnetic signals passing by. Channel 17. How, he wonders, do TV transmissions know when to stop; which antenna configuration is best? Are they beckoned? Do they know, in some way, which is correct, just the right length of rod to admit them congenially like insects to a flower? He can understand, perhaps, how an element might be too short. But too long? Why should that be a problem? Just take what you need.

The whistling doesn't coincide with the buzzing of the weather stripping; the buzzing comes after. First a sound like breathing from the antenna then the buzz from below–low and resonant like a signal received and amplified. He's getting cold. The evening light is almost entirely concentrated along the horizon now. The rooftops are still illuminated but there's no warmth–they really do look like patches of snow. Below the roofs it's so dark he can't sense depth at all. It's as if the houses had vanished leaving just dark earth and snow, glacial fragments like an ice-age prairie–what it might have been, in fact, thousands of years before. There's a strong gust and one of those conchlike blasts, buzzing into a rattle then breaking to a higher note and holding it for a long time. He can feel a vibration in the antenna but all he can hear is that long note–unlocatable if he hadn't already known what made it–rising, it seems, from the cold prairie like an animal call of some kind. Something one might have heard actually long ago: animals like those on TV, on that Himalayan ridge, whatever they were, so still and primitive-looking. Or the unidentifiable dead animal by the curb. What sort of sound would it have made? Thinking of it, he can almost smell it. He thought it had a smell. Not decay but an animal smell. He feels terribly uneasy. He really wants to get down but it's hard to let go of the chimney. The light is practically gone–only a thin bright line at the horizon–and the clouds as well, leaving the sky so clean it's already almost black, about to produce stars. He doesn't want to be up here when the stars come out. He feels he's allowed himself to get caught outside after curfew or something, caught outside some boundary. Still he hesitates to move as if it were too late at this point and his best hope were concealment. He knows it's crazy but he doesn't move. His eyes have adjusted now to the reduced light and he can see the ground. The streetlight at the corner has started its preliminary glow, a greenish circle of pavement beginning to appear. He hates that. He doesn't want to look at the softly illuminated circle in the street. He simply doesn't want to consider it at all, being up here on the roof having to anticipate something walking into that circle of light. It doesn't matter what. He's got his ear against the antenna pole and he can hear the hollow whistling even as the wind dies down a bit. A strange, dreamy noise like a seashell makes. He thinks of the quiet; of the lost-pet notices. He remembers once at the seashore finding himself chest-deep in the surf surrounded by small leaping fish all headed the same direction. There must have been hundreds of them, a number of different kinds, some very colorful. He was delighted until he realized something must be pursuing them. And then he couldn't move. He was afraid he'd attract whatever it was; so all he could do was stand there waiting for the fish to go by and then slowly walk from the deep water, like in a dream, back to the beach.

Right now the wind has slacked off completely. It's so quiet. He can see house lights but it's so quiet it's as if he were the only one. No one else left. No cars, no voices. No movement in the houses–they could be empty for all he knows. He can't help looking down at the pavement under the streetlight–a section of curb, a patch of pale grass. If he could make himself stay here long enough something might show up. He might find something out and his uneasiness would be explained, a reason for it discovered from this viewpoint, from right up here on top of the roof removed from the world just enough to see something otherwise obscure or untranslatable as when children imagine that by sneaking a look at a familiar object in the night–suddenly switching on the light at some forbidden hour–they might discover a terrible secret. But he doesn't want to do that. The stars are out and he wants to go back down. Slowly and quietly. How odd and difficult it was trying to explain to his wife about the fish. "What kind of fish," she asked. "How big were they," she kept wanting to know as if that were the point. It was hard for him to express, somehow, the obliqueness of the threat. What felt like the inevitability, perhaps. Unspecified, it became generalized and permanent. He retained a fear of the ocean after that. Such a small event. If he had actually seen something it would have been all right; his fear would have collapsed around it and it wouldn't have been a problem.

He can see other streetlights farther down–one at the end of the next block and another beyond that, just a glow through the trees. Slowly, quietly as he can he disengages himself. He gets down on his hands and knees then rolls over into a squat, trying to keep his shoes from scraping too much against the shingles as he makes his way down. He recalls how his wife looked as he waded toward the beach in slow motion, how her face looked like the center of a flower in the colorful shade of the big umbrella, such peace and quiet, smiling at him with her eyes half closed.

5

When his wife was alive Mr. Delabano liked to read in bed at night. How curious that's changed, he thinks. How quickly he goes to sleep now, unable to read more than a sentence or two before drifting off. It's as if her presence, asleep on the window side, her breathing, kept him afloat for a while. Right now it's quiet. No wind at all and a clear sky. The moon is up. It must be almost full–he can see it shining on the curtains even with his bedside lamp on. He pulls another pillow behind him to prop himself up a little more. It's a heavy book, not the sort to read in bed but he's determined to have a look at it in spite of the hour, afraid he'll have to purchase it, the cover is so badly torn and stained from nearly two months in his car jammed under the front seat adjustment mechanism. The paperback garden manual, of course, is undamaged; this one looks like real leather. Probably shouldn't even have been on the checkout shelf. Green leather with the emblem gold-stamped on the cover. A rarity no doubt; misshelved, priceless. *Amazonian Biotoxins.* He wonders why, climbing down from the roof, it should have occurred to him after so long, the thought of it holding him still for a moment in the kitchen in the dark, sending him looking until after midnight. Outside his window the abelia rustles softly–a residual breeze. The approach of morning. He doesn't want to know what time it is. He turns back to the front of the book. There's a sepia-colored photograph–turn-of-the-century or thereabouts he guesses–of a man in a forest clearing in bright sunlight holding a large white hat and standing beside a peculiar-looking plant somewhat taller than he is, from the center of which emerges a short, thick stalk with a big thistlelike flower or fruit on top. It's the plant on the cover, in the emblem where, schematized and with nothing to indicate scale, it looks more like the ones he remembers from the newspaper ad. The same symmetrical, spiky structure at the base anyway; not the flower or whatever it is. "Cupidia eberhardi," reads the caption in an ornamental cursive, "a living fossil whose sap tribesmen value both as arrow poison and aphrodisiac." In the background, standing, barely visible against the dark wall of trees, are the tribesmen. Bowl-cut hair like helmets, looking straight ahead at the back of the bearded man, Mr. Eberhard perhaps, buttoned up in a white suit, immaculate and vulnerable, it seems, so near the seat of passion. On the facing page, centered and insulated from the photograph by a glassine tissue, is an explanation: "Facsimile of the frontispiece to the 1911 edition of *The Golden·Path* and the only photograph of Dr. Eberhard's discovery."

How about that, he thinks. Dr. Eberhard in fact. He looks at the emblem on the cover again, trying to read the tiny print in the circle around the plant. "N. M. Eberhard Pharmacognostic Foundation." "Pharmacognostic"–he tries to pronounce it, an awkward word. It sounds made up. He flips through the book looking for other photographs. Mostly there are maps or line drawings and the few scattered photographic plates aren't very interesting at first glance–no old sepia-colored ones like the frontispiece. What there are look like discards from someone's vacation album. Black-and-white, accidental-looking shots of bushes or thicket, stands of trees. A few show dirt roads through the forest or brush without recognizable subject matter unless it were dirt roads or the brush and weeds that grow along them. These look to him altogether arbitrary–they could have been taken almost anywhere it seems, somebody's unpaved alley–yet they are so specifically captioned ("Dynastes satanas"; "Golofa pelagon, 1200 m") as to suggest any sufficiently expert or keen-eyed person might pick out the essentials like an Indian guide. These are the pictures he keeps flipping back to, looking for something to explain them. The Latin names don't sound like plants somehow. They sound too heavy. Even threatening. But maybe they are. "Devil weed" or something like that; a patch of it photographed at a respectful distance on a dirt road in South America. Or maybe it is an animal–there could be tracks not clearly visible in the photograph. A poor reproduction. But there should be a close-up of a print or a bush or whatever. Something to let you know it's intended, not really arbitrary; that there is something there and what it looks like. Otherwise it seems like one of those children's games in the backs of comic books teasing you to find the hidden monkeys. Nor is the text immediately helpful. He flips to another photograph–this one through dense forest, a canopy of trees but, still, a dirt road with nothing on it, a fringe of weeds. He turns to the front of the book. There's the emblem again on the title page–Occasional Papers Number One; The N. M. Eberhard Foundation; Buffalo, N.Y.; 1961. Then back to the dirt road through the forest. He imagines the photographer standing there. A fairly long exposure. A tripod probably. He closes his eyes and leans back. The abelia is brushing the window again. It might be getting close to morning. He glances at the curtain. It's still dark but there's no moonlight now. He should be asleep. He looks at the book on the white sheet beside him. So intensely green it seems likely to cause a stain. He looks at his fingers then picks it up again turning to the photograph of Dr. Eberhard, somewhat overexposed in his white suit in the forest. Looking at the photograph, he experiences a sort of after-image green, the color of the binding, which tends to invest the jungle behind the white suit. He really must be tired, ready to drift off surely. He turns to the first page of text. This will do it, he thinks. "Paths of Resistance." It's the preface. He thumbs past the first few pages:

> . . . that organisms tend to "recline" into cooperative systems and that, in the broadest sense, toxins may be understood to function much as fragrances, to map the lines of interdependence, mark the seams of contact among the principal elements Professor Eberhard called biothemes.
>
> Shortly before the final Brazil expedition, in the Epilogue to *The Golden Path,* he wrote, "I return to the tortoise—the ancient Hindu cosmological foundation whose cobbled back supports the world, the segments of whose great carapace I feel are descriptive of the real, transtaxonomic structures of life which are essentially enduring and within and even between which, species and genera flow and ebb, express themselves and withdraw as guests in a house or wind across a pond."

There may be the faintest gray light beyond the curtains. Ambiguous, no color in it. He reaches over and turns off the lamp. Now it's definite. It must be five-thirty or six. It makes him almost dizzy to have to think of the world spinning without interruption, the light coming back around the other side. He has no sense of a new day. It's like the same one returning. In a minute there will be shadows on the curtains. The abelia bush and the ivy. Like an accidental photograph. He's watching for it, waiting for it to develop. The first indication. There. He can see the shadows when they move slightly; the feathery branches, no depth and silent like the neighborhood. He listens for something–birds, whatever–like trying to visualize the world beyond the shadows. There's nothing; white curtains; but he imagines something anyway. He's not at all sleepy. He's watching the curtains and listening, sitting up, still holding the book against his chest. The shadows are quite distinct now. English ivy at the top and the abelia to the left and at bottom waving a little, shifting the pattern as elements drift across each other and toward the window briefly into focus, leaves and tiny blossoms. The room feels cold. And there's a smell again or he's imagining it–something in the house or the memory of the dead animal. A confused memory. There's no smell. He has to be tired and his back hurts from sitting straight up, hugging the book and watching the window. The leaves are fluttering, swaying every now and then. The nearest ones make the sharpest shadows. The paler, hazier shapes are farther away–fainter and more blurred the farther away they are until it's like smoke in the background, waves, just barely there like a mist. It can't be heat and there are no trees that way. It looks like steam. He imagines rain forest. A leafy canopy. He can hear light rain or water dripping if he's perfectly still. Pit pat on fallen leaves or dirt. It's not a familiar sound, not the usual sound of rain. It makes him think something's wrong, a broken line or a clogged window unit overflowing but he doesn't move. It's too cold for air-conditioners. He puts the book down and pulls up the covers. All the way up to his face, holding them there with his hands underneath. Like a child he thinks; and he thinks of the little girl next door. It's hard to imagine his neighbor's house so close. The shadows are like jungle, denser as the curtains brighten. There's too much for the little space between houses. The hollow, leafy drip and the mist or whatever it is–his room's light glows and fades with it, darkens when the swirls collect. He's caught in it. Like someone hypnotized in front of the television; captured; helplessly exposed to whatever might come along.

Something leans into view periodically in the intermediate distance between the precise shadows of the abelia branches and the uncertain, hazy background–solid and rather pointed like an elbow as if someone were standing there next to the window with his hands on his hips, shifting his weight from time to time. Its movements don't coincide with the waving of the foliage. It's part of something heavier off to the right out of view. Still it moves a little, enters and withdraws from the picture with its own rhythm like a person or an animal. It's not someone's elbow. It twitches every now and then. Purposefully, it seems. Little jerks. Twice it seems to approach the window and its shadow darkens briefly, still only barely intruding but darker, almost touching, brushing aside the branches perhaps; he can't tell. Then its whole configuration changes. It appears to shift around, its main bulk visible now from the right, very hazy, farther away than the rest of it and coming around behind as, he imagines, it redirects itself toward him, the nearest part–the part like an elbow, pointed, what he thinks of as the nose–quite near and black, pressing the window he thinks, and pausing like that.

He can hear water dripping very clearly, more slowly than before but very distinctly. Pit, pat–a slight echo. There's definitely a smell. If his wife were here he could reach over and touch her and say, "What's that?" He could say, "Open the curtains and see what that is." And it wouldn't be much–construction or something next door, loose trash. There's a sort of thump from the window and the arrangement shifts slightly–the "nose" moves up a bit, then a twitch to the right and now there's another part of it–sharp, very pointed, not like an elbow. More like an ear, he thinks. Some kind of ear. He puts out his left hand for his glasses on the nightstand but strikes the lampshade which rattles with a springy sound and won't stop, it seems, buzzing and rattling as, suddenly, the smell becomes overwhelming. He throws off the covers, flinging himself around in the bed at the threat of it, what instantly he feels is the threat–the rattling and the smell. It's like when the cicada went off under his bed that night. The lamp is still buzzing. He has an image of cicadas again–like the rattling, swirling shapes beyond the frosted bathroom window. He's on his hands and knees on the bed, facing the curtains and unable to determine what's going on. The unpleasant shape that was there before is gone but now it's very confusing–the mist or steam is much denser, really whipping around and the foliage is flapping violently. He can hear it now as the lampshade settles down–the abelia shaking and batting the window and a sound like blowing rain spattering across the glass and then onto the siding under the eaves, a couple of times against the glass again and then up under the eaves and against the shingles, it sounds like, as if directed. As if by a fire hose.

He reaches over to the curtains and lifts them from the bottom, dazzled at first by the flash of sunlight. It is steam. It looks like steam. Clouds of it drifting down from his neighbor's house, rolling off his neighbor's roof and sweeping into the gap between their houses as if drawn by a wind, sucked in by the spray. Where is that coming from? Someone's shooting water onto his roof, playing it back and forth and under the eaves again. He jerks away as the water hits the glass. Now it's stopped. He listens. Or it's spraying his neighbor's house. He gets his glasses then pulls the curtains all the way open. The air is still brilliant with spray but the steam's not as thick and he can see Mike Getz with his back against the cyclone fence in the space between the houses adjusting his nozzle and directing the stream onto his own roof. He's got it down to a narrow jet, arcing it high up onto his roof, back and forth in a careful pattern, wetting it down thoroughly. The water is racing off the cedar shingles and overflowing the gutter at the near corner, pouring onto a blue plastic tarp with a sound like rain on a tent, now slacking off gradually as Mike Getz makes his way around to the front. The loud patter reduces to a dribble, then a steady drip. Pit pat like drizzle off leaves onto leafy ground. Coils of stiff plastic hose jerk past through the gate, an occasional wave of mist from the front then it seems to be over. The smell is gone as well.

Mr. Delabano stays at the window for a moment gazing at the plain brick wall–simple red bricks all the same color, white mortar, a trim green boxwood hedge. Then he reaches up to find where the curtain rod is attached to the brackets above the window, locates the little set screws that hold it in place and lifts it clear, sliding off the curtains and folding them carefully before placing them in the empty bottom drawer of his dresser.

6

Just like a pile of kindling on top of your house waiting for a match," says Mike Getz, standing on Mr. Delabano's front porch holding in one hand a scorched cedar shingle and the hand of a little girl in the other. She's about five years old, short blond hair. The younger one.

"Anyway, you've got composition but I didn't want to take a chance; there were a lot of sparks flying around there for a while. A whole lot of sparks weren't there, Janie," he looks down at the little girl, disengages his hand and gives her a pat on the shoulder as she puts both arms around his leg, half hiding behind him but continuing to regard Mr. Delabano with one eye, "and a few of them were blowing your direction so I figured I'd better give you a squirt as well, especially on that side. Hope I didn't wake you up or scare you to death."

"Oh no, I was awake," says Mr. Delabano, watching the little girl who has retreated even farther behind her father's leg, practically concealed except for her arms and, occasionally, an eye. There's a silence. Both men are looking down at the child who is entirely parasitic now, completely attached and nearly invisible from the front.

"Janie," says Mike Getz gently, "this is Mr. Delabano." Instantly the small arms constrict. "Janie's the one who decided we needed to have a fire in the fireplace this morning." Mike Getz is still looking down at his daughter, a constrained smile. "About four o'clock in the morning, wasn't it, Janie?" He laughs and gives her another pat then looks up at Mr. Delabano, "We never used it, not once all year–all our fires are on the grill; I had no idea they could do that; it was dirty. Do you use yours?"

"Not this year," says Mr. Delabano, looking back down, trying to catch Janie's eye, "not yet this year; I haven't bought any firewood." And immediately he realizes his mistake.

Janie isn't inclined to detach herself even when it's awkward. Backing Mr. Delabano's overloaded garden cart with one hand through the narrow side gate, Mike Getz has to guide her through with the other, keeping her feet clear of the wheels and out from under his own. It's a fairly demanding operation yet one to which, Mr. Delabano senses, he is not invited to contribute. They seem to have an arrangement. Sometimes she places a stick on the pile but always with the left hand, hanging onto her father with the other and leaving him only his right to swing or roll the larger logs onto the stack as best he can. It doesn't really amount to very much–a load and a half, not enough to constitute a significant eyesore stacked next to the glass door in the corner of the patio. Maybe he'll use it. He's getting pretty cold standing around in his robe and slippers. To the north it looks like a new line of clouds coming in. One front after another.

Janie has her father in a headlock now, holding him down with her arms around his neck. It's a communication. He's taking the opportunity to stack logs with both hands but he's listening to her. She's whispering and he nods. Mr. Delabano walks out into the yard trying to keep warm until he can go back inside. The clouds are really moving across. Soon, he thinks, the grass will stop growing but not yet. It's pretty shaggy right now in fact. There's grass in the rose beds too. They look neglected. Only a few late blooms and not very spectacular. From here, by the chain-link fence between his house and Mike's, he can see through to the front past his bedroom window and the boxwood hedge–lawn and sidewalk then a narrow section of street. Someone is pushing an old-fashioned reel mower; he can't see it but he can hear the gentle scissoring noise passing between the houses like a breeze. It reassures him. He closes his eyes for a minute and listens to it, leaning against the fence. If it weren't so cold he might fall asleep like this. It's the proper sound of a neighborhood. It's like the smell of roses.

He opens his eyes and there's Mike Getz with his daughter standing at the edge of the patio waiting for him to revive apparently. They're not ready to leave. There's something else.

"Maybe we ought to check out your fireplace just in case," calls Mike Getz, taking a step toward the back door as Mr. Delabano approaches. "This wood's real dry; you don't want to burn more than a couple at a time until you get some green. If you've got a flashlight I'll stick my head up in there for you."

"No, thanks very much," says Mr. Delabano, sliding the glass door open about a foot, "I'm sure it's fine; I'm sure it's all right but thanks for the wood; that was a lot of trouble; I'm sorry about your roof." The clouds have moved across the sun and Mr. Delabano pauses in the grayness, looking down at the little girl, in full view now, facing him and tugging on her father's arm. For a moment Mike Getz seems not to notice; then he reaches down and picks up his daughter and smiles at Mr. Delabano. "Janie wants to smell your flowers," he says. "She wanted me to ask."

"Oh, yes," says Mr. Delabano.

"The big blue ones," says Mike Getz, "or purple; whatever they are."

Mr. Delabano slides the door shut behind him. "Do you like flowers, Janie," he asks, vastly surprised at himself; imagining himself through her eyes for an instant and appalled for some reason.

"No," she seems to whisper or maybe only moves her lips.

"Oh yeah," says Mike, "she and her sister even planted a flower garden this spring; they just sort of forgot to water it didn't you, Janie." Her head is turned away now–buried in her father's chest. "You've got to give them water if you want them to grow. Isn't that right, Mr. Delabano."

"That's right," says Mr. Delabano after a second. He's looking around for his pruners but settles for a pair of grass shears on the brick sill under the kitchen window. "Here," he says softly, walking over to the antique rose. "Here's a decent one; one good one." He clips a small apricot-colored bud, blows it open a bit and pinches off the thorns. "Here's a nice one," he says returning with it, holding it toward the little girl. "It has a very good smell. It's very old. It smells like an old garden." She turns her head slightly and he hands it to her.

"What do you say, Janie?" asks her father. "Can you say thank you?" But Janie has nothing to say. She wants back down, twisting to get free and losing one untied pink sneaker which her father kneels to retrieve. The lawnmower has stopped, Mr. Delabano notices; it's quiet now. He wishes it had continued and wonders whose it was. Goodness he's tired. He wants to sit down but then he might not want to get up and it's cold and he needs to go inside.

He slides open the glass door again but no one's paying attention. Mike is tying Janie's shoe while she appears to have fastened on the big blue flower by the fence. She's trying to squirm around to look at it which makes it difficult for Mike to get the shoe tied. He keeps having to shift his position, finally noticing Mr. Delabano by the open door and giving him an apologetic smile. "There," says Mike, standing up, free for the moment to put both hands in his pockets and approach Mr. Delabano with a sad shake of his head: "It has been one hell of a morning; I hope you didn't hear any of it."

"The water?" says Mr. Delabano.

"No, before that–Janie. I guess you didn't; that's good, anyway the pyrotechnics were bad enough. Boy it's getting chilly." He looks at the sky, flat gray now all the way to the horizon. "I didn't mean to keep you out here; I'm sorry. She just wanted to have a look at one of those big flowers."

Mr. Delabano is watching her. She's standing at the edge of the patio looking up at the blue flower, simply standing there and looking at it.

"Janie's been having a real hard time lately and we're doing just about anything we can . . ."

Mr. Delabano's face must show concern because Mike turns around. She's still looking at the flower but her body seems very stiff, her arms straight down and tight against her. She's locking and unlocking her knees. Such a strange, jerky little movement. So regular it looks involuntary.

"Oh, jeez," says Mike rushing over and kneeling in front of her, holding her carefully by the shoulders. "Come on Janie; come on let's go." Now there's a faint gasping noise. Mr. Delabano takes a couple of steps back through the open door as it escalates–almost an animal sound. He feels the warm air passing around him as it pours out the door but he doesn't close it. Janie is resisting being picked up, lifting her arms straight over her head and slipping out of her father's grasp, collapsing on the concrete and crying; only crying now. The other sound has stopped and so has the jerky movement. For a minute Mike stands there just watching, his hands at his side, looking as though he were witnessing her misery from a great distance.

Mr. Delabano is stunned by the bleakness of it. The little girl crying in his garden. The bleakness of the garden itself, the rose bushes like twigs, sticks in the ground, and the perfunctory, desperate-looking chain-link fence. Nothing has seemed as threatening as this. Janie is crying more quietly now as if she were, in fact, in the distance, on the prairie abandoned. He hardly notices when Mike picks her up and takes her away. He can hear her, it seems, for quite a while. The faint sound carries as if no structures intervened, as if it came to him across a field.

He waits until finally it dies away; then he steps outside again, sliding the door shut behind him. For a moment he stands on the patio looking at the backyard trying to understand the shift, the devaluation of everything. Even imagining it all trimmed and tidied up–removing his glasses to blur away the neglect–doesn't help; makes it worse in fact. There's nothing of consequence. It's as if a dam or some sort of membrane had burst, let everything out; all the particulars, cultivated affections, right out through the chain-link fence.

How permeable and hopeless it looks. Every yard running into every other, finding the same level. Wire fences like fish traps.

A cold spatter of rain sends him back inside; into the living room to look out to the north through the big picture window which seems much bigger with the curtains down. A few drops hit the glass–the edge of a shower, nothing ominous. Just gray sky. He transfers the heavy, folded curtains from the couch to a chair and collapses on the couch, pulling his feet up, propping a couple of brocade pillows under him and gazing out the window, allowing himself to feel inert, suspended between the hum of the furnace and the intermittent patter of rain against the glass.

7

Mr. Delabano wakes up because his stomach hurts. It's hunger and a little heartburn. He sits up in the dark, manages a belch and feels somewhat better. He's completely disoriented however; overloaded with contradictory notions of his whereabouts. He can see the streetlight, the one at the corner near his house but it's a long time before he can understand why. He just sits and stares at it for a while waiting for the facts of his situation to resolve and finally they do but he's disturbed. Mostly by the light–the glow on the pavement and the light itself. And he hesitates to move. He knows he's in the front room on the couch but he feels terrifically precarious as if he were on the roof again; as if, in a dream, he had awakened on the roof and any movement might send him tumbling or initiate some other disaster. Attract something terrible.

His nose is stopped up and starting to run but he doesn't even want to raise his hand. The light is so strange. It has a pinkish or an amber tint. And there's a shimmer to it–even to the air above the illuminated street as if the concrete were steaming.

He stands up and waits for his right foot, which has gone to sleep, to stop tingling, takes a Kleenex from his robe pocket, wipes his glasses, then his nose. The light seems to fluctuate, ripple across his eyes when he moves. He thinks at first it's standing up too fast or he's catching the flu–he's cold and he wishes the furnace would come on. He moves his head a little left and right and the light flickers–a visual analogue to the sensation in his foot. His optical nerve or the world has gone to sleep. He wants to adjust the window like a TV set.

He steps around the coffee table, limps over to the window. There's something on the glass. Condensation or something; dust in the air, precipitating out, shifting the light toward red and fogging the window just enough to receive a sort of projected ripple of leaves or grass from somewhere. Inexplicably he has a feeling of disaster unattended; something leaking or left open: burst water pipes, refrigerator door. It makes no sense; there's no problem; it's just that feeling seeking a place to attach and, finding none, expanding. He thinks of the abandoned farmhouse beyond the shopping center, out there by itself on the pale dirt and dry, yellow grass. He finds the thermostat on the wall by the door, shoves it all the way over listening for the delayed thump of the gas igniting. Then he makes his way to the bedroom in the dark, gets his camera from the top of the dresser. There should be a time-exposure setting–a little *B* or *T* on the film speed selector. He snaps off the case and returns to the living room, taking off his glasses and standing by the window to see the numbers on the dial.

He pulls the sofa away from the wall and rests the camera on the back of it, crouching down behind, trying to find a comfortable way to keep his eye at the right level without cramping his foot. The window is so much larger than the field of view it feels like he's outside peering through the range finder. Or the outside has leaked in–a flickering across the screen like blades of grass as if he were crouching in a blind and waiting for something. It's an uncomfortable thought, bringing with it the feeling of precariousness once more, delicate balance. He's breathing as quietly as he can through his mouth, trying to focus but finding it difficult; the ripply light frustrates the little split-image focuser. It's like looking through some sort of infrared device. A CAT scan of the neighborhood. What might not become visible under such scrutiny? Show up in the shadows like a spot on the X ray–a case for not looking for what you don't want to find: "Oh, it's been there for years more than likely, just never caught it." He remembers white walls and fluorescent lighting and the darkness of the X-ray film like looking out a window at night.

He rotates the focus to infinity–surely the streetlight is far enough away–and holds his breath. He'll just guess for the first one. He won't even count; just hold the button down and don't breathe for a few seconds, but he counts in his head anyway. One. Two. There's a sound and he stops. A thump like the furnace coming on but softer and farther away. He advances the film and braces himself again. This time a long one to make sure. Three. Four. Five. It's like trying to force it, squeeze something into visibility, make it come out and it seems the longer he holds the button down the more difficult and uncertain it is, the greater the risk, the rosier and more luminous the image seems to become–saturating his eye until it really does look like some specialized portion of the spectrum, a glow of possibilities. There's a flash of bright light and he almost drops the camera, barely catching it against his chest and holding it there with both hands for a minute waiting for his dazzled right eye to adjust. Then the sound again but more of a rumble. Thunder. And then another flash, prolonged like a flare, crackling across the sky to the north and finishing in a great clap and roll as the first heavy drops hit the window.

The light in the kitchen is too bright. Too cool and brilliant at first. It takes several minutes to recalibrate or whatever; for the light to become familiar again and for him to feel comfortable so conspicuously illuminated in the rainy darkness at five-thirty in the morning, setting out the breakfast table–the blue-rimmed white bowls, a small one for sugar and a big one for the shredded wheat; two spoons and a glass and a carton of milk. No paper though. It's raining pretty hard and he's not sure it's come; he can't tell if it's out there on the driveway getting soaked or not. He listens for it through the rain and now and then takes a look out the picture window. Everything now looks perfectly normal. The pale greenish glow of the streetlight and the flat shine of the street.

It's an electrical storm. More or less steady rumbling and booming all around, once or twice causing the kitchen lights to flicker and the refrigerator to skip a beat. He pours milk into the bowl first to keep it from splashing, takes a seat and opens the green book to his mark. He's got the box of little shredded wheat biscuits ready to pour when the lights flicker again and go out for a couple of seconds, catching him there holding the box of shredded wheat and watching, in the darkness, the reflection of the lightning in the milk.

8

"Ascending the Rio Negro above Manáos, a great unraveling takes place. Water and earth relax and withdraw from their customary relationships, unwind from each other, exchange properties and form, losing all constraints in the complex, horizon-wide effluence that seems to emerge from some primary impulse less chaotic than experimental.

"Here forested islands take on the quality of streams, meander and flow, separate and diverge between watery banks whose red-stained, black stillness stiffens into onyx or, at sunset, deep gold. For a moment, in the evening light, these lakes and pools are burnished to solidity, become the more stable element resisting the jungly torrent, the rushing forest, broccoli-thick, braids and rivers of it overflowing, like ink onto glass, some unimaginable burden, some dark, essential reservoir. Here traditional definitions break down as if in the presence of a superior axiom whose permutations are yet undecided, unresolved into the fixed components of the world. And here (although among us there were those whose pragmatic character of mind seemed to have innoculated them against the experience) there arose, like unhealthy vapors, a sort of dizziness of the spirit, the uncertainty of the outer world having spread to the inner, rendering most of us–and Harkness expecially–immobile and silent at our little island outpost in the rain for three days waiting for supplies to arrive in increments as incrementally we arrived, ourselves, at a condition of stasis no doubt compensatory for the inner vertigo, the sense of purpose lost in the blackwater maze past which our hopes refused to navigate.

"Like children at a game of adventure stopped short by darkness or curfew, we seemed to confront a point of suspension, a limit beyond which our activities ceased to apply and from which, to our enquiries, no response might be anticipated; all, I must say, the more bewildering inasmuch as we were none of us inexperienced and long since had crossed the psychological threshold, the moment of civilized dislocation upon insertion into the primitive wherefor my wakeful night upon the directionless waters of the Purus years before. But here in relatively comfortable circumstances, no more than a hundred miles upstream of a bustling, if isolated, metropolis of fifty thousand, we had foundered in a way, come upon a tear in the fabric of our suppositions which, absent any physical danger or other insurmountable difficulty, one might think reducible to a matter of aesthetics; and, to be sure, no similar discomfort was to be observed among the aboriginals who, innocent of aesthetics in all but the most rudimentary sense, went happily and stolidly about their business judging our behavior no more mysterious than usual. Aesthetics, then. Broadened and stretched perhaps by the long passage up the Amazon; preconditioned, as it were, to engage the whole geographical canvas and recognize its terms well enough to respond to what seemed a vision of their disintegration; aesthetics as a sort of civilized superstition, rendering us sensitive and vulnerable, enthralling our spirits as surely as any tribesman's under the influence of a spell.

"It was not, of course, that the labyrinth was unnavigable; our pilot knew the way somehow–a combination of instinct and, I suspected, a lack of peripheral vision for I was told the solution might change from year to year and even month to month in the rainy season as sandbanks shifted and the streams changed course. Imagination, surely, would be disastrous. What was needed was the mind of a laboratory animal trained in the pursuit of immediate possibilities, incapable of curiosity or calculated risk, immune to the beguilement, the drawing away of one's attention and purpose, their dispersion, as if onto a blotter, along every tangled channel and stream, entrained in the general mingling of substances.

"Amazonia, I had come to believe, could be understood as an essence which, diluted, might yield all the natural properties of the world and within the concentration of whose center one might find these clarified, distinctions and relationships made luminous and precise as graphite compressed into diamond. Yet here at the approaches to the center itself, the unexplored regions between the Negro and the Yapura, one sensed an opacity, a mixing of the colors of the world into black to which the colorless, anaesthetic character of the natives seemed responsive–an evolutionary benefit without which we despaired. For it was despair that seemed to gather each morning as the February rains erupted from a sky dense as forest and merged with the earth along the up-river horizon in such a confusion of elements, such rich, ambivalent interchange of fluvial and meteorological substance, one might not determine the direction of flow, doubted one's habitual notion of rain as too refined, too decorous a segregation of the constituent phenomena inapplicable here at such energies and densities where forces converged shed of all polite categories, where no calculus might penetrate much less our poor surmise.

"When at last we set out aboard the little wood-burning steamer, I was relieved to secure for Harkness and myself a tiny cabin on the upper deck whose only window was provided with a curtain and whose situation directly above the engine room admitted a resonant and continuous surging of mechanical noise sufficient to insulate our senses altogether from the circumstances of our passage. Ironically, in this din we found it possible to recompose our thoughts as both storms and silence were equally drowned out leaving us, except for meals which were taken on the foredeck, an almost womblike space wherein to recover a sense of our mission as gradually we convinced ourselves that our recent indisposition was less psychic than malarial. Nevertheless, for the three days it took to reach Moura, I preferred to keep the little curtain closed especially in the evenings when clouds tended to dissipate and the rosy light of sunset turned the forest black and the streams pink-gold and the feeling returned of some primeval ambiguity.

"Perhaps it was an antidote to ambiguity that I sought, merely a therapeutic exercise which engaged my thoughts as we lurched and chugged through the darkness modulated by the strange harmonics of engine noise combined with the snoring of Harkness who, by now, seemed more at ease than I. Or perhaps it was a subconscious response to this biomechanical melody whereby, having locked myself away from the very center and source of fecundity and growth, I began to conceive a notion of the regimes of life entirely transcending, as I imagined, the functional taxonomies and phylogenies of Darwin and Wallace no less than the divine heirarchies of the Middle Ages. To the sound of engines and Harkness sleeping, quarantined from the incomprehensible vitality around me, my intuition seemed altogether disengaged, wildly receptive to forms of evidence more compelling for their poetry than their logic. I fastened, especially, upon the image of my boy, Baltasar, the day previous after he stepped on a tucandera ant–a solitary glossy black creature an inch and a half long whose sting, though rarely fatal, brings hours of misery. This one had probably come aboard with the last load of wood and I recalled the look on Baltasar's face after the initial yelp of surprise and pain, the look of a child discovered in some transgression, submitting to the consequences as if he and not the ant were the interloper, as if the ant were no more than a passive agent, a marker for some treacherous and complex membrane between incompatible modalities or themes. It seemed, in fact, to present an allegory–powerfully descriptive in a way I had yet fully to understand.

"At some point I emerged to the realization that the engines had become quiet. Harkness was peaceful and I could hear the chirping and drumming of thousands of frogs. I extinguished my lamp and opened the curtain, thinking we must be approaching the little port of Moura, for I could see lights ahead and, at first, I thought a celebration must be underway because of the impression I had of torches or lanterns. A procession, I thought; thousands of lights flickering among the trees in tiers and ranks as if descending from a height some distance beyond the riverbank. Then, as my eyes adjusted, the sense of order and distance vanished and, despite my efforts, I could not reclaim it nor impose any reasonable interpretation whatever upon the phenomenon into the midst of which by now we had drifted.

"With some difficulty I managed to lower the window part way, in the process waking Harkness who, without a word, joined me at the little opening presenting our astonished faces to the moist darkness, the sounds of frogs and the rich, strangely comforting odors from the animal pens below–which latter combined with the glittering arboreal display to synthesize, no doubt by association with traditions of the Nativity, a sensation of the spiritual more powerful for its removal from traditional settings.

"There was no question that the engines were stopped–far from any port, in midstream silent as a log except for the gentle dripping of the stern-paddle and the shifting about of the cattle below us. 'Lampyrids,' whispered Harkness; 'Photinus probably.' And with that I felt adrift, severed from any residual suspicions of human agency, overwhelmed by the accident of our presence and the isolation of what we witnessed, the starry twinkling for hundreds of yards, perhaps a mile, along the bank as if some celestial marvel had descended to complete the primordial mixture.

"The extent to which the jungle beyond the riverbank was involved I could not tell except to observe a sort of rippling glow that seemed to issue from regions further in. And, in fact, there appeared to be an undulatory quality to the whole display, reminding me of reports I'd heard from time to time of coincident behavior among Asian fireflies–fantastic demonstrations but supposedly limited to a few densely illuminated mangroves at most and, in any case, nearly perfectly synchronized if the stories were to be believed. This, on the other hand, was evanescent; a tissue of light developing gradually out of the darkness, the constituent flashing, golden points appearing to float independently among the trees while nevertheless responding to one another or, sequentially, to some exterior stimulus thereby creating an impression of waves or currents not unlike, I imagined, the effect of a breeze across a field of candles. The air was motionless, however, our forward progress having now practically ceased, and I became aware of the extraordinary quiet that enveloped our vessel; even the animals now were still and apparently the steerage passengers as well for I could not detect the customary flow and ebb of evening chatter among the Caboclos and Indians on the lower deck. We were enthralled, the entire company somehow chastened and brought up short–no less, I suddenly realized, than poor Baltasar in his agony and I was deeply struck by the implicate equation; pain and light, fear and love, in this vast confluence of phenomena, were commingled quantities like any other, here compressed not, as I had imagined, into crystalline agreement with our presupposed categories, but toward a deeper form, a primitive order indistinct and unavailable unless to some specialized intuition, a connoisseurship of some sort; for what appealed, strange to say in such a stillness, was the music, or rather the sense of music inaudibly conveyed–a luminous notation, as it seemed, that raced its reflection along the bank. If only a transcription were possible, I felt, one might have a map accessible as melody, a seamless gathering, a continuum, of all one's arbitrarily differentiated senses toward a description, a thematic apprehension of the world bypassing the interpretive confusion, the muddling, sympathizing compulsion to invest experience with all the personalities of the mediating organs.

"I thought of Baltasar and the clarity of his encounter, his grace, the pain itself transcending the character of its reception, overflowing discrete sensory channels, a tide of misery like the great pororoca; like the waves and currents of the firefly lights. I thought of him down below with the others, clinging to the rail like a beetle in a web, caught in the presence of some great distinction. 'The Golden Path' I said to myself and with some fervor, apparently, causing Harkness to turn. It seemed profoundly appropriate–a Pythagorean term I believed at the time although I have since been able neither to verify it as such nor even to recall precisely what I imagined its meaning to have been. Perhaps it is Gnostic. In any case its sense evaporated with the spectacle for, as we watched, the waning yellow moon appeared above the jungle to a chorus of howler monkeys and one by one, all up and down the riverbank, the glittering lights went out."

9

Mr. Delabano's camera keeps fogging up. Standing in the garden he holds it under his coat for a minute, then tries to withdraw it, focus and snap the picture as quickly as possible but the lens fogs too rapidly and the viewfinder as well; the only presentable bud on the old rose fades as he watches, disappears before he can release the shutter. So he just stands there for a while with his camera under his coat looking around at the grass, still icy and soon to yellow with the early freeze, at the neighborhood and the quiet, the airlessness of it, clouds so high and wispy they belong more to space than the world. The neighborhood is empty. It's Monday morning. He's got about five shots left and he wants to drop off the film when he goes to get the groceries. But the lens keeps fogging. He tries again–just testing, scanning around to see how quickly it fogs, looking through the camera at the alley, the rows of fences, Mike's red cooker almost glowing in the condensation on the viewfinder. He snaps a picture of that for no particular reason and goes back into the house, drops his coat over the recliner and waits for the camera to warm up. Then he takes the discarded cut blossom he retrieved from the patio yesterday, lifts it up to the kitchen window light and takes a picture of it. He looks through the camera into the backyard for a moment but he doesn't take a picture; he moves the focus back and forth watching the split image–the real one, as he thinks of it, and the ghost one–separate and converge and separate again. This is what she feels, he thinks. What Mike Getz's daughter cries about. The doubtfulness. He takes a deep breath and puts down the camera. How terrible for a child to feel it.

To the south, three or maybe four alleys over, there's a flash of bright orange in the little space between houses where they all happen to line up. He can hear the whine so far away it sounds like mosquitos, the faint banging of garbage cans and the whine again as it moves out of sight. He's never sure which days they'll come–Thursdays usually but sometimes Mondays or both. He thinks of the whale shark again, the one he saw on TV years ago–scuba divers hanging onto the back, hitching a ride on the dorsal fin as the fifty-foot shark descended into darker and darker water, filter feeding, passing everything through on its way down to wherever. He wonders if it made a sound. If the divers could hear it. At one point, he remembers, the head of the shark had disappeared beyond the glow of the camera lights but the tail was still visible and the divers also, just barely, still hanging on and soon to let go before they were taken too deep; but at that moment right at the edge of the light they were still holding on to this thing–the wide-angle lens made it look like a train–and any second they would have to let go; but how easy not to, he thinks. Especially as they passed outside the light, just then to hold on for another second to feel the pull in the dark, just to really sense where it was going, the inevitability of it.

On the table in the kitchen, next to Mr. Delabano's camera and the used roll of film, are three library notices gleaned from the month's accumulation of junk mail before he took it to the trash. "Did you forget?" each asks on the front of the card, then below in smaller letters, "Someone is waiting." He's still got his coat on; his car keys and billfold and two handkerchiefs in the pockets. He's going to return the books on the way to the supermarket and he should probably take one of the overdue cards–the most recent one. It's not true though, he thinks; no one is waiting. Not for the paperback garden manual and certainly not for the green book. Imagine somebody waiting for that. What kind of person would that be? *Amazonian Biotoxins.* No one's ever checked it out as far as he can tell. A little foil sticker in the back says donated in memory of somebody or other and it's probably not been looked at since. Who would want it? Not even specialists he suspects.

He puts down the garden manual and takes the green book over to the kitchen window, flipping past the pages he's read to the back where most of the photographs are. Almost at the very back there's an entire page of photographs he hadn't noticed. They're just regular black and white–not sepia like the frontispiece–but they look old nonetheless, grainy and with scattered blemishes like old neglected family photographs. And, except for the blemishes, they're identical–or identical pairs it seems, five side-by-side pairs of old photographs showing the same little field or clearing, bare dirt fringed with grass and a tall, dark stand of trees in the background. He takes off his glasses and looks at the caption:

"A typical 'parallactical sequence.'" They look like old-fashioned stereoscopic pairs but they're all the same, no difference whatever.

It takes a while for the station wagon to warm up. The colder it gets the longer it takes and he hates waiting for it–having to gun it a little now and then to keep it going and having to sit still in the cold watching the white exhaust swirling around and drifting back over the car. His house looks strange to him now. All the curtains down and all the windows gaping as if it were in a kind of shock. He guns the engine a couple of times and gets out, waits for a second to see if it's going to die, then crunches across the grass to the holly hedge below the picture window. He reaches across the hedge to the glass, presses it lightly, slides his fingers down and along the ice at the bottom then brings them to his lips. He cannot recall such an early winter. He turns at the sound of the station wagon laboring, shaking a little as the engine kicks past each moment of peril. If it dies he has to wait forever to start it again but he gets to it in time to tap the pedal and interrupt the cycle. He guns it once more, turns on the defroster then puts it in reverse and waits for a car to pass before backing out and heading down the street in the wrong direction, following his thoughts.

The wind's blowing so hard it's difficult to steer. The station wagon catches it like a schooner even along the small streets, twenty-five miles an hour whistling softly in the gusts and lurching slightly this way or that. He's driving very slowly now, unconsciously lifting his foot off the gas like someone passing an accident, slowing down, he's surprised and baffled by the image that occurs to him, seems to slap into him like something blown, completely out of nowhere and for no reason yet striking him, fastening his attention like a memory, urgent but forgotten and suddenly recalled. He's barely moving now, easing over toward the curb to let a car go around, sliding a little on the ice and stopping there finally, his foot on the brake and the engine running, trying to understand it–the scene from the back of the green book, the common scene presented by the series of old photographs. But now it's alarming, as if it contained a threat. And altered slightly. Something added. How remarkable he should hold it in his mind like this; he feels it should vanish under examination any second like a dream–unconnected to the world, to his experience so, like a dream, it should disappear, an imaginary terror. His foot slips off the brake and the front wheels twist into the curb with a jolt causing the engine to stall with the right front wheel up on the grass. Now it's quiet; he's holding his wrist where the steering wheel spoke hit it, looking down on the seat beside him for the green book but it's not there of course–he decided to pay for it, find out, at least, what it would cost. Tell them he lost it. The quiet and the pain in his wrist make it worse–the silence like the photograph, like apprehension, and the pain like a symptom or a premonition of something. In the photograph, the image he has of it, just at the edge of the grass surrounding the bare patch of earth there's something like a shadow or an object blurred and it's as if the pain and the threat refer to that. That darkness right there he hadn't noticed before–subtle, unresolved. He's got his eyes closed. He wants to keep it isolated, separated from the world, the neighborhood; as if, were he to open his eyes, it might get out, he might sense it out in the daylight blurred and subtle like a dark spot on the X ray and he doesn't want to think of that: looking at photographs after his wife died; vacation photographs it was impossible to believe contained, somewhere, a dark spot. You couldn't see it in the sunlight. And only barely in the X rays–he could almost have blinked it away it was so vague to the untrained eye. He actually almost felt he might–revise it, unrealize it. A spot on the X ray like a dream. So hard to believe in that. He's got his eyes open now but the windows are fogged. He needs to back his car off the curb. Someone might call the police. It must look like he's had a stroke or something; and maybe he has. What if he has? A mild one. There's a regular ticking from the engine as it cools–every couple of seconds, the sound of the metal adjusting; and outside, the rattling of dry seeds on a mimosa by the sidewalk, soft and ghostly, almost like cicadas. He breathes in deeply and holds it for a moment waiting for a pain, something critical and obvious but there's only his wrist. And the other thing–the disturbing memory or vision. Whatever. It's very dim now against the light outside, diffuse, almost gone but not quite. No longer threatening exactly; but confused and unpleasant. Physically, he feels okay. A little shaky but basically all right. His wrist is better. On the other hand he's not sure where he is. He's looking around, moving his head and testing a soreness in his neck. There are no conspicuous blanks, no gaps in his memory as far as he can tell–the sequence of recent events seems intact. But he's unable, at the moment, to locate himself or even to recall which direction he's facing and neither the ancient and untrustworthy gimbaled compass on the dash nor the gathering high overcasts are helpful. Obviously he can't be far from home; he's in the neighborhood certainly, the same sorts of houses, the same kinds of brick and siding; small trees and grass and sidewalks and a straight, flat street that goes to someplace he's been, has to have been sometime. And yet he has no sense of it. Like waiting to remember someone's name or face and it won't come–a kind of darkness descends. He should back off the curb and get out for a minute, stand outside in the air and get his bearings. It won't take much, just a hint and it will come back. He can feel it. Right at the edge.

He takes a handkerchief and wipes his glasses, blows his nose. The car rocks slightly in the wind. There's a dog or something in the road maybe a block and a half away–dark brown or black and just standing there motionless in the middle of the street. It's hard to tell at this distance and because it appears to face either away or toward him, but he thinks it's a dog. He opens the car door and it catches the wind swinging forward violently out of his grasp, bouncing back and allowing him barely to grab the top of it to keep from falling out, one foot in the street and the other caught under the brake pedal. He's got to hang onto the door with both hands to get free, pull himself up and out, holding on for a minute to gain his footing on the ice. Immediately both feet start to go out from under him and he grabs the side of the door frame with one hand, reaching with the other for the handle but striking the lock and swinging himself around to the outside as the door begins to close with his weight, his feet slipping gradually down the grade toward the curb. He can tell what's going to happen but he can't do anything; if he lets go he'll fall under the car and the door will close anyway. He'll be locked out just the same. He remembers to lift his fingers clear as it shuts.

Now there's just the rustling of the mimosa tree and a sense of great emptiness. How thoroughly uninhabited all the houses seem to be, even the ones with cars in the driveways. Such stillness. Not a lull; not the ebb between the leaving of some and the rising of others but really empty–no one to think him suspicious, no one to watch. It seems colder than before. He can see through the window all the door locks down, his keys hanging from the ignition still swinging slightly; the garden manual on the seat and the roll of film. Like the belongings of someone who's died. He feels insubstantial, his balance slipping away and his sense of direction. The animal in the street hasn't moved. Maybe it's not an animal–just something dark so far away it could be anything. He's shuffling around the back of the car, bracing himself against it, moving toward the sidewalk; it's not too bad. He can walk slowly. A pile of stuff, he thinks. Something fallen off a truck, lying in the street exciting unpleasant interpretations. There are oak saplings planted along the easement just ahead, leaves brown and yellow obscuring his view as he walks. It could be a dead animal again although it would have to be quite large–much larger than the other one. That one might have been a piece of tire, he remembers thinking at the time. He stops. He can see it framed between two little trees. It's like a dog. But there's such an even shine to the street–the luminous overcast reflected in the glaze–such a whiteness to everything it's hard to see because of the contrast; the animal is so dark. He doesn't want to get any closer though. It might be injured or sick. It might be rabid. But one never hears of rabid animals in cold weather. That's something he remembers from his childhood–the threat of rabid animals in the summer. It always frightened him terribly although he was never certain what was meant–animals that acted strangely, too friendly. Like strangers with candy he imagined. Mad dogs. Out there in the heat somewhere, wagging their tails and waiting. In those days such thoughts might interrupt him now and then, disengage him from his friends, make him pause for a moment and look around, standing in some vacant lot on a hot afternoon and thinking of the possibilities, appalled at how easily such terrors could be invoked in broad daylight on a summer day with the insects humming. And sometimes he would want to go home as he would like to now. The wind's getting under his coat. The oak saplings are whipping back and forth, losing a few leaves–the yellow isn't normal this early; it looks like iron deficiency–pale yellow leaves scattering down the street and blowing past the black dog which is what it obviously has to be.

Mr. Delebano's heels encounter the rise of icy grass at the edge of the sidewalk and he falls backward more or less spread-eagle on the lawn behind him. He twists himself around on all fours, pushes himself up and does his best to run, stumbling once or twice but making progress across the yards and driveways. If it were a dream he would hardly be able to move; his legs would respond as if they were asleep, no circulation, and the greater his effort the greater his frustration at the inevitability of his being caught from behind by whatever it might be. But awake and unconstrained he feels out of control as if he were slipping down an incline, an old body jerked along, propelled by childhood instincts unexamined, ungoverned, simply activated–full-on, a rusty coil in the spring popping loose the will to run home without reflection, without looking both ways, right across streets, across people's lawns and shrubbery. He wants to dart between two houses and get to the alley but he stops himself in someone's front yard, completely out of breath, standing by a redbud tree with a white glazed ceramic kitten attached to it. The kitten's head is turned as if apprehensively; as if it were part of some dramatic tableau, the other part missing. Something to be imagined. But back down the street there's nothing. Beyond his car, maybe two blocks away, there's nothing in the street or anywhere else. And rather than feeling reassured, he imagines the possibilities have metastasized and he's unwilling, for the moment, to leave the redbud tree with the ceramic kitten, unable to determine the safest route. He's captured, it seems, within his peripheral vision–hemmed in by glimpsed movement at the corner of his eye. All around him at right angles to wherever he looks there's a suspicion, now, of something. How glossy and obvious, on the other hand, is the ceramic kitten against the dry, black trunk of the redbud tree. He wants to reach up and touch it but he'd rather not take his hands out of his pockets. It looks colder than the air around it. White and shiny and permanently afraid on the half-dead trunk. Redbud trees, unless they are very young, seem generally to be dying. He's shivering more or less uncontrollably now. If it were a dream he would have a false dream of waking up, catch himself and try again until he managed it. Then a great exhalation, a kind of sigh to make sure; a kind of shaking himself. There's no dog; nothing definite. Up and down the street how empty of everything the neighborhood looks. How pale and apprehensive. He steps across the icy grass to the sidewalk, looks both ways and begins to walk, slowly on the pavement to keep from slipping, constrained steps like in a dream or in water, like wading waist-deep back up the street the way he came originally, toward home he supposes but with no sense of it and trying not to look, in any case, except down at the sidewalk, watching the seams and cracks like a child and not stepping on them.

10

It's disconcerting to Mr. Delabano how gradually he has arrived home, how gradually he has come to recognize his whereabouts. It should have been sudden: "Oh yes, here we are." Circuits abruptly functioning; lighting up the map. But it seemed to come so slowly; he has arrived in increments without surprise or relief, some strangeness still adhering and making him hesitate, stopping him to look at Mike Getz's house for a moment; he's reluctant to enter his own, wanting to gauge the dislocation, the sense of familiarity withheld, and hoping for it to disperse, perhaps, permit the resumption of whatever's missing–if not familiarity exactly then something like that; conviction or belief. He's afraid of going home now, opening the door and not being certain in some way. Even Mike's house seems so removed; just down the walk to the front door, the dark windows and red brick. He can't imagine going there or what sorts of things might be inside. But at this point the front door opens and there's Mike's wife in a colorful, striped bathrobe walking straight out to get the paper, catching Mr. Delabano standing at the end of the walk looking right at her, the newspaper practically at his feet and no chance to move or turn away. She stops at the bottom of the steps, pulling her robe around her and regarding him cautiously, looking for a clue. He thinks how red his face must be, how red it gets in the cold and the knees of his trousers and the bottom of his coat dark, wet from falling on the ground. He pushes his hair back then picks up the paper and holds it out, intending to deliver it but, realizing her confusion–that she has not yet recognized him–holding back and so finding himself in the unbearable situation of seeming to entice her, standing at a distance, extending the newspaper and tempting her with it. He should speak, it occurs to him, say his name and let her know it's all right but it seems at this moment impossible; he's too cold, the separation too great and his identity insufficiently robust to constitute an explanation for anything, inadequate to validate even such an ordinary gesture. He's overcome with embarrassment and isolation, losing control now altogether on the sidewalk in the cold in front of Mike's wife and beginning to cry, softly and with no hope of preventing it. He lets the paper drop and gropes for a handkerchief in the pockets of his coat, then his pants pockets front and back all the while looking down, thinking he must have lost both handkerchiefs and that now he is lost indeed, exposed entirely without a handkerchief, wiping his face with his hands, telling Mike's wife he's sorry and that he must be ill; that his car broke down and he had to walk so far it must have been too much for him. He should go home immediately, turn away and walk into his house but he stands there, immobilized by his discomfort and, suddenly, by the realization he's without his keys and unable to get in. Locked out completely.

"Mr. Delabano," says Mike's wife, pronouncing it correctly and approaching now, saying his name again and bending a little.

His legs are shaking. He's holding his glasses and wiping his eyes. He can't see very well except to make out that she's smiling and the bright, blurred colors of her robe.

The TV is on; there's a children's program with people dressed up like giant stuffed animals, but no one's watching–no children around. Mike's wife places him on a big white sofa in the front room, gives him a cup of coffee, makes sure he's all right and excuses herself. He can hear her in another room speaking quietly. On the telephone perhaps, then to someone present, maybe a child. His coffee mug is plastic with cartoon characters on it, enhanced with indelible marker, carefully embellished. Mickey and Minnie and Donald have all been improved–re-outlined and filled in with colored scribbling. There's a sort of drama taking place. Mr. Delabano takes a sip and turns the mug. They're being pursued round and round by something that may have been a skunk originally but has been altered beyond recognition with black marker, violently and unpleasantly transformed, no attempt to stay within the lines at all. He puts it down, leans back and closes his eyes. The giant stuffed animal show is going off the air and there's a weird theme song–just a mouth harp whanging away and a jumble of tiny voices.

"Mike's on his way," Mike's wife reappears in a gray jogging suit. "We're down to one car, I'm afraid; but he's not far. How's your coffee?" She's got the coffeepot, reaching for his mug. "Oh good grief, that's Janie's; here," and she's back in a second with an undecorated ceramic one, filling it, apologizing and gathering up the scattered sheets of paper from the floor and the coffee table–a child's drawings, the ones on the tabletop mostly facedown but a number of them he glimpses and they all look the same: a narrow band of blue at the top with a big yellow sun in the corner, and at the bottom green grass, a house with a chimney and next to the house something black like an animal of some kind. All pretty much identical. Maybe fifty of them, now in a neat stack on the wet bar with the telephone placed on top.

"It's a battle when you've got one home all the time," she's pulling a large, exotic-looking cane or wicker chair closer to the coffee table, seats herself in it cross-legged, hunched over, resting her coffee on her legs. "Do you have any children, Mr. Delabano?"

"No," he says, looking over at the TV. The mouth harp music is trailing away ever so gradually.

"Goodness," she sighs and she's up to turn off the television then back to her chair. "Janie keeps it on all the time; I just don't hear it. Can I get you anything; we've got some cinnamon rolls still warm."

Mr. Delabano can smell them. After everything, he must be getting over his cold.

"Really, if there's anything you need or someone you need to call . . ."

"No," he says, preparing to say more, something to deflect her concentration on him. He knows how it should sound but he can't produce it. "I'm sorry," he says, "it's just the keys; I locked them inside. You shouldn't have called Mike."

"Oh, Mike's a master at that; it's happened to us so many times he keeps a coat hanger in the car which, of course, is crazy except he loves to help somebody else. He's always ready–you know the kind of guy who likes to direct traffic when he sees an accident. He'd never forgive me." She pauses for a minute with her cup raised, still smiling but looking beyond him, listening for something, then excusing herself once more.

Mr. Delabano closes his eyes again and it seems he can still hear the mouth harp music confused with the wind outside–a thin, twangy sound like weather stripping, unpleasant children's programming blowing like leaves; the sound of wind through TV antennas. He's drifting asleep when Mike's wife returns with Janie, guiding her into the room, holding her hand and asking if she remembers Mr. Delabano.

"I lost my flower," says Janie, holding onto her mother with both hands now but looking at Mr. Delabano, her mother glancing back and forth, watching closely but not saying anything.

Mr. Delabano stands as if some balance were tipped, such a slight addition to the feminine presence having triggered some balky reflex. "I know," he says, "and I have it; and when I get my keys you can have it back."

Janie looks at him for a moment longer, then breaks away, dashes out of the room and reappears with a drawing that resembles the others.

"Oh Janie," says her mother. Then there's the sound of a car door slamming and Mike, both arms loaded with fried chicken boxes, kicking his way in and loudly announcing salvation's arrival as his wife makes shushing noises, urgent calming motions. He stops and leans the door closed with his back. Janie gives her dad a quick glance then approaches Mr. Delabano and hands him the drawing. "Do you know what that is?" she asks.

"Well," says Mr. Delabano, "it's a little house with a chimney on a bright sunny day."

"No," she says. "What's that?" And she pulls on his arm and jabs at the black object. "Do you know what *that* is?"

Mike has unloaded the chicken boxes onto the table by the door; his wife has moved closer to him and they're both very quiet.

"Yes," says Mr. Delabano after a minute. It's like the altered cartoon animal on the plastic mug, densely scribbled with so much pressure there are ridges of crushed crayon; he imagines a little hand pressing down that hard, trying to form such a notion, so violent and obscure it's hard to tell anything's there but there is, buried in the effort, a suggestion of a head and a mouth. Eyes possibly. "Yes," he says again, "I think I do." He's looking at her now. "I think it's a very bad dog."

Janie looks over at her mom and dad, then turns back to Mr. Delabano, beaming, smiling so broadly Mr. Delabano smiles back. "I know," she says; "I know, I know," then twirling out to the center of the room and rotating there with her arms outstretched, happily turning and repeating the phrase till her father picks her up from behind. "What do you know, babe?" He's laughing and spinning her around as her mother looks on, apparently astonished. "What do you know, huh?" but now Janie's just giggling as he prances around with her, swinging her onto his shoulders, retrieving with one hand a box of fried chicken and galloping, thus encumbered, to the kitchen.

"Jackpot, Mr. Delabano," says Mike's wife quietly, taking his arm, giving him an odd, mock-suspicious look and leading him to the big round pedestal table where Mike, still in his overcoat, is dealing out paper plates.

Janie carries her plate and a single drumstick over to sit by Mr. Delabano, her mother following with a carton of milk and the decorated plastic mug. "Is it a really old flower?" Janie asks, looking up at Mr. Delabano, taking a huge bite and, nearly incomprehensible now, "Is it really, really, really, really . . ."

"Janie," says her mom.

". . . really, really old?" Mr. Delabano has never seen his house from inside someone else's. It's like an out-of-body experience. He can see most of his backyard, three of the four blue flowers and, for a minute, he thinks they're what Janie's referring to. He tries to see them that way, at a distance like memory, ancient; wondering what she could mean. Wondering also at his inclusion in all this, the spontaneity of it and what sort of jackpot he is perceived to have won.

"Mr. Delabano saved Janie's rose," her mother announces. Mike pauses with a scoop of mashed potatoes above his plate, looking at his wife, then at Mr. Delabano and back to his wife. "No kidding?" he says. "How about that, Janie?"

"I know it," says Janie, "I can have it back, is it old?" she asks again.

"Oh," says Mr. Delabano, "the rosebush is, yes. We found that in West Virginia where an old house used to be. It might be a hundred years old."

"How old are you?" asks Janie.

"Oh my," says her mom.

"About a hundred years old," says Mr. Delabano, looking down at Janie and widening his eyes to emphasize it.

"No you're not," she says. "How old can flowers be?"

"A lot older than that, I imagine." He notices, a little uncomfortably, he's been given the floor, Mike and his wife having withdrawn into a sort of attentive disengagement, smiling and sitting back in their chairs, waiting for him to continue and watching Janie with great interest. Janie is watching Mr. Delabano, grinning at him, somehow, past an entire roll she has stuffed in her mouth–a demonstration apparently worthy of comment although Mr. Delabano is at a loss to provide one, feeling suddenly disconnected in the silence and incapable of an appropriate response, terrifically conscious of the wind whipping past and the sense of discrepancy it carries, the fragility of the situation. He's unable to keep his thoughts from drifting outside to the flat, unimproved backyard with tricycles and a swing set and the partial view of Mike's white frame garage off to the left–plain white board siding right down to the ground with no plantings, just a narrow concrete walk along the side, turning left behind it, between the garage and the alley, drawing Mr. Delabano's attention to that space and the suspicion that something could be there, just around the back, something having gone behind it, sensed, perhaps, a few seconds ago and felt to be there now.

Janie knocks over her milk in a rush around the table to her mom. And immediately Mike is up as well, leaning over them and asking what's the matter as if habitually, not expecting an answer, simply attending them, Janie locked around her mother's neck as they leave the kitchen and the spilled milk pooling at the edge of the table, dripping pit pat onto the floor.

II

Mr. Delabano has the green book open on his kitchen table. The sun has come out now in the late afternoon, slanting through the window above the sink and across the table and the page with the stereoscopic photographs. He's still got his coat on as he has all day–his keys in the pocket again; he's aware of them, fingering them occasionally as he looks at the page of identical photographs, every little imperfection now illuminated in the direct sunlight–the screened texture of the printed reproduction itself like a curtain, a mask. There's nothing. In this light he can even see the weave of the paper. What could be there? He can feel the texture of the paper with his thumb; holding the book up, bending together the front and back covers with his left hand and holding the single page up to look through it toward the sunlight, speckled paper, darker at the edges, brown but still translucent. Like frosted glass.

He needs to put the groceries away. The ice cream will melt. He closes the book and sits there for a moment facing the sun with his eyes shut, the rosy light flickering a little, the sun behind a tree. He's tired and a soreness in his neck has spread down his back and across his shoulders. He gets up to put the ice cream and the TV dinners in the freezer; the rest can wait. Then he walks out on the patio. It's still cold but there's no wind and it feels warmer–looks warmer as well, the sunlight reddened, dust in the air or residual haze. Everything glows. He passes through the garden and the gate to the alley. Mike's garage looks gold in the light. White-painted wood but radiant now, shadows beginning to ascend from the bottom. His own shadow appears and rises near the corner of the garage, runs off the edge and across the back of Mike's garage in the sunset, horizontal white boards, about a foot of concrete foundation and the shadow of the chain-link creeping up. In this light, the sun shining down the alley and across the yards at such a low angle, he can see the old dog paths–not just in Mike's yard but the next yard also. Depressions along the fence line, a couple of diagonals running between and, from Mike's back door, one long arc to behind the garage where Mr. Delabano is standing. It's like a blur–a prolonged old photograph through which something has wandered. He remembers old pictures like that; nineteenth-century family groups across which someone's pet has taken an excursion leaving a blur like a trail of smoke.

It must be warming up. Water has begun to pool in the alley, channeled down the middle and dazzling him as he turns back home, gold sunlight flashing off the little stream and shooting down the alley as he walks.

Such weather, he thinks, waiting for the microwave to ring and hoping the light will last for a moment filling the whole back of the house with a pink glow sustained and reflected by every surface it seems, even the ceiling–shadowless right into the corners, luminous as if it were summer and making him imagine cicadas again chattering outside like generators, all their noise now gone to light, invasive and uniform. Nothing could be hidden in it. He looks at the page with the stereoscopic photographs, at the text, flipping back toward the front and scanning:

> North of the Maku Igarape the Waikano move cross-country with the greatest reluctance, preferring to cling, past all practicality I believed at first, to the brooks and streams, skimming their canoes up the merest trickle before portaging to another . . .

A gust of wind and Mr. Delabano looks up. A faint buzz from the window.

> . . . the sensation more than once as I traveled with them up the Piripini and its vanishing tributaries, motionless as baggage in the center of the boat, that, still paddling, we had left the water behind altogether, progressing by faith and habit alone across the forest floor, kept in motion by balance and instinct so perfectly regulated to the properties of water that water itself had been effectively evoked. Nor dared I look over the side to correct this impression for I had learned that my slightest departure from the inert condition—indeed, so much as a sneeze produced by a white man—were sufficient to capsize us; and enough in any case, I felt at such twilight moments, to wake us as from a dream.

It seems too warm. Mr. Delabano gets up to adjust the thermostat and open the patio door a little, then all the way–it's like summer almost. Indian summer. He stands in the doorway feeling the air. The microwave dings but he's looking at the red sky and the big flowers nearly black in this light, and huge–stretched open, expanded. Each one maybe a foot in diameter. They look like antennae. He leaves the door open, goes to attend his TV dinner, rotating it once, resetting the timer and returning to the table. The light is fading but he can read by it–a deep rose color now and a faint breeze through the open door lifting the pages of the book and suggesting a scent or the possibility, the color of the light and the warm air combining to suggest it. He's lost his place. He flips to the middle, one of the arbitrary-looking photographs with mysterious captions, this one darker than the others but otherwise similar: a dirt road through brush with a few scraggly trees that look like mesquites. The caption reads: "Luminescence." But there's nothing luminous. The trees are so dark they're practically silhouettes, the sky barely lighter, everything gray with tiny flecks of white here and there like imperfections on the print. And nothing in the text.

The light and the breeze have vanished together. Outside everything's still–no sounds at all, gray light, all the rosiness gone completely right down to the horizon. Mr. Delabano gets up and walks out to the edge of the patio. All the shadows of the houses and garages overlap now like louvers; twilight sudden as shutting the blinds or maybe the opposite–like curtains blown open. With no breath of wind the nightfall seems to borrow that quality. Blowing across unimpeded, rushing across the prairie and right through the house if you leave the door open, forgetting the lights. There are lights on in Mike's house–a light in the kitchen and one bedroom on this side. Mr. Delabano goes back in to get the keys from his coat, walks out to unlock the garage, glancing back at his darkened house for a minute before feeling his way to the garden tools and an old heavy pick which he bangs on the concrete till the head slides off, leaving him with just the handle.

It's worse than gophers, he thinks, standing now in the garden, in the dark with his pick handle. He notices Janie's bedroom light wink out and for a while he just stands there wishing he had eaten his dinner and looking across the rows of fences and between all the houses and listening for something carried along the grid of the neighborhood like noise through the plumbing–something audible at a great distance in such warm air like the sounds you can only hear with your ear to the pillow; like a ringing in the pipes.

12

Faint dreams all night, inaccessible even as he sleeps; thin, rudimentary dreams like an infant might have, a screen of static with something behind it coming and going and waking him periodically like sand in his bed, the grainy anxiety of it, over and over until morning and even then for a while the feeling stays with him till he's showered and dressed and moving about, removing cold Salisbury steak from the microwave, dropping it in the trash and rinsing his hands and looking out the window at the flowers. They're still black. Even in the morning light; but drooping a little it seems, not quite so huge. He looks in the refrigerator for another lemon to grind up in the disposal but there isn't one; no baking soda either. Nothing for the smell which is quite noticeable.

He hears the clatter of the TV trolley next door, rolling over the threshold and onto the screened porch, plastic wheels making a racket on the concrete. He places a bowl and a fresh box of shredded wheat on the table, goes to unlock the patio door but it's half open. He slides it the rest of the way–still air, even warmer than last night and humid, just like summer–then he gets the milk and a glass and sits at the table using a knife like a letter opener on the cereal box, running it under the flap to pry it up then pulling apart the interior bag to open the seal without tearing. The smell of fresh shredded wheat overcomes him. It seems to entrain the smell of the house, the unpleasant smell, amplifying it, informing it with a sense of dustiness or static–shredded wheat like static, a bad taste and a hot sensation at the back of his neck. He closes the box and looks at it for a minute, then down at his arms resting on the table–a sticky, grainy feeling; he raises them a little and turns his hands up. They're red. His forearms also, a deep brownish red; and there are red fingerprints on the milk glass.

He backs away from the table without touching anything, knocking his chair over and standing in the middle of the kitchen looking at his arms and hands, staring at them as if he were wounded, bitten by something and uncertain what to do. He thinks for a moment he might have bruised himself somehow. Something he did yesterday. But it's like a stain. Sticky; and there are dark smears across the table. He moves to the counter and lays his arms in the sink and stands there like someone waiting to be sick, waiting for something else to happen. He can hear the TV next door flipping channels, continuously flipping, blurts and rushes of noise like a crystal set. He hits the cold water knob with the side of his hand, places his forearm under the tap carefully like an injury as if it were going to sting. But the water carries most of the color away. And with a little soap it's gone completely, no injury, nothing left except little rings on the countertop where the water splashed. Tiny red circles around the droplets. He can produce them by letting water drip from his fingers onto the counter–a reddish circle appears each time; all the way across the counter he makes little drops and little rings, getting more water from the tap and continuing past the toaster to the edge of the counter nearest the patio door. Each time the effect is more distinct, the red circle darker. He walks to the kitchen table–a slight movement of air and a ripple of TV laughter through the open door; the smears look like blood. He lets a drop of water fall and it's like one of those spectacular chemical reactions that magicians use. The water hits the table and turns to blood. Not just a ring but a perfectly red spot that makes him imagine a pain in his finger, a sharp smell like alcohol.

Air seems to move back and forth in the kitchen, gently in and out through the door like waves, the sound of the TV drifting, coming and going. He dries his hands on his pants and runs his finger along the top of the table leaving a clean mark with reddish brown borders and an accumulation of dust the same color where it stops. He looks at his finger, bringing it close but holding his breath; holding his hand over his nose and mouth. Still he catches an edge of it–more like ammonia than alcohol–and just the edge, a sense of being grazed, brushed by something massive. Immediately he holds his finger away but keeps the other hand to his face, grasping a thought, trying to hold it and not daring to move until it's retrieved and played out: a picture of a dust storm. One of those huge ones he's seen in books or magazines rolling across parched landscapes like something solid, a mudflow or even an animal, vast and inescapable like some Japanese movie monster above the houses and farm equipment, so big it's possible to imagine people in its path on the ground–people not situated in an airplane or removed to some elevation with a camera–unable to recognize it, not being able to tell what's happening, its extent too great for it to be distinguishable, exactly, from surrounding features it has replaced or engulfed. How difficult to resolve this. The thought of it. Not quite to see it because it's too big. Or only dimly, obliquely, to sense the approach, the alteration of some part of the sky–something looming imprecisely, incomprehensible to people visible as little specks in the fields and around the houses, much too small for comprehension to fit into yet standing around looking toward it. He imagines them immobile like animals in the glare of headlights, sensing it like animals, the way animals on the highway seem to sense the traffic as something subtle, hardly there at all but terrifically disturbing. He thinks of the dead animal again. And how squirrels, especially, go crazy at the last moment darting this way and that, abandoning safety two or three times to turn around and race back under the wheels. He's washing his hands now and looking out the window again, holding his finger under the tap much longer than he needs to, waiting to calm down but having a hard time and just holding his finger under the water until his thoughts recede a little. He doesn't even want to look at the kitchen for a minute. He's staring out the window with the water running looking at nothing in particular, gazing at the light.

The doorbell is ringing but Mr. Delabano doesn't want to answer it; he's in bed, sitting back with the pillows stacked up behind and his legs stretched out and the pick handle next to him, looking out the curtainless window into the little space between his house and his neighbor's. It's his neighbor at the door. Mr. Delabano glimpsed him coming across, carrying something–touch-up paint, probably, for Mr. Delabano's car door where the coat hanger scratched it. He insisted on that, refused Mr. Delabano's dismissal and now he's here waiting at the door, certain Mr. Delabano is home and not likely to leave without ringing once or twice again. He might even walk around back looking for him, passing between the houses and coming upon him here in the window. If that were to happen Mr. Delabano would close his eyes and pretend to be asleep, displayed but deeply removed like Mao or Lenin, profoundly unavailable. He imagines that. Tensed and waiting for a tap on the glass. Wondering how long before he can open his eyes. The doorbell again. This time he's holding it down producing, between the ding and the dong, a prolonged buzzing sound that's vastly irritating to Mr. Delabano, making it difficult for him to lie still as if he were itching all over or being menaced by some large insect. Maybe that's it now. Maybe he'll leave. Mr. Delabano leans his head against the window, looking down the side of the house toward the front, waiting for Mike to walk back across. But not yet–just the narrow bright space and beyond it, washed out in the brightness, the street and the sidewalk and the houses on the far side. Mr. Delabano continues to look and after a while he imagines something or the possibility of it. Like the possibility of fragrance last night, the merest suggestion or anticipation (but in this case unpleasant) of something, not his neighbor but something else, perhaps the dog but not exactly that, intruding into the space, simply moving across, silhouetted. And with the thought, something like a bad taste and a hot feeling again at the back of his neck. He closes his eyes tightly and leans back. Something interrupts the light. He opens his eyes immediately and looks outside. It must have been Mike. He adjusts the pillows and leans back once more as the doorbell rings, buzzing like a short circuit, bringing Mr.

Delabano up out of the bed and into the hall to reach up and place his hand over the plastic bell housing, listening past the final thunk for sounds from the front steps, Mike turning to leave. But there's nothing, so Mr. Delabano waits for a minute, imagines him gone, then walks to the picture window and there's Mike looking back–standing in the grass with a can of touch-up paint and looking at Mr. Delabano with a sort of wince. All he can do now is get outside as quickly as he can to try to keep it in the yard. But Mike's already on the steps as Mr. Delabano opens the door and it's impossible not to let him in, deflecting him into the front room and taking up a position, standing still to anchor his pacing, discourage his drifting toward the den or the kitchen which look like a murder scene, stained towels everywhere and a bucket of red water in the middle of the floor.

Mike's talking more or less nonstop, pivoting around in front of the picture window with a nervous oscillation that gradually subsides, reduces to fiddling with the touch-up paint, rolling it back and forth one hand to the other as he apologizes for leaning on the bell like he did, hoping he hadn't awakened Mr. Delabano, telling him how Janie would have had him come over at the break of dawn–in the middle of the night in fact–to get her flower back and suggesting Mr. Delabano ought to be glad he never had to deal with kids, ought to feel lucky, although he really shouldn't say that and didn't really mean it but he's about at his wits' end with all this, whereupon he proceeds to recite, like a forensic argument, the details of his daughter's affliction, its development over the summer into something resembling a network, an entanglement of little terrors and aversions impervious to professional psychology, culminating in the pictures and the guessing game, all the drawings with the scribbly black figures and keeping him up all last night with that in fact, having decided sure enough there was a bad dog like Mr. Delabano said; and what produced that particular idea anyway? Where did that come from? He's looking at Mr. Delabano now as if waiting for an answer but not really expecting one, turning to gaze out the picture window for a minute, then back around examining the paint can, smiling slightly and rolling it back and forth.

"I'll get the flower," says Mr. Delabano and Mike nods, continuing his routine with the paint can as Mr. Delabano waits for a second to see if he's going to say anything else, making sure he's not inclined to trail after him, before he goes into the kitchen, stepping across on the towels and holding his breath until he's back in the front room with the rose which, after three days, is fully open, barely wilting and faded nearly white, translucent in the light through the picture window as he hands it to Mike, exchanging it for the touch-up paint as if some sort of transaction had been made.

"There aren't any dogs, are there," says Mike, turning to look out the picture window again then back to Mr. Delabano.

"What?" says Mr. Delabano, standing as still as before; inert, he hopes, but not impolite.

"No bad dogs or good dogs," says Mike, still smiling, "no dogs at all or cats for that matter," he pauses, looking at Mr. Delabano. "And you'd think somebody would say something–people would talk to you walking down the street. They'd say, 'Hey, have you seen my dog; my little girl's going crazy because the dog ran off,' and you'd say, 'No kidding, my dog ran off too; maybe there's something funny going on,' and you could figure something out. But it's all kind of dead. You don't hear anything really or it's just sort of obligatory, just the usual thing and very restrained except what Carol said about you yesterday and what you said to Janie. So what was that?"

Mr. Delabano had been prepared for him to go on for a while longer, had steeled himself for it so now he's surprised and unable to respond, caught in the stillness, battened down with nothing to say. His neighbors' TV is even worse from the living room, barely audible like a toilet running. Mike's smile has broadened a little, his head cocked slightly as if he were going to make a joke. "You know what she did last night?" he says. "After we got you fixed up you know what she said? She said she knew where the bad dog was and she could show us if I could move all the furniture out of her room. She already had most of her stuff dragged out in the hall but she needed me to carry the bed. How about that. I mean everything out in the hall–toys, clothes, everything. You couldn't get past it. Looked like a disaster. Carol said she thought it was best to let her go ahead but it was incredible. I had no idea she had that much stuff." He shakes his head, looks at Mr. Delabano again, "So, what was that about the bad dog; was that like a joke or something?"

They're flipping channels again next door and the sound affects Mr. Delabano like the buzzing of the doorbell circuit. "Just a minute," he says, and Mike follows him as far as the hall, waiting there for him to return from the kitchen, this time with a brown plastic medicine bottle half full of cinnamon-colored powder. Mike gets a whiff as he's handed it, jerks away and brings it back toward his face slowly, "Jesus!" then, holding it away again, glances at the mess in the den and back to Mr. Delabano, just holding it now and looking apprehensive as Mr. Delabano moves past him into the living room, over by the picture window. "I'm sorry," says Mr. Delabano, "it smells terrible," and after a minute, "I forgot to close the door and this morning it's all over the back of the house. I think it's the flowers."

Mike continues to look at him for a moment. Then, still holding Janie's rose and the medicine bottle, he walks over and seats himself carefully on the edge of the sofa and brings the bottle deliberately quite close, right up to his face.

"Don't," says Mr. Delabano softly. But Mike's got his face right in it now. It looks like a ritual, the rose in one hand and the bottle in the other. It's hard to see his face, bending over the powder, very still, no movement at all except for the hand with the rose which he's extended out to the side, that arm now absolutely straight, holding the flower as far away as possible as though isolating it, protecting it from contamination. It's like waiting for a diver to surface, scanning the water and starting to worry. Mr. Delabano moves a little nearer but he still can't see Mike's face; it looks like maybe his eyes are closed. There's an ID badge clipped to his shirt with a large, surprisingly good photograph as if for reference–as if to compare with whatever emerges; a picture of Mike on a good day, so unlike the usual mug shot, more like a tiny studio portrait, capturing the best moment, an easy smile, completely natural like evidence of a happy life as if that's what were being attested. Mr. Delabano leans closer–"Thorsen-Reich Chromatography Group" it says underneath, then his name and some information in small print. Mike's arm has come down. Still holding the flower but limp on the couch. It must be ten-thirty or eleven. It's very bright on Mike's side of the room opposite the uncurtained picture window; then dramatically darker as a cloud passes over and Mike's head jerks up, his eyes wide open startling Mr. Delabano who retreats a step, thinking for a second he's alarmed or angry, about to get up and take some sort of violent action. Then Mike's face simply falls, his eyes drop, all the stiffness seems to leave his body; he just places the bottle on the coffee table and leans back looking immensely sad as if remembering something terrible, some sorrowful piece of information he already possessed but had managed not to think about until now. The room lightens and darkens again. Mike raises his eyes to look toward Mr. Delabano but past him, staring toward some point in his direction–out the window at the fluctuating light, still holding the rose but with both hands now in his lap.

Mr. Delabano fears he may have done some damage. For a while he stands there waiting for Mike to move or say something–afraid to say anything himself. It could be like sleepwalking, he thinks; perilous to interfere. Then Mike straightens up, puts his hands on the table and starts to speak. But he's unsuccessful and has to try again. He's like someone overcome by illness or grief. Once more he tries and stops, then looks at his watch, picks up the medicine bottle again, holding it with the rose in the same hand, smiles and in a very soft voice that Mr. Delabano can barely hear says something about the time and having to get to work and then he's gone. Up and out the door without another word, leaving Mr. Delabano standing by the picture window watching puffy clouds move by, west to east, the whole neighborhood glowing and dimming with the shadows which, unlike the clouds, have no movement, simply occur, darker and brighter everywhere at once, like the hands of a clock the moment at ground level changes without visible progress or is felt to have changed.

He sits on the couch at the end opposite where Mike sat, leaning against the bolster. How abrupt and hard-edged the light is coming into the room with no curtains to soften it even at the sides–everything outdoors fading into it, lost in the intermittent glare. He thinks perhaps he has never been so hungry. It's hard to remember the last time he had a proper meal or exactly why that should be the case. He thinks about the cafeteria out on the highway by the new shopping center. He dislikes cafeterias generally but it appeals to him now for some reason–the idea of it out there like an industrial site, potent and automatic.

In the bedroom he makes a list. He needs cleaning supplies, paper gardening masks and Lysol and he wants to pick up his pictures while he's there. He stands the pick handle in a corner and straightens the bed. He can see Mike's back door propped open–the screen door, with some bulky object projecting past, hanging out over the steps and jiggling a bit as if someone inside were trying to dislodge it, bring it in or out. Then Mike appears stepping sideways around it, reaching one hand over the top and grabbing the bottom with the other, hoisting it through, his wife on the other end; they're walking it out to the garage–a set of box springs it looks like. And there's Janie on the steps now, her back to Mr. Delabano, watching their progress.

13

Mr. Delabano has made himself light-headed cleaning house wearing a paper dust mask soaked in Old Spice aftershave. Like sniffing glue, he imagines, sitting on the edge of the bed, carefully removing his clothing, placing it in a plastic garbage bag and lying back to stare at the ceiling and listen for the return of the oscillating sprinkler playing against the side of the house as it washes down the patio. In a minute he'll take a shower, have a piece of apple pie and look at his pictures but first he'll wait for the dizziness to pass and listen to the sprinkler which comforts him like the sound of the push-mower. Like a voice, he thinks; someone whispering; as if there were information, a short sentence or a word the utterance of which he can recall but not the sense exactly. Like almost remembering something–spattering gently against the house–something spoken.

In the kitchen in his bathrobe he leans on the counter and looks at the soles of his feet; he does this several times as he sets out the package of photographs, the pie in its styrofoam container from the cafeteria and a glass of milk on the table which retains one small reddish blotch at the corner. The smell of the Lysol should be oppressive but he finds it reassuring. He watches the sprinkler for a minute before sitting down at the table, checking his hands and examining the milk glass, turning it a few times, then picking up the envelope of photographs still sealed with a gold sticker. He wanted to save them till things were in order, had to keep them away from the young man at the camera shop who wanted to give him pointers on "special effects." Now he slips his finger under the seal and withdraws them in a neat stack, closing the envelope with the negatives inside and placing the photographs on top. He regards the first one for a moment, takes a bite of apple pie and looks at it again. It's a wasted shot. One taken accidentally while winding on the film but he wonders what it is: a diagonal line separating a pale and more or less featureless lower half from the mottled greenish brown at the top which looks like it might be grass or weeds although badly out of focus. The one under it is similar except the pale area at the bottom is gone, replaced by a bluish white triangle at the top left–he thinks of it as the top, sky-colored. A tilted horizon. It's the prairie beyond the shopping center parking lot, dry grass and brush coming into focus farther out. In the first picture the lighter section is pavement. He places that one to the right and the second to the right of the first, next to the glass of milk. His wife used to hate this and would leave him alone when the vacation shots came back–his meticulous, sequential examination of the pictures like a game of solitaire; reading the tarot. They seem to be in order. The next one is intentional, the farmhouse–mostly horizon but the farmhouse is there, just barely, a dot beyond the highway, the windmill sticking up to mark the spot; otherwise one could miss it, such a small house right at the intersection of prairie and sky, slipping over the edge. This one he places below the main stack, starting a new row from the left and now looking at the next. It's the dead animal. It looks like another random shot, accidental like the first two but it's the animal. Something by the curb; it could be anything, a rag or a piece of clothing. The photograph conveys nothing of its presence there, how he remembers it, the mysterious generality. Nor is the close-up any better–the one from a low angle, kneeling to see the teeth and the black nose still moist; none of that is in the picture, not the way he remembers. Here it could be someone's dog or maybe nothing much at all. And then shots of blue flowers–nine, ten, eleven; lining them up, a third row now, moving his pie out of the way. They're all the same like seed packages. And unpleasant repeated like that one after another; he looks at his hands again, gathers all the flower pictures into a single stack and lays out the rest quickly without really looking at them, like finishing a hand, flicking them down with a slap each time like cards: four red ones and four black ones, the red ones only more or less red out of the corner of his eye, generally tending to shades of red or amber, but the black ones quite black, pictures of unexposed film. They printed everything as he asked but it bothers him they went so far to think the series might grade into nothing. That whoever ran the photo machine couldn't be sure, deciding these events were so faint and uncertain as to be indistinguishable from failure, degrees of accident. Yet there are images.

Placing the remains of his pie in the refrigerator, then standing by the counter and finishing his milk he can see them–not in detail at this distance, but as a sort of pattern.

They make a pattern the way vacation photographs–similar moments in different locations–usually don't. Vacation shots spread out on the table look like confetti. Celebratory and uniform. These, on the other hand, suggest progression, tendency. Even the black ones, now, seem like potential. Things about to happen. Things to come.

His clothes are ready. The dryer is dinging away but he's looking at the photographs, appraising them from afar, the two in the middle especially, and preferring this distance, the sense of reconnaissance which the dinging, however, makes too urgent as if there were a time limit. The first six make a group culminating in the flower; if he were to flip through them rapidly they might seem to move, he thinks. Become a sort of lurching approach–the rising and falling angles of horizons and curbs like someone stumbling or like waves–and then the flower, dazzling like a flashbulb going off. After that the pictures are darker, then black. These are the ones he laid out quickly without examining as if, like medical photographs, like X rays, they might reveal something disturbing. He wishes the dinging would stop. He imagines it sounds like a hospital now, announcing some emergency. He moves quickly to the table, turns the eighth photograph facedown and stands back to look at the others–first the black ones at the end, stepping nearer again and bending down to gaze past the satiny nonfingerprinting surfaces to make sure nothing's there, nothing subtle to explain their having been printed. He remembers years ago a psychic on TV or maybe in a magazine who produced foggy pictures, clairvoyant photographs, by staring into a camera; how silly and impossible it looked the way he held it right up to his face, one eye against the lens and the other wide open, visibly and ridiculously intent, physically straining, forcing his will upon the camera, a fat thin-haired man on a stool with his legs braced far apart, and the photographs so vague after all that effort–the one he remembers like looking the wrong way through a telescope, or some early photographic experiment, dark around the edges and just a vignette in the center, a faint and hazy picture of a bridge.

Mr. Delabano sits down, bracing himself with his feet hooked around the legs of the chair, studying each black photograph again, then the preceding ones in reverse order, backing up one by one: Janie's rose–his hand is in the picture more than he thought, holding it up to the window and the light that catches it just right, just enough in a very shallow focus to leave the background, the interior of his house, indistinct and dark, his hand and the rose emerging rather artfully. Then Mike's red cooker in the fog. It looks like fog, and it gives the cooker an absurd feeling of mystery, glowing red on its tripod in the mist–a clairvoyant photograph. Next, the one he turned over, a white rectangle, and preceding that–the first one after the stack of blue flowers–is a view from the picture window, severely underexposed except for the streetlight itself way over to the left; he can see the shape of the globe, no glare, like a lamp with a rheostat, like a stage light, dramatically red, just starting to come up, grass and street and sidewalk detectable right under it but the rest of the picture almost as dark as the unexposed frames although not dead black and not entirely featureless as he looks more closely; he can trace the sidewalk nearly all the way across and there's a shadowy suggestion of houses. It's like an infrared photograph, clinical somehow or military, deep red and grainy as if taken through a sighting device from a considerable distance. Even without its companion photograph, the one turned facedown, it would impart a sense of threat, he thinks; apprehension regarding the object of such scrutiny.

He leans back, unhooks his ankles from around the chair

legs and rubs them together to relieve the soreness before arising to attend the clothes dryer, opening and shutting its door to stop the dinging, then stepping outside to turn off the sprinkler, returning to his chair, checking his feet again and sitting back, still for a moment, listening. There's absolutely no sound now except the refrigerator. It's getting to the time of day, the final glow of late afternoon, when he might ordinarily hear a redbird–a single one somewhere with that slightly sad, repetitive little song which he associates with the hour just before sunset, whether because it's their habit to produce a song at that time or simply his to be quiet and more receptive he didn't know.

He flips over the photograph that was facedown, rotating it until it's right side up. The streetlight's now like the sun in Janie's drawing, yellow-orange, a brilliant round ball of light in the corner above the houses and pink grass and whatever it is that's smeared across the foreground, a dark streak, a blur, from the right bending back on itself at the center, twisting around there like a swirl of smoke, a crayon scribble out of which there emerges–toward the camera it seems–a repeated form, a sequence of three or four overlapping but reasonably well resolved images like the front end of an animal, a snout and stiff ears, a stuttering reiteration of it like rapid motion in a comic strip, and eyes like stars–four pairs, two pairs streaked, smeared together as if the first flash of lightning caught the head as it twisted, then another flash and then again like a strobe light although he remembers it as a single event, a single roll of thunder. He turns the photograph over again, staring at the white reverse, the blankness of it. Did he cry yesterday in front of Mike's wife? He can't imagine it. The white rectangle is like a room. Like having turned away from the X-ray display into a white room, absolutely silent, withholding all comment. Fluorescent lights and somewhere a hum.

This time it's the phone. It's been ringing a while, waking him slowly–the bedside ringer is turned down and he can hear the one in the kitchen. He has no idea what time it is but it's cold and moonlight is pouring in across the quilt and angling partway up the wall by the door. He's having trouble disengaging from whatever he was dreaming, interpreting the situation. There's no one to call him in the middle of the night.

"Hello." There's no response but no click, it's not hanging up and he can hear something like breathing, sniffling, and a beep as a button is depressed as if accidentally at the other end.

"Hello," he says again softly, and there's an intake of breath. It's a child.

"My daddy says you can see it."

"Janie?" says Mr. Delabano.

"Yes?" says Janie.

"What did you say?"

"You can come see it."

"See what?" says Mr. Delabano. Heavy exhalation now as if she's exasperated, preparing to try again.

"My daddy says you can come see what I made."

Mr. Delabano reaches over to the nightstand for his watch; holding it in the moonlight–3:20 A.M.

"There's a very bad dog. Do you know which one it is?"

Mike's house is completely dark, this side in shadow–no lights at all. He wonders how she can see to use the phone and where she got his number. No one's awake there except Janie, he feels certain. No one is awake anywhere probably. He wonders if this is habitual–how ghostly that would be, her wandering around the house all night in the dark, doing the things children do but in complete darkness. How strange and sad that would be.

"Do you know which one?" she asks again–such a tiny voice at such an hour.

"No," says Mr. Delabano. "Which one is it?"

"It's my Scotty dog. He has red eyes. Really red. Can you come?"

"Yes," says Mr. Delabano. "Now you should go to sleep."

He holds down the button with his left hand, the receiver still on his chest–he's awake now and watching the pattern of moonlight, the lattice of the window withdrawing across the floor and the foot of the bed. When the phone rings again he can feel it like a shock.

"Tomorrow," he says, "in the daytime; I'll come over then, all right?"

"Okay," says Janie, "but it's moving."

"What's moving?" says Mr. Delabano.

"The bad dog," says Janie. "Bye."

Mr. Delabano unclips the phone jack and turns on his side, facing the window and the shadowy side of Mike's house, clear moonlit sky like a halo around it, or a mist. It's cold again. He reaches down and pulls up the covers. It's like fall now.

14

The phone's been ringing all morning–three or four rings at a time usually with five or ten minutes between, then maybe an hour's relief before the pattern starts again. It's the pattern of a child's concerns, urgency forgotten then remembered again. It's like her voice as well–all that ringing in the midst of such quiet like her voice at night, hearing her voice in the dark like listening to something secret, normally hidden, the telephone like a stethoscope and ringing now, in fact, as he looks out the picture window searching for movement, activity of any sort. He can see the newspaper in the grass and it seems surprising it should be there; it's hard to imagine the conspicuousness required to throw it, the conspicuous activity of slinging newspapers or even retrieving them. Yet his is the only newspaper left. Doors must have opened and people emerged. He places his hand against the glass, holding it there flat for a moment as a car passes down the street. He thinks he should feel it against the window somehow, the car passing by as a slight vibration, the window like a tympanum, but he can't and it's as if he were deaf. Even though he heard it pass, some sense of it fails to reach him. What if he were to go for a walk, put on his coat and just stroll around the neighborhood? Would there be encounters? A few people, mothers and children in the yards, carrying groceries and nodding hello? Might that be enough; or would it be, like Mike said, dead in some way?

Just inside the little entryway, behind the wingback chair where he tosses the mail, is a narrow built-in bookcase with scalloped trim and knickknack shelves inadequate for books but about right for shoeboxes full of loose photographs–culls, duplicates and, especially, black-and-white ones from the fifties which he finds it difficult to look at anymore. They are too personal for some reason, the black-and-whiteness too final, too emphatically the past. But it's a box of these he takes down and decants on the coffee table, spreading them out, separating clumps that have stuck together, turning them all faceup and shuffling them around in a generally circular fashion allowing him to scan without dwelling on them. They are dry as grass. Desiccated it seems, without power to affect him–empty as the view out the picture window and as arbitrary, a pile of leaves he's rustling through, faintly yellow, iron-deficient. Deficient in general. All the way through from the beginning–pale and deficient continuously. Unlike the Amazon. Exactly the opposite and beyond remedy. Some of the older ones have wavy white borders, scalloped edges like the trim around the knickknack shelves, as if to suggest a fancy picture frame, confirm that these events were significant, these people standing in front of houses and school buildings, posing beside automobiles, were not arbitrary and accidental, might not without loss be exchanged for any other photograph or a glance out the window. He picks out one and gathers the rest back into the box. In the kitchen he leans against the counter and looks at it, then walks over to the glass door to stand there holding it up. It's a picture of his wife in the rose garden. The tiny date on the border at the bottom reads, "Jun 54." The blossoms are hardly detectable, lighter shades of gray or flecks of white here and there like small imperfections on the negative. He looks at the photograph then the garden itself and the four huge stalks with their flowers quite black now and beginning to curl, imagining it like jungle, trees and vines arranged so densely he has no sense of the neighborhood beyond it, the commonplace streets and houses and yards; just his wife there–plump, in a big hat–in the clearing by the roses, unconcerned, holding a pair of clippers and smiling back.

The phone's ringing again. He picks it up without thinking, still looking at the photograph. There's nothing at the other end. He's just listening and looking at the photograph but no one's speaking, only background noise. Television music. The kid show with the giant stuffed animals, twittery voices and a mouth harp but reduced and drawn over the telephone wire into something primitive and aboriginal-sounding, a wrong number from some exotic place. Otherwise silence, then a child's whisper: "Wait a minute," followed by a loud bang as the receiver is dropped and Janie's mother telling her to stop playing with the phone as more loud knocking about of the receiver compels Mr. Delabano to hold his slightly away from his ear until the commotion subsides. He listens for a while to the kid show theme music fading away and a commercial that follows, kitchen sounds, a brief jangling of silverware, then footsteps approaching and a click as the receiver is placed back on the hook.

By noon it's completely overcast again and there are snow flurries (the earliest on record according to the TV weatherman), discrete, tiny flakes mixed with sleet swirling and clicking against the windows, blowing across the patio into little drifts against the house. The TV reception is lousy; he flips through all the channels then switches to the antenna to see if the networks come through any better but it's the same. Channel 17, though, has brightened. He checks the setting and sure enough it's coming over the antenna, something showing through the static; nothing identifiable, just movement, a sort of waving back and forth, something swaying behind the snow. He puts on his coat and steps out on the patio, almost slipping on the ice where water pooled from yesterday has frozen. He knocks a couple of logs against the steps to shake off the ice, standing them just inside then retrieving another before closing the door and pausing there for a moment looking out past the ghost of the cat decal on the glass, snow hissing off the roof and swirling into the yard, really starting to come down now, whiting out everything and making the cat face easy to see: an indelible adhesive silhouette where the decal pulled off leaving just a yeowl, more afraid, now, than fierce; though still enough to frighten birds. Maybe scarier like that, he thinks, sitting down at the kitchen table with his coat on his lap as if waiting for something, someplace to go or something to happen, ignoring for the moment the wet logs on the linoleum and watching the TV screen, the pale snow-colored light like light through a window, like snow blowing through tall grass.

He collects himself after a minute, gets up taking his dishes over to the sink, pouring out the coffeepot. He can hear something now; like a cat or a child. Crying or laughter; possibly something electrical–there's a sputtering noise. He goes to turn up the volume, leaning close to the screen as he does so, peering into the glare and feeling the brush of static electricity like leaves against his face, now jerking back suddenly at a terrific thump, continuing to stare at the TV for a moment then spinning around at the second impact–a great splatter of snow against the glass door, obscuring his view of the patio and something bright red, someone giggling. At first he imagines it's the weird sister from next door returning, crouched down out there in some aggressive and incomprehensible fantasy. But it's a child's laugh–he can see her now, jumping and slipping a little as she meets his eye, enveloped, almost spherically encased, in a stiff red parka and vastly amused as she flings a poorly formed snowball like a handful of feathers. A much better one launched from further back in the yard explodes against the door frame hard enough to make it rattle.

Mr. Delabano opens the door about a foot. "Hey," yells Mike, "what do you think about this weather? Is this crazy or what?"

He hurls his remaining snowball away down the alley as Janie, given a clear shot now, lets go another mittenful of unconsolidated particles, kneeling to scoop up another as her dad arrives to restrain her, slapping the snow off her mittens and the knees of her pants.

"You can come over now," she says above her father's back as he bends to pull her jeans down over her boots. "We have a fire."

"Completely under control, I swear," says Mike, straightening up, grinning and a little red in the face, struggling to prevent Janie scooping up another snowball, lifting her by both hands now and swinging her a little. "We're all playing hooky today and your presence is requested." He bounces Janie away across the yard to the fence, hoisting her back over. "Demanded, in fact," he yells, watching as Janie runs back into the house, then returning to the patio.

"I'm sorry she's pestering you. How many times did she call?"

Mr. Delabano shrugs, opening the door to let him step inside, then standing out of Mike's way as he automatically picks up the three wet logs and sets them carefully into the fireplace, opening the damper and squatting down to peer up inside the chimney. "I think she's better today." It's hard to hear him–he's twisting around and craning his head back; his mouth remains open and it's as if his breath were being drawn out, his voice vanishing up the flue. "She really wants you to come"–sort of a whispery echo. He's got his keys out now–a flashlight key ring, shining it up inside, leaning further back and extending one leg for balance. Mr. Delabano moves around him to turn off the television.

"I'll be glad to," he says.

Mike's got himself all the way back into the fireplace with both hands braced against the sides, keys dangling from his right, the little penlight still on. He looks ridiculous now; simply gazing out into the room, unfocused as if having found a reflective moment there in the fireplace.

"I'll be happy to come," says Mr. Delabano.

"Shh," says Mike.

Mr. Delabano can hear the refrigerator humming and the snow.

"Listen to this," says Mike. "Here, listen." Mr. Delabano walks over and leans against the mantle, bending a little, unable to imagine anything adequate to reward such contortions; Mike's hands and the sleeves of his jacket are filthy. "Come here," he says and Mr. Delabano inclines a little further, nodding, aware of nothing but a draft, a slight rush of air. "Huh?" says Mike looking for confirmation, compelling Mr. Delabano to nod more vigorously lest he be required to join Mike in the fireplace. "We don't get this channel in my fireplace," says Mike, climbing out now and grinning at Mr. Delabano who directs him to the sink.

"It's like a bottom-of-the-well effect, isn't it," says Mike, wiping his hands on a wad of paper towels, walking over to the glass door and looking out at the snow. "You get down at the bottom of a well and up at the top you can see stars in the daytime; except in this case you can hear something." He's holding the dirty towels and watching the snow, quiet now. Little whirlwinds of powder are lifting off the steps, whispering against the glass, breaking up and recurring.

"You know what that stuff smells like?" he says after a moment.

"What?" says Mr. Delabano.

"I mean do *you* know," says Mike, "what you said to Janie–had it occurred to you?"

"I don't know," says Mr. Delabano, uncertain at this point whether it had or not.

"Well, it smells like a wet dog, doesn't it?" says Mike. "A component of that; you ought to wear a mask." Mr. Delabano nods. Snow is swirling in a great spiral up from the patio and out into the yard, lifting puffs of white from the black flowers and shaking the stalks, leaving them swaying stiffly–all together for a moment, oscillating at the same frequency, their heads, quite dark now, bobbing in unison and suddenly anthropomorphic, reminding Mr. Delabano of the choreographed flowers in old animated cartoons but in the present instance unpleasant and even faintly alarming.

Janie's waiting for him bundled up and all by herself in her front yard, taking Mr. Delabano's hand with a cold wet mitten and leading him into the house without a word. Mike's rearranging the fire, the older girl looking on. "Under control," he gets up brushing his pants and smiling at Mr. Delabano, "no pyrotechnics today; what do you think, Janie?" But Janie's paying no attention, towing Mr. Delabano right past.

"Let Mr. Delabano take off his coat, honey," says her mom, but he's on his way down the hall now, pausing at the door to her unlit room awaiting further guidance as his glasses unfog and his eyes adjust. He can see his bedroom window through the open blinds, and on the floor, spread out over most of it, an elaborate construction of toys and blocks.

"Come on," she whispers. He looks back down the hall thinking others might be following but apparently not. No sounds from the living room. He keeps near the wall, following Janie around to a point on the opposite side. "See," she says still whispering, looking down at something on the floor, part of the construction, but he can't tell what. The construction is all there is; no furniture; a clean, unfaded rectangular patch of carpet where her bed must have been.

"See his eyes," says Janie. Mr. Delabano looks more closely. Parallel rows of plain wooden and smaller brightly painted blocks run this way and that, intersecting at more or less right angles, converging here and there on more complicated structures of books and shoeboxes, wooden puzzle pieces and so forth–all spreading over the carpet like a little town complete with tiny pine trees that look like borrowed Christmas ornaments and a selection of toy vehicles, not always to scale, placed at intervals along the streets. The blocks, then, are houses; and Janie's pointing to something just outside the nearest row, just at the edge of the town, black and therefore hard to see–a paperweight-sized dog like a plaster carnival prize with glass eyes, bright red, catching the light from the window slightly.

"It's my Scotty," says Janie. "He started over here," she indicates a position two or three feet counterclockwise around the perimeter of the construction; "and here's our house," she points to it, close to the center, a more realistic structure than its neighbors, snapped-together plastic components with a roof and a chimney and a little human figure standing in front.

"That's all," says Janie, racing out of the room, her nylon parka grazing the wall with a sound like a whip.

He can hear them talking now, Janie getting unzipped. How cold it is in this room. The snow has started coming down more heavily and quietly in big flakes. It seems to transmit more light through the blinds which allows him to see more clearly the drawings on the wall–what he thought at first was grime and haphazard scribbling but in fact looks quite coherent, more like a primitive mural, somewhat smeared and obscured apparently by an attempt to remove it. It goes all the way around as high as a child might reach, skipping the closet door and passing behind him where the design is less distinct, where she seems to have begun with crayon, changing to marker it looks like as she worked her way along–entirely in black and the same motif throughout. Rakes, is his first impression. Garden rakes or hay rakes with no handles or handles broken off arranged this way and that, side by side, at odd angles to each other or sometimes overlapping–and rather menacing it seems to him, a great flock of rakelike shapes hovering over the town, looming all around at the horizon. Some of the effect–the atmospherics of it, the sense of something emerging from a cloud of dust or smoke–is due to the scrubbing that has stained the wall while abrading certain areas of the design more than others causing them to recede as if into haze or distance. But it's the shape itself, the repetition of it, that's most disturbing–the intention to reproduce it like this, like an obsessive and unpleasant idea, like spray-painted swastikas, something like that, over and over, and that a child should have intended it. He looks down at the plastic house Janie pointed out as hers and the tiny figure standing in front of it. He can see no other figures, no representations of life, not counting the trees, except this little one–schematic, without gender, featureless except for round black eyes–and the black plaster dog in whose direction it faces. The dog, he judges, would not be visible to it; various structures are in the way. It can see the wall, though–the encircling cloud of drawings–and he tries to imagine that, the view from that point, eyes solid black, noncomprehending.

It's terribly cold. He can hear Mike poking the fire but he needs to think what to say before he goes back in, some remark; he's been in here too long and it will be awkward now. He looks up. Janie's mom is in the doorway.

"Might as well leave your coat on, I guess," she gives a little laugh and an exaggerated shiver, clasping her arms as if to warm herself. "What do you think?"

There's a soft clunk as Mr. Delabano's shoe knocks over a wooden block, causing it to strike another. He kneels to replace it as Janie's mom makes her way around the room.

"I'm Carol, by the way. I don't think we ever made it to introductions." She's standing above him, arms still clasped across her chest, looking chilly and a little uneasy in her thin white sweater. Mr. Delabano rises, not knowing whether to extend his hand, remembering his embarrassment two days before and feeling captured again now and somehow disreputable here by himself in this little girl's room. He looks around at the mural. He can sense Carol studying him for a moment; then she turns. "That came first," she says, "before the scribbly pictures like the one you saw. They're birds." Now she's looking at him again. "What do you think?" she asks.

"What kind of birds?" says Mr. Delabano.

"Just birds," says Carol; "she won't say what kind or what they do or anything. I just shouldn't have tried to clean it. Now it's worse. Now it looks like a cave painting," she gives another little laugh.

And it does, he thinks. It has that quality: the deteriorated surface and a sort of carelessness about the overall arrangement–he thinks of spray-painted swastikas again and an image he has from somewhere of handprints or stencils of hands held flat against the rock, red hands or red outlined as if sprayed over with red paint covering some cave wall or a cliff. The rakes are like that; the tines like fingers or wing feathers spread apart. Like vultures, he thinks; the jagged broken stumps of handles resemble heads with stiff, splintery ruffs of feathers, beaks in some cases.

The snow is starting to stick to the window, darkening the room gradually, making it seem even colder. Mr. Delabano licks his finger and touches the glass behind the slats of the blinds. He pulls it free like removing a piece of tape.

"You used to teach, didn't you?" says Carol. Mr. Delabano looks at her–she's smiling and really shivering now. "I'm sorry," she says, her voice shaking a little, "I've been snooping; I taught for a while–just the little ones–but you did, didn't you; when? The fifties? You taught the big ones right? Blackboard jungle?" she laughs again. "What did you teach?"

"General Science," says Mr. Delabano, "just two years, grades eight and nine." He takes a half-step as if to leave the room, to indicate his intention, but Carol doesn't move–she's standing there looking at him and smiling, rubbing her upper arms and shivering. He can hear Mike furiously agitating the fire again. The room has become quite dark.

"Did you ever see anything like that?" she says.

The drawings are too dim, now, to make out clearly; just a haze like a layer of smog: grimy walls, fingerprints and scribbling.

"Anything at school like that?" she asks again. "They had spray paint then, I guess?"

"They certainly did," says Mr. Delabano, looking at her, expecting this must be a joke but unable to verify it–her smile and her discomfort seem to cancel.

"No," he says, "nothing like that."

They're both looking at the opposite wall now, Carol silent, Mr. Delabano waiting for her to move, as Janie reappears–backlit, standing in the doorway like a museum guard. Carol regards her for a moment without saying anything, turns briefly to Mr. Delabano. "All right," she says softly, "now I have a science question: Why is this room so cold?" Then she makes her way carefully back around the construction, pausing in the doorway to brush back Janie's hair before guiding her up the hall. Mr. Delabano moves to follow but stops for a second by the floor vent near the closet, bringing his hand down close to the grill and feeling the warm air pour up through his fingers.

"We've got celery with cheese stuff in it, little round crackers with some different kind of cheese stuff on it and, yes," says Mike, displaying a brass tray bearing tiny glass tumblers, a bottle of liquor and a quart-size paper carton, "we have eggnog."

"Eggnog?" asks Carol.

"What's eggnog?" asks Janie.

"It's like buttermilk," says Janie's sister, reaching to examine the carton and nearly upsetting the tray.

"Eggnog," says Mike, recovering his burden and regarding his wife with faint defiance, "we shall be festive."

"My God," says Carol, taking Mr. Delabano's coat at last, "that has an expiration date you know."

"It was in the freezer," says Mike, handing Mr. Delabano a cup and motioning him over by the fire to an upholstered chair into which he sinks uncomfortably and more or less helplessly to a semi-reclining position from which it will be difficult to rise or even lean forward without effort. The side table is beyond his reach as well–his shoulders having settled to a level with the arms of the chair–so he must hold his drink and, thus immobilized, confront the proceedings more directly than he would like. On the other hand the fire is rather soothing–the sound as much as the warmth, Mike turning the logs and poking the embers again, absorbed in this for the moment and leaving Mr. Delabano to examine the contents of his cup as Carol and the girls withdraw to the kitchen. The smell strikes him as an appalling combination of apple pie and the doctor's office–the sprinkle of cinnamon or nutmeg perhaps disposing him to unpleasant associations. Mr. Delabano lifts his eyes. Mike's looking at him, holding the poker and gazing down at him as if paused in his intention to say something. Caught between thoughts. "Listen," he says at last in a portentous tone of voice, "don't worry about the expiration date. Nothing gets past one-fifty-one Jamaican." He gives Mr. Delabano a wink and turns to replace the poker, missing the hook with a great clatter of iron on brick. "Drink deep or taste not, Frank." He picks up the poker and makes it the second time, retrieving his eggnog from the mantel, smiling and raising his cup to Mr. Delabano who is compelled to lift his own. The whipped cream acts like a valve–sealing the mixture until, inclined beyond a certain point, the topping breaks loose, obstructing his nostrils and flooding his throat with rum which he swallows to keep from choking. For a moment, in a sort of shock, he imagines he has been tricked, got back at–recalling how Mike looked yesterday on the couch bending over the little medicine bottle, submerged in it, lost for a while, even injured it seemed.

"So what do you think," asks Mike. He's got the poker again, playing with it, looking at the floor and tapping the poker against his shoe, "are we under alert?"

"Pardon me?" Mr. Delabano manages a whisper. "I'm sorry?" he tries again. Carol is back with the girls. Janie has her flower in a glass of water. Three or four petals remain.

"Oh, don't make him drink that," says Carol, stepping forward to take the cup. "Let me get you a beer or something."

"No, I'm fine thanks," says Mr. Delabano, recovering his ability to speak and deciding to keep his eggnog, holding it against his chest and feeling not at all unpleasant having got past the initial surprise, letting Mike's question float for the moment. The crackling of the fire is like the sound of the sprinkler playing against the house, the fumes of the rum more congenial than aftershave.

"I mean the Situation Room," says Mike. Mr. Delabano looks at him–from a considerable distance it seems–Mike's smiling again and twirling the poker, point on the floor, spinning it and about to drop it a second time; Mr. Delabano is anticipating that, regretting the noise it will make; there it goes but Mike grabs it, just holding it now and sitting down finally, crossing his legs and tapping the poker against the heel of his shoe. Carol and the girls are seated also–all three in the big throne-like wicker chair across from Mr. Delabano, Janie in her mother's lap and the older girl balanced on the arm.

Mr. Delabano has the sensation he's sinking even deeper into his chair, subsiding at a steady rate, gradually and, to his hosts, unremarkably as if this were no extraordinary thing–only Janie is paying any attention, gazing across at him, studying his decline with the sort of detached appreciation one might extend to serene and established natural spectacles like sunsets or the flight of geese.

He's going right through the floor; although closing his eyes delays the process, even reverses it if he keeps them shut–the chair reinflates and he feels himself recover. The fire sounds like a blizzard, like snow blowing against glass. Someone's munching a celery stick.

"Did you call the Gooch sisters?" It's Carol's voice–almost a whisper. They think he's asleep. More munching of celery or crackers. It's like being a child imagined to be asleep, within yet withdrawn from events like a rock in a stream, status suspended–such a sense of kindness in this, the softening and rerouting of intentions; Mike has stopped tapping his shoe. How long, he wonders, before he must open his eyes–or what if he doesn't. What if he should remain here like this, asleep in the chair on display indefinitely like the body of Lenin. He thinks of that again, the respectful rustle, the changing of the seasons.

"No, maybe I should," says Mike. He's getting up; a clink as he replaces the poker. "She seemed pretty definite this morning."

"Which one?" asks Carol.

"Lillian, I think. The older one," says Mike.

"Nobody else?" asks Carol.

"Gosh, no."

"Not from the lab?"

"No. What's that going to do?"

A gentle crash of logs collapsing.

"Shh, don't," whispers Carol.

"I didn't," says Mike.

Mr. Delabano opens his eyes. It's Janie who's asleep. Her sister is gone but Janie is where she was, curled up in her mother's lap, something tangled in her hair which Carol is trying to remove, fanning Janie's hair across her leg and pulling strands apart carefully a few at a time then giving up, smoothing it back away from her face and just looking at her. "We should let it grow," says Carol quietly. Mike's standing in front of the fire, hands in his pockets looking at them.

Mr. Delabano's sinking spell has passed. He leans forward slightly, experimentally, then far enough to reach over the arm of the chair to place his cup on the table, bracing himself like that for a minute, turning to look at the snow. Everyone's watching as he settles back; Janie also, her head still resting on Carol's leg but eyes open. Carol glances down. "Did you keep Mr. Delabano awake all night?" she asks, rearranging Janie's bangs again, receiving no response. "I'm sorry," she says, looking across at Mr. Delabano, up at Mike and back to Mr. Delabano–once more alternating her gaze like that before returning her attention to her daughter who appears to be asleep again, breathing softly. Mr. Delabano can hear her breathing. The fire has quickly burned down to nothing so there's only the brush of snow against the window and Janie's breathing through a stuffy nose–she has a cold, he thinks; children have colds.

Janie's sister is in the kitchen opening and closing the refrigerator, looking for something, drifting away finally down the hall. "Your roses," says Carol just above a whisper so that Mr. Delabano has to lean forward a little. "Your roses," she begins again, placing both her hands over Janie's and leaning forward also, "were so wonderful this summer." She looks up at Mike again then back to Mr. Delabano, shifting a little to reposition the child on her lap. "They were just so lovely. . . ."

Mr. Delabano has managed to gain the edge of his chair, leaning toward Carol without having to strain now, hands folded. ". . . and Janie thinks so too, everyone does–do you know the Gooch sisters next door?" She's become animated, using her hands, extending them as if to touch him, as if to reassure him. "You should put some out front, really–you should put some in our yard," she laughs. Mike is expressionless, standing rather stiffly and Mr. Delabano wonders if he might have had too much to drink as Carol glances up at him quickly then, holding Janie with one hand to keep her from sliding off, she reaches toward Mr. Delabano with the other, extending it, leaning as far as she can and keeping her hand there poised, protective like a crossing guard, holding open the path for something yet to come, something almost at hand as the position must be difficult to maintain. "We just have to be careful," she's saying, "Julie has asthma and Janie's been so upset anyway and you never know, especially with chemicals or sprays or whatever; especially with Janie–she still puts things in her mouth. I know you understand." But Mr. Delabano doesn't; he missed the shift from roses to something else–she's talking about insecticides, pesticides; withdrawing her hand now, looking up at Mike then leaning back and gathering her daughter into a more comfortable position. "We just have to be careful," she says very quietly, looking at Janie who is fast asleep and breathing more easily now with her mouth open. Carol lifts her, placing Janie's head against her shoulder, looking at Mr. Delabano again with a thin smile, "She's a random sampler," she says, then shifts to the edge of her seat as if preparing to get up and carry Janie off but pausing for a minute, turning to gaze out the window and rocking slightly, making the wicker creak. "Oh, Mike," she says at last, rising and carrying Janie out of the room.

Mr. Delabano senses he's missed something critical, failed somehow to respond. It's colder now. It's nearly four o'clock and it's not letting up–coming down steadily and quietly. Hardly any wind. Outside it's so evenly lit, like a big room–indirect and perfectly even light like fluorescent coming in through all the windows as if outside were a cold white room. Mike hasn't moved–he looks somewhat adrift, gazing toward the wicker chair. Mr. Delabano looks around for the pint bottle of rum but it's disappeared. He moves to get up but changes his mind, settles back again, watching Mike who seems altogether removed, lost in some sort of reverie. It's like a waiting room now–strangers suspended in the fluorescent light.

Mr. Delabano clears his throat. "I don't use insecticides," he says.

"What?" says Mike after a couple of seconds.

"I don't use insecticides," says Mr. Delabano again. Mike's looking at him now, squinting a little as if with the effort. "I don't use anything like that at all, not for years," he continues, "not since Grace got sick." Mike's just squinting. "My wife," says Mr. Delabano.

Mike comes over and sits in the wicker chair, arms resting on his knees, no longer squinting. "So what was that stuff you gave me? Was that fertilizer or what?"

"I don't know," says Mr. Delabano.

"You don't know if it was?"

"No, I mean it wasn't but I don't know what it is."

"Then what do you do with it?" Mike's got his hands together making a steeple in front of his face, resting his chin on his thumbs, speaking clearly but without moving his mouth very much.

"I don't do anything with it," says Mr. Delabano. "I cleaned it up–that was the mess. I had to spray the back of the house and wash off the patio too."

Mike is simply looking at him now as Mr. Delabano begins to feel implicated in something awful–some vague but hideous perversion. He has the urge, once again, to examine the soles of his feet, the bottoms of his shoes. He looks at his hands, then up at Mike.

"I'm fairly certain it's the flowers," he says. "I think they produced it."

"Those big ones," says Mike.

"Oh yes," says Mr. Delabano. "Roses don't do that."

"They aren't roses?"

"No," says Mr. Delabano, aware that what's wanted at this point is a full explanation, a history of the matter–something at least more than simple responses which he knows must sound like he's being difficult, as if he were in fact guilty of something, involved in something unmentionable, each question pushing him along only so far before he balks, reluctant to have the facts assembled as if he were a criminal or as if it were a medical interview and he were himself afraid of some terrible revelation: just a few more questions and there it would be, out of his hands, obvious and inescapable.

There's no expression behind the steeple of Mike's fingers; he drops his hands to his knees with a slap and leans back in the chair with much creaking of the wicker, placing the entire tray of goodies on his lap and starting with the celery sticks, crunching away and gazing out the window to Mr. Delabano's left. "Boy," he says, watching the snow, "is this something."

Mr. Delabano watches the celery sticks go, then the little round crackers until Mike's left with an empty tray, his hands resting beside it, looking sad, Mr. Delabano thinks–even tragic, his face without shadows, perfectly illuminated, pale, snowy light in his face and no expression really: empty light incapable of supporting expression; completely joyless.

"Did you know about the gophers?" asks Mr. Delabano quietly, bringing this forth with considerable effort at the particular moment when hope seems finally to have bleached away almost to the point of vanishing and beyond which, he senses, nothing might be done–a whiteness having descended, like that of the hospital he imagines, like the blankness that accompanies a shock.

"What gophers?" says Mike.

Mr. Delabano wishes Carol would come back and offer him a beer again, make some noise in the kitchen. He feels flushed and there's a hum in his ears like the sound of the weather stripping but faint and internal. Mike has put down the tray and shifted around to face him. We had gophers, Mr. Delabano thinks to himself, imagining the sentence and how silly it will sound–like a metaphor: a symbol or euphemism for something; too simple to stand on its own; too small a fact, reduced in the cold to insignificance.

On the sidewalk in front of his house Mr. Delabano stands for a moment, looking up and down the street in the pale darkness, yards and houses like cloudy sky, vague and unpicturesque–a little more snow might erase everything, not actually cover it up but generalize it beyond retrieval. He thinks of the rose in the liquid nitrogen, the famous cyrogenics demonstration, but it's not like that, that doesn't say much about roses: how, before they're shattered against the flask, they steam in the air for a second as if it were the fragrance escaping, condensed but still volatile; like seeing your breath.

He's going for a walk, shaking a stocking cap out of his pocket, finding the pom-pom and pulling it right side out; he can't bear to go directly home without transition, without seeming to put some distance between his house and his neighbor's; and the footing's not too bad–maybe two inches of dry snow on the sidewalk and none falling, under the streetlight a few stray flakes but that's all. He can hear voices somewhere, children possibly or possibly not, it's hard to tell and hard to locate like echoes in a large room, a darkened gymnasium, they come and go as he walks, excited children he thinks, up ahead somewhere to the west and maybe a couple of blocks over; but none to be seen. The side streets are empty, snow everywhere pale gray and clean as a carpet, no cars to track it up and no one else walking. He might just keep going for a while, the crush of the snow is so easy underfoot and it's such clear sailing–nothing to snag his thoughts, it seems, even subconsciously; an absence of detail, no points of interest. He might slip right out of town this way, into the undeveloped no-man's-land between the houses and the highway and beyond that who knows what–gray-white prairie as far as he could see. What must that be like? Outer space, he imagines, sky and ground practically indistinguishable.

To the west there's a pink glow on the clouds from the

sodium lights along the interstate. It fluctuates a little now and then, ripples with the traffic, with the interruption, he supposes, of the reflected light. It's like an aurora the way it shimmers, brightening block by block holding his attention, keeping him going much farther than he really intended. This is the last street, a cul-de-sac with a playground at the end--all the east-west running streets along this edge of town, for reasons unclear to Mr. Delabano, are cul-de-sacs, bringing the neighborhood up short against the weeds and bare caliche that span the half mile or so between the last houses and the highway. It's as if something were planned but never funded or the surveyors for the interstate were off by a few degrees, sighting between larger cities, deflecting inadequately for the smaller ones and leaving, in this case, a gap too large to fill. He can see the utility pole with its single hooded light by itself out there beyond the turnaround, silhouetting the slide and the swing set and the cast aluminum animals on giant springs. What an uncomfortable place for a playground, even in the best weather–right at the edge of the world like one of those bleak, obligatory little playgrounds they have at cheap motels, a sort of consolation more than anything.

Now there are footprints around him. He can see them as he passes under the last streetlight–smaller than his and indiscriminate, scattered about across the lawns and into the street, individual trails here and there terminating in parallel skid marks where they tried to skate on the snow. It's as if they fled at his coming. He listens for voices again but all he can hear is a faint thrumming of snow tires on the highway. He's decided the little park is his destination–just that far, to stand under the light by the swings and look at the highway. But now he stops. There's a child beside one of the spring-mounted animals and he can imagine how it would look to someone–some parent who surely must be nearby (the child not much older than Janie and probably belonging to one of the houses nearest the park)–for this child to be approached out of the darkness by a strange old man with no business in the area. Surely someone is watching even now, someone who's used to living here at the boundary of the habitable world, standing by a window and watching her child playing here, insensitive to the uneasiness of it; maybe even the risk–for it seems to Mr. Delabano that beyond a concern for appearance, there's a need for caution here as in the presence of events too delicately balanced, as when rescuers find themselves paralyzed by an infant on a window ledge. He wishes he could tell what the child is doing, standing there looking at something on the ground–transfixed apparently. There's a call from somewhere close–the next street over; a woman's voice, sharp and unpleasant. And for a moment the child seems to pay no attention, continues to stand there at the edge of the light looking at the same spot. Then the sound of a door slamming and the child races off, disappearing at top speed behind the last house on the left.

Mr. Delabano's feet are getting cold but he waits a moment longer, listening for the door to slam a second time. Then he proceeds to the playground, half stumbling where the sidewalk stops and making his way more carefully across the uneven ground to the slide where he stands in the light, leaning against the steel ladder and looking at all the footprints in the snow, wondering how many children there might have been, how many actually participating in the creation of what the younger child was looking at–the single monstrous print near the edge of the illuminated area, placed just right to catch the shadows, throw its contours into relief.

These children must have been older; it's the sort of notion an older child might have and be able to execute with some competence, all of them pitching in at some point, one or two having seen pictures, certainly in books or on TV–how the Glen Rose tracks looked for example, how the rock still looks like mud squeezing up around the outside of the tread, recording the weight, the massive unlikeliness. Here they've done the snow like that, heaving it up at the edges to deepen the impression and marking the tips of the claws just so–three of them, fairly delicate triangular pits beyond the toes–and the whole thing much larger than a real one might be, five or six feet long like what you'd see in a movie, big enough to be altogether incredible, a true monster. And leaving just this one impression under the light as if his stride were that long, coming by at a lope, the rest of his trail out there in the dark. Or as if having made this one they were frightened; pleased and then frightened. He can imagine that. Having placed it so near the edge of everything, backing off, delighted then quiet with the realization of it, the real possibility, the feeling of having spoken aloud some dreadful suspicion.

He can see no cars on the highway now at all, yet the pink glow still seems to shimmer as if the clouds were moving, racing across, sweeping low and very fast across the highway. At ground level it's still; just the lightest breeze and not really uncomfortable except for his feet. He knocks his heels against the side of the ladder to shake the snow off his shoes, then walks back toward the street, stopping just outside the light and glancing back at the pattern of smaller footprints, how frantic they look churning up the snow like splashes in the water, circulating around the gigantic impression then radiating away from it, scattering across the playground to the east and disappearing into the dark. It seems real in a way, or as real as such things might be–in whatever sense a thing like that could be possible at all. This is what it would be like. A false track, an indirect impression like a photograph or an X ray; accessible to rumor or prognosis. It might go away, then again it might not.

15

"It's just that we had a little problem," says Mike, "no big deal, but I wanted to make sure you had the negatives so I can get you another set."

"A set of what?" says Mr. Delabano–he's got the phone cord stretched over to the sink, rinsing out his cereal bowl into the disposal which is whirring away making it difficult to hear; in addition he's distracted by the goings on outside, the strange perambulations of the sisters next door (the Gooch sisters, Carol said) who have been ranging about in their backyard all morning in housecoats and fringed shawls on a sort of inspection tour as far as he can tell, pausing here and there as if to study the lawn at various points, the pale dust-dry grass that emerged from the snow which seemed, like dry ice, to sublimate over the last few days rather than melt.

"A set of prints," says Mike.

Now they're standing a few feet apart, facing the sun (still rosy, it's not yet eight) and allowing their shawls to inflate with the breeze. They look like birds. Huge lawn decorations. He places his bowl in the sink and flips off the disposal without looking down; they're turning now, how bizarre; rotating slowly. Whatever for, he wonders. Turning like that as if to dry themselves out–like moths, he thinks, rather than birds; emerged from the chrysalis.

"Frank," says Mike.

"Yes," says Mr. Delabano.

"I need to make you another set of pictures," says Mike. "Should I call you back?"

"No," says Mr. Delabano, retreating from the window and leaning against the stove, "I'm sorry. You need the negatives?"

"Your pictures got ruined," says Mike.

"Okay," says Mr. Delabano, still able to see just the top of one sister, just head and shoulders at the edge of the kitchen window, rotating slowly. "That's all right."

"I'm really sorry," says Mike.

"That's all right," says Mr. Delabano approaching the window again and noting how rapidly the light loses color, how dry and pallid things have become, not just the grass, as if the snow had somehow bleached everything. "What happened?" he asks.

"Have you talked to Janie?" asks Mike.

"No," says Mr. Delabano.

"Well, she burned them."

The sisters are walking back into the house now, passing out of view. He can hear the screen door slap behind them. He imagines Janie burning photographs and how dangerous that would be, especially, it seems, under the circumstances–such a dry spell following the snow, even his skin is dry, waking him at night with the feel of the sheets. He imagines her doing it at night; and that, had he been awake, he might have seen a flicker like light from a candle or a TV. There's the trolley, now, from next door, clattering out onto the concrete. "My goodness," he says.

"Just tossed them in the fireplace," says Mike, "except for two; she kept that one of the flower, the rose, and the picture of my grill. She thought those were fine. They're up on the mantel."

Mr. Delabano is looking at the snapshot of his wife now pinned to the bulletin board next to the phone, wondering where the negative is and thinking about taking that picture, what the young man at the camera store had said, suggesting there was something remarkable about seeing the moment with no mechanism intervening, seeing through the little window and bringing the two images together, body and soul in perfect focus. He becomes aware of the telephone again after a while, that he's still holding it without saying anything. And nothing, apparently, on the other end–no dial tone, just a sort of hollow sound and occasionally faint noises somewhere away from the phone. "Hello," he says.

"Yeah," says Mike like someone answering in the dark, still awake, "I guess I better get to work."

"Okay," says Mr. Delabano.

"Have you got any more of that stuff?"

Mr. Delabano isn't certain what he means. He's listening to the whining of the garbage truck away down the alley somewhere; he can hear it over the telephone also–an odd sort of stereo effect.

"The red powdery stuff. It's contaminated. Or if you can remember what used to be in the medicine bottle–but you have to be sure."

It was something his wife took but the label was gone. He should have washed out the bottle. "I don't know. Something for pain."

"No more of the powder, then?"

"No."

"How about if you heard the name of it–Demerol or something like that?"

"I don't think so."

"Or maybe if it was very strong–I guess you could check the medical records."

The garbage truck is getting louder, he can hear the banging over the phone now, hollow thumping of plastic cans like drums.

"Maybe we could do that," says Mike. "Was it something really strong? I bet it was codeine. That's what it looks like. Was she in pretty bad shape?"

"Eventually," he says, although it can't possibly matter–some trace of her condition lingering in the bottle, a residue of her discomfort now confused with something else.

A short while later Mike comes by, hangs around the kitchen for a minute then follows Mr. Delabano into the backyard to look at the flowers, moving from one to the other but keeping his distance, speculating that they might be dead, then standing by the fence and looking across into his own yard for a while with his hands in his pockets before hurrying away with the negatives and a small collection of old prescription bottles. Mr. Delabano can hear him roaring off, backing out too fast, scraping his car and gouging the pavement in front of his drive, suggesting to Mr. Delabano the passage of events beyond his control, the likelihood of something more invasive which is a prospect like that of getting the arrow pulled out, or an old piece of shrapnel slowly working its way upstream toward the heart; a splinter some little child would rather die than remove and over which he would prefer to cry softly for an indefinite period of time, for the foreseeable future in fact, than risk the concentration of his anguish beyond some critical point.

He steps out on the patio through the open door; the temperature is the same outside as in. He can still hear Mike's car heading out all by itself–he's going to be late–racing off to work, receding finally and merging with the general hum and the soft hissing sound coming from the back porch next door where the sisters have settled in for the morning. He can see them through the screen–shadowy, a faint glow from the TV. He listens for the sound of flipping channels but they're just sitting, hypnotized apparently, watching the static, bluish light flickering slightly across them like candlelight or light reflected from a pond. He's standing among the rose beds now, pressing his foot into the dry bark, wondering what happened to the moisture and finding himself bothered by the sound from the TV, increasingly disturbed by it, the sense it seems to carry of emptiness and pallor like fine white dust settling out over everything. He gazes down the rows of houses, most of their backyards visible through the chain-link and which contain more or less similar equipment, odds and ends–things that, taken as a category, tend to look the same when installed behind the house (never in front), things people keep in their backyards to reassure themselves backyards are truly congenial and habitable; are not bleak, exposed regions, transition zones between the house and the alley, tending always toward the latter, toward sadness and dissolution.

It should be possible, he thinks, to let the four plants decay. It may turn out there's nothing to discover, no need to pull one up for a specimen and he can simply let them collapse and disappear naturally without having to do anything; let things get back to normal on their own. Let the gophers come back if they want, and everything else. He kicks at the yellow grass between the beds raising a puff of dust that settles on his shoes–the runners are brittle; he can see where he kicked right through. The whole neighborhood is like glass or like parchment, thin and bleached out. One can see through it a little–to the prairie or maybe the limestone or whatever; like a faded Ektachrome slide, he thinks, backing to the fence and looking down the rows of houses again, all the sad backyards and the TV antennas that he imagines must be receiving, in a sense, that same noise all the time, taking it out of the air and just humming with it, hissing quietly. It's like a noise produced by insects. A whole field of them, invisible but everywhere at once, as if the neighborhood were like that, a field of insect noises, perfectly still except for that; like vacant lots from his childhood, one of those open fields in the summer where the grass had grown up, infused with the oscillating whisper of insects, charged with it to an alarming degree, he felt, as if vacancy were a sort of potential ready to produce whatever terror was current–mad dogs or whatever. They might appear any moment. They could be just out of sight in fact–or in plain view, for that matter, but somehow illusive, not yet fully resolved. In a certain frame of mind, at the right time of day there could be an open field, absolutely empty, and he would be afraid of them. The conspicuous absence of mad dogs in a field seemed as threatening as anything because it held that possibility; the noise seemed preparatory. He looks down the alley. How bright the morning is; and so still now he can hardly feel the air around him as if it had no temperature; not a cloud in the sky and not a breath of wind and all the antennas like tall grass, exactly like tall grass, functionally identical. He remembers waking up last night to the sound of his phone ringing in the kitchen–even more urgent at that distance, like someone else's phone, a siren in the night. It would have been Janie but he couldn't bear to listen to it, all the portent brought to such a tiny focus, such a small voice at three A.M. when he had no defenses.

The sound from next door has changed, a new component emerging from the hiss, separating out of it like a gasp, a prolonged expulsion of breath at the verge of a scream but unvoiced, only breath and fastening his attention on the air itself, how incredibly bright it is, clear as vacuum and hardly adequate, it seems, to support a sound so heavy with physical implications–a kind of rattling of the throat, at first not so loud, then pitching up an octave or so, finding its note and shrieking across the neighborhood like a civil defense warning, a tornado alert, and periodic like that, declining every few seconds like one of those sirens, descending a little before each intake of breath as if each outburst despaired individually, entirely summarized the situation from terror through hopelessness over and over, and all the while someone else calling his name, a woman's voice intermittently audible. "Mr. Delabano," it says flattening the second *a* like the middle *a* in banana; "Mr. Delabano," it calls again and again from the screen porch next door where the TV is flickering like a strobe light across a confusion of forms above which only one face seems to be visible closing and opening its mouth at intervals either screaming or calling, he can't tell which. There's no letup. It's not going to subside. It's like the alarms of zoo animals cascading from one species to another. He looks around amazed to find no one has come out to see what's going on; the backyards are empty as if evacuated. He takes a couple of steps past the rose beds–it's very hard to tell what's happening, just the one face still visible, the rest indistinct as he approaches the fence now, breaking into a little trot, intending to leap over as Mike had done but losing all his momentum when his toe jams in the chain-link then slips out causing him to bang his elbow on the rail. The commotion seems to have accelerated–there's a great flapping motion now, something fluttering up and down. He's trying to force open the gates across the driveway and feeling a touch of panic at this point, unable to work the rusted spring latch, throwing his weight against the gates to pop the chain but only bouncing off, bending the posts a little. He should simply run through the house but that seems impossibly indirect; the cries are more frantic, coming with greater frequency–almost sexual in this regard, suggesting some imminent and catastrophic termination of events. He flings himself at the fence again, throwing one leg clear over the top and straddling it for a second before sliding off on the other side, his right foot hanging briefly by the cuff of his pants; then across the yard to the screen door, yanking on the handle to no effect, punching at the plastic button with the side of his fist. Her voice is just about gone–all breath again. He can see her through the screen paying no attention to him, standing in front of the TV and producing that cry while the other–Lillian, he thinks, the one who must have been calling him–makes vigorous shushing noises and fluttery gestures in her direction. With a loud snap the door swings out sending Mr. Delabano back down the steps where he decides to remain for a moment. There's something wrong with the TV for sure, beyond just the tuning; he can see it irradiating her yellow housecoat, popping and hissing and flashing into her face as the older one–having drifted into a kind of shock it appears–approaches and withdraws, holding out a shawl which is refused repeatedly, fended off as she keeps trying to toss it over her head it looks like, wrap her up, as Mr. Delabano interprets the gesture, exactly as one might attempt to rescue a person on fire.

He steps up onto the porch generating a small reaction from Lillian who quits her matadorlike presentation of the shawl, holding it now to her chest and watching him from the opposite side as he makes his way around to where he can see the TV screen. It's flashing erratically, going dazzling white every so often with a popping sound as if there were a short circuit, then settling back to its former level as the hiss returns and what looks like some old black-and-white movie behind the static: horrified close-up Oriental faces alternating with landscape or something–a city skyline, fires and explosions then zap goes the screen, blinding for a second (her cries are very rapid now, right next to him, like someone gasping for air or in some sort of passionate frenzy) then terrified Orientals again and back to whatever it is–something looming over the city making showers of sparks as it hits the power lines, the TV popping and flashing like crazy. He reaches over and flips it off. Instantly there's silence. It's like a clap of air, a change in the atmospheric pressure. The younger one is just standing there with no expression whatever, perfectly quiet and looking at the TV as her sister approaches to guide her away into the house without a word.

There's a faint breeze now. Mr. Delabano waits for a while to see if he's needed, watching the screen door as it closes ever so slowly, the spring drawing it around finally past the angle of best leverage and slapping it shut. There's no sound at all from inside, no further trouble apparently. Still he waits a bit longer just in case, standing on the steps and fiddling with the broken latch for a minute or two before going home.

Mr. Delabano has a funny taste in his mouth and a sort of buzzing in his ears he can't seem to get rid of although the vacuum cleaner drowns it out. He leaves it going between passes as he straightens up and puts away all the curtains he's stacked here and there about the house. He could put half the furniture in storage, it occurs to him, and not miss it–most of the stuff in the living room probably and the dining room as well. He could store it in the garage and open things up considerably, give himself some space–something like a firebreak or a defoliation in the military sense of a protective simplification, a radical reduction in the confusion, the domestic complexity which he suspects must constitute a hazard somehow, innumerable points of obscurity and concealment. Especially offensive from where he stands right now by the picture window with the vacuum cleaner howling in the next room are the ruffles along the bottom of the sofa. What are they really he wonders. A little curtain at the base of the couch as if there were something under it requiring formal containment. An official sort of darkness, a precinct of shadows beneath the couch. He gets down on his knees. He can put his hand right under it of course; right through the ruffles, the little pleated curtain that looks as if something were intended to emerge theatrically from behind it. Dust ruffles is what his wife called them. To keep the dust from escaping into the room perhaps. To retain lost objects; here's a quarter–he sweeps it out–and a piece of candy or something wrapped in cellophane, no something else. He jerks his hand out then reaches back under, accidentally knocking it away so he has to get down on his stomach, reaching all the way under now, gathering cobwebs, then he's got it, holding it between his thumb and forefinger, turning his hand carefully so the ruffles don't catch as he withdraws it, a dead cicada with its wings outstretched, covered in cobwebs; it rustles like cellophane as he pulls the cobwebs away trying not to break it, taking great care with the wings which are perfectly spread–both sets front and back–like a mounted specimen. He turns around to sit cross-legged on the floor facing the picture window, leaning back against the couch and looking at the light through the wings then turning it over to examine the underside. There appear to be no mouth parts, just something like a stinger or a feeding tube folded underneath and very large eyes like pearls right at the front and so far apart it probably sees stereoscopically, overlapping yet peripheral fields of vision which certainly can't be for flying, they're so erratic; like little bottle rockets, little buzz bombs screaming off more or less out of control it seems in whichever direction they happen to be pointed. Such big eyes though; faintly metallic and still shiny, in perfect working order he imagines like a camera without film or without a battery. Without something in any case although it's hard to think what by itself could go wrong inside such a small and mechanical-looking creature that might not go wrong with a watch for example, might not involve simply running down at last, stopped at half-cycle with the wings locked open. It's all mechanism; nothing deeply mysterious surely, no mortality as such–at least not like with people, the mystery and mortality you get with soft tissue and bulk, declining inevitably from a sort of imprecision.

He places it on the coffee table. He's never really seen one like that in life. In the trees they're nearly impossible to spot although you'd think, making such a racket, it would be the simplest matter. In fact they're always on the opposite side of the branch–they inch around at one's approach, all of them, at least according to something he read, the entire population within some critical radius, flattening themselves against the side away from you so all you get is a glimpse at best but usually just noise. That's what the eyes are for, he suspects–getting around to the other side in time and keeping out of sight. They're probably designed exactly for that, eyes in front and way out at the edge so unless your eyes, like the cicada's, precede you into view, it always sees you first, the blind outer margins, like being seen before you're quite there, lagging behind yourself half a second, caught slightly in the past or in the future, whichever. He's seen woodpeckers do it also and even squirrels although not until you get pretty close. They'll skitter around a tree trunk making all kinds of noise; you can hear them perfectly well as you circle the tree but there's nothing to be seen and you wonder how they can know which way you're moving or how fast–obviously they must key on your shoulders or your feet but it still seems odd until they appear finally out of reach in the upper branches. Cicadas, though, stay hidden until you're too far away to see them at all except maybe with binoculars. Or a periscope, he thinks; a pair of periscopes–how would that be? A couple of toy periscopes, one for each eye, held out to the side (if one could maneuver with such a thing, keep one's balance with one's eyes, in effect, a yard apart); what would that be like? Depth perception to beat the band for one thing–and all those cicadas, what could they do, buzzing and chattering away in the heat; you could walk right in among them and there they would be, covering the branches, thousands perhaps right where they were all the time; squirrels and woodpeckers too for that matter and who knows what else, lost dogs; who knows?

He takes the cicada into the dining room and places it in the cut glass compote in the middle of the table, stands and looks at it for a moment then turns off the vacuum cleaner and goes to rummage around in the drawers below the kitchen counter until he finds an old pair of heavy culinary shears with deeply serrated blades and red-painted grips with spurlike extensions for additional fingers. It's sort of unpleasant; so explicitly surgical.

Kneeling at the corner of the couch he takes an experimental snip where there's a slit in the ruffle, a carefully hemmed gap where the front and side panels are allowed to overlap like the back of a coat where it parts at the waist. The complexity of it is incomprehensible to him. It's hard to evaluate–the soft edge of the couch meeting the floor with such protocol, such complication; how much would it cost to replace it, a damaged dust ruffle, one that had been compromised in some fashion (might it be one of those specialized skills whose practice, like the caning of chairs by the blind, requires some traditional affliction?). It's like the edge of some organism; there's a clam or an oyster that looks like that, ruffly at the margins, so elaborately evolved. He continues the cut, keeping the shears just under the frame, trimming closely as he can but having a hard time with the seams and the pleats where the cloth doubles, adjusting his grip so he can press the blades together to shear cleanly without fraying. Then there's the recliner which is easier–plastic flaps without pleats–and the bed and a little overstuffed chair with ottoman where he likes to hang his pants at night. The buzzing in his ears has stopped. He's got an armful of ruffles now, standing in the kitchen and testing the silence, the absolute quiet, and watching the evening light projecting agitated shadows on the wall above the stove–very faint leafy patterns shaking this way and that as if, invisible against the glow when he turns to look and located apparently at a point quite distant between the window and the setting sun, a tree intervenes and, in otherwise still air, tosses violently in the wind.

16

He keeps waking up waiting for the phone to ring in the kitchen, lying in the dark anticipating it, then drifting off to dream that it's raining and waking up again over and over like that, unable to break the cycle until he decides to go disconnect the possibility altogether, taking the kitchen phone off the hook then discovering he left the groceries out last night. The refrigerator light is dazzling, making him squint as he puts away the milk and the once-frozen dinners, noticing the time over his shoulder as the light sweeps behind him across the clock and the stove and the two fancy packages with red yarn bows and little folded cards attached–so peculiar and unpreventable, the sales lady beaming and wrapping them automatically: "It's the only way to avoid bloodshed if you've got two the same age," she said, tying off each glossy pink sack with a bow like a suture. "There," she said, "the batteries are inside."

He closes the refrigerator; his legs are getting cold. Batteries? he wonders, sitting down at the table; it'll be light in an hour. There's a hint of dawn already in fact–just like Christmas morning, he thinks, the strangeness of the packages in the semidarkness. Why should he need batteries?

He gets up to go put the receiver back on the hook, standing there next to it for a moment before sliding open the patio door and stepping outside. It's cold and there's a breeze; pale gray to the east above Mike's garage but overhead there are stars and a waning crescent moon high in the south. He takes a seat at the edge of the patio, watching the progress of the light for a while and listening to the gentle slapping of the sisters' screen door. He can see Canis Major very low above the rooftops–not really the whole constellation but just the big star, Sirius, starting to dim now, fading along with the yellow backyard lights across the alley. He closes his eyes. There's a phone ringing somewhere. Not his–he turns to make sure the glass door is open–Mike's or the sisters' probably, ringing and ringing, making the air seem thinner as if it were harder to breathe until at some point it stops, replaced by the whisper of traffic from the highway.

The stars have disappeared. He gets up carefully, favoring his left side and standing for a minute with his hands on his back before going inside to start the coffee, bringing the pot to the window to see as he measures it out, then transferring the gift-wrapped packages to the table and flipping on the light. He removes the red yarn and the presentation cards embossed with little rocking horses, placing these on the counter before opening the sacks and withdrawing the boxes, each with a round cellophane window imprinted with graduated crosshairs giving a glimpse of the contents. "Spymaster Periscope," it says at the top, "With Ultrasonic Communicator"; and below the window, enclosed in quotation marks, the cryptic motto: "What do they see when you know you are looking." On the other side of the box are instructions in Japanese.

He takes out the periscopes and lays them on the table next to each other: as a set very purposeful, very military-looking dark gray plastic and altogether more complicated than what he had in mind; extendable apparently–he picks one up and telescopes it all the way out–with a pair of hand-grips, one of which is provided with a big red button of the sort he associates with the firing of machine guns from fighter aircraft. He pushes the button but nothing happens. He places the viewing end against his face, standing and turning toward the window and the faintly rosy light now coming off the side of the garage. One eye, then the other–it's too small for both and it's not working right; he pushes the red button again to no effect. There's something but not very clear; he leans forward and back, raises his hand and waves it around–a sensation like that experienced by amputees: a ghost limb; he can see right through it, a wall or something, the clock behind him inverted. He's got it twisted around. He turns the upper half, continuing to look as portions of the kitchen rotate in the tiny field, wheeling around 180 degrees until he has it forward and everything right side up, bending his knees a little then sitting back down to bring the garage into view. It seems to him significantly less interesting than, say, merely looking through the window although a child's imagination, he supposes, might be sustained just by the elaborate extension of himself, the removal of the person from the actual site of some perilous observation. He scoots his chair over closer to the window, tilting the periscope and scanning across his garage to the sisters' yard and down the tilted line of backyards and garages, the light already bright and colorless against them. It's true, someone with a rifle emerging now from behind one of those garages might not see him even if he looked this way and what if he did–one of those terrible things you hear about from time to time, someone goes crazy and starts shooting one morning (he can still hear the screen door slapping in the breeze, lightly tapping now and then, barely audible)–if he did what would happen? How would it look if he were far enough away to be quite small even in such a constricted field, maybe four or five houses down, the tiny flash of the rifle and a fraction of a second before the bullet strikes the mirror jerking the periscope back in his hands.

He returns the chair to where it was and puts the periscope on the table, looking now for the batteries, rummaging through the sacks full of purple tissue paper and finding them at last taped to the boxes–little ones like hearing aid batteries about the size of a dime to be inserted with considerable difficulty into the base of the handle. He has to slide home the little plastic covers with the flat of a butterknife, each compartment closing with the same loud click as if designed to require such force, become armed as it were with great finality. Now when he pushes the button there's a beep.

In the front yard he keeps the periscopes tucked under his robe and studies the grass until a couple of cars pass out of sight, then quickly steps to the curb producing his instruments, inadvertently beeping a few times as he brings them horizontally to his face, trying to find the right grip. He wants the long empty view straight up the street to the west but doesn't really know what to make of it, angling the periscopes forward and back; the images merge without much effect, slip apart, come back together with hardly any gain beyond a vague sense of emptiness compounded, of depth and distance gone slack as if somehow strained beyond limits, or as if the limits were psychological the way a certain student he remembers could never manage to use a telescope–a conceptual problem he had finally decided, a sort of fundamental disbelief. He goes back inside, gets his coffee and stands in the open patio door for a while feeling the breeze more faintly, everything settling down toward noon and averaging out, the sun now well above Mike's garage. How sweet his wife's voice was, he thinks; how fragile and soft, hardly more than a whisper.

> The "one-eyed ceremony" among the Pogsas requires the initiate to submit to having both eyes sealed with an aromatic plaster whose composition is closely guarded although it seems certain to include among its active ingredients a measure of their mysterious arrow poison. Regarding its properties they will say nothing except that, after a while, the pain goes away; although on this point my interpreter wished to note that, according to a Desano acquaintance, relief, when it comes, is not so much from the pain itself as from certain constraints upon the affections.

There's a ding from the toaster and Mr. Delabano marks his place, returning with a tuna sandwich and a glass of milk now cold and apparently none the worse for having been left out. There's a thin, hazy light like light through gauze; cool, milky light coming in through the windows and a faint smell of roses–just for a moment, from the open door, a pale imaginary trace of one, the old rose perhaps, although they're just sticks now, not even a leaf. He turns to the photograph captioned "luminescence," the very dark one with a dirt road through spiny-looking trees and scattered flecks of white like fireflies but without the streaking one would expect were this the case. He gets the magnifier from the little velvet bag next to the dictionary where his wife kept it, holding it just above the photograph and bringing his head down until he can see the pattern of the photographic screen. The white flecks are painted on. Applied to the printing plate somehow, very carefully like asterisks overlapping the screen with hair-thin radiant lines. He flips to the "parallactical sequence" at the back–ten views of just grass and dirt with some trees in the background as if maybe they forgot to paint something in. He takes a bite of his sandwich and leans back tilting the book against the edge of the table.

> They are the "beast men," the naked "wild men of the forest" with whom intermarriage is unthinkable nor contact sought for whatever reason excepting the occasional taking of slaves.
>
> Such is the scorn in which they are held that their name has gained currency as an epithet whose indiscriminate application further deepens the obscurity of these illusive forest-dwellers, enveloping them within a penumbra of indistinct loathing and apprehension till they seem metaphorical, sad personifications of some generalized regret. Nor, it should be admitted, do such notions automatically vanish with the fact. So profoundly rudimentary did their society seem initially that I found a period of acclimatization was required, as upon entering a darkened room, before I could see well enough to discard or at least substantially to modify the impression that the Pogsas in fact represented no culture at all but rather a sort of indeterminate state, a preliminary condition, pre-cultural,

uncatalyzed and undeveloped like those neotenous insects whose subterranean immature forms having evolved upon some fortuitous advantage spend all their existence grappling hidden in the earth, their brief, foreshortened emergence deferred to an afterthought or a dream.

None of which is to deny a certain evasive cunning evident from the first even in the smallest of transactions—the distinctive long skull with its protruding jaw and receding forehead tending to take a strange, oblique tilt upon consideration of the simplest matter, eyes darting this way and that above a smile in whose furtive complications might be read the subtle politics of sitting and sleeping and the taking of meals.

Nor could one fail to observe, here and there, demonstrations of craftsmanship and skill, most notably with regard to their weapons which were the equal of any I had seen among the Waikano and in whose use the Pogsas are unexcelled, having, according to Manoel's Desano informant, been the inventors of the blowpipe and the source, long ago, of its dissemination among all the Betoya tribes. Yet, somehow, like those half-finished marbles by Rodin, earth clings to them. They are, I could not help but feel, in some essential way unrelieved from the forest, incompletely differentiated from the darkness, the jungly process which seems to subtend all their attitudes and desires with its secret instruction to the exclusion of sentiment and even simple curiosity.

It occurred to me however, as I sought to habituate myself and to retreat insofar as possible from

> whatever preconceptions might deflect my judgement, that what had been characterized by others as dullness or apathy among all the Pogsas was an altogether distinct behavior unrelated to the conditioned lethargy of the Caboclos or the stolid indifference of certain acculturated tribes. Rather it seemed a withdrawal toward precisely this dim priority, this essentially primitive intuition whose call is no more audible to us than that which a housecat may suddenly attend, quitting the dangled string to crouch immobilized and unresponsive.
>
> To our eyes, to our developed and segregated sensibilities, the fire of the Pogsa at night is joyless for within it no festival inheres, no ritual is ignited, no metaphor, no image of the soul. It is primordial, clear and remote; the fire, perhaps, of Dubois' Pithecanthropus . . .

Mr. Delabano brings the book to his chest. It's the rose. He can smell it, the antique one as if it were blooming, the perfume drifting in with the light; pale fragrance like light through lavender-colored tissue–there's a mass of tissue blossoming with a soft crinkly noise out of the sack on the table, uncompressing like one of those time-lapse sequences of buds springing open. He watches it for a moment, placing the book on the table and finishing his sandwich and the glass of milk. The purple tissue, the richness of it, seems inconsistent with its surroundings, the great bloom of it there still barely unfolding, slowly now, almost fully expanded with the light from the patio door glowing through the edges so densely colored everything around it pales–the light in the kitchen and the light outside as if whatever ambient sensation remained were drawn out in this effect, color and fragrance reduced in it. He takes his plate and his glass to the sink, rinsing them out, watching the swirl of milky water and thinking of the horrified Oriental faces, the smooth pale faces with unwrinkled eyes, their mouths wide open, coming and going in the static. He goes over to the door and stands looking out at the garden, the sticks of the rose plants and the black flowers. The smell seems evenly dispersed without a source as if generated internally like the sound he experienced yesterday, something at the back of his mind almost like the old rose but, actually, not quite. The taste of milk is unpleasant. He goes to rinse out his mouth, gazing down into the sink with the water running, holding his hand under it for a minute and feeling how cold it is, like tap water in the winter after dripping all night to keep the pipes from freezing. He's been here before, he thinks, and done exactly this–the water running, trying to remember or isolate something, a sort of chemistry involved in letting the water run as if to purify, render something like a photograph or a stain, develop something against the whiteness of the sink. He can imagine a purple stain spreading away from the drain cover, like a potassium permanganate stain or a phenolphthalein reaction–the magic trick to use on the first day of class, the clear solution poured into another clear liquid to produce–what? Wine, he would say to them. Wine from water. And some would want to see it again, standing closer and bending over the flask to give it a sniff: it's not wine; it smells like the clinic. And it did; the wrong sort of smell for such a color, sharp and unpleasant, the wrong sort of alcohol. Perhaps wine in a broader sense, though; like blood in the broadest sense (one boy was Catholic–right up there with the others, a smooth, pale face, wide-eyed and his mouth open as if expecting something more, an expression better directed toward some catastrophe, something out the window truly monstrous). He turns off the water and in the silence imagines the sound of static again but just for a second. He looks out the window down the line of garages to the west; there's no one out, no rifleman, nothing threatening although the fragrance makes him uneasy, the density of it, the concentration–he looks at the palms of his hands–beyond some threshold like a little too much artificial sweetener; just that little bit too much changes the character, casts the whole thing into doubt and compromises the original sense–in this case that of a moment preserved, as he thinks of it, the tenancy of those whose fence rail it was in Virginia where the roses grew. Such a notion as presented now, as carried upon the fragrance, seems false and incomplete as if the intensification of the fragrance revealed, like a lab test, unpleasant complications (the simple rosiness rendered more potent, more active by combination, say with some other essence and there is something else; he looks at the floor and the bottoms of his shoes), bringing out flaws, dark areas, in the notion itself, that moment he likes to think transmitted and, by extension, every moment like radio waves, old programs radiating forever. Something unfathomable is entailed. Such thoughts entangle something else like a coelacanth in the net, squirming among the bright moments, detectable close under the sweetness like a consequence or, rather, preceding it, driving the fragrance like bees in the flower or what comes before that, what comes before the bees?

The back of his neck feels hot. He turns on the faucet and splashes cold water on his face and neck, soaking his shirt collar, reaching for a paper towel and looking out the window, down the backyards to the west with the water running. There, he thinks, leaning over the sink with the side of his head touching the window, above the rose trellis in the gap between the houses and the garages where the chain-link fences recede against the horizon is a dark area, a sooty patch of sky as if there were heavy construction somewhere out beyond the highway, dust and diesel smoke suspended, gathering and hanging above the spot.

He turns off the water and goes to the west window but the sisters' screen porch is in the way–he can see the TV still where they left it; and he can see pale sky through the screen, through both screens, rippling with faint dark lines as he moves his head to one side or the other, the screens overlapping, shifting in and out of phase. He returns to the window above the sink for a moment, then to the kitchen table, opening the book to the stereoscopic photographs again, the "typical parallactical sequence," hooking his ankles around the chair legs and picking up the magnifier. The little flecks and streaks here and there appear to be damage to the original prints or maybe stains on the negatives printing white–actual blemishes in any case, not painted on, some frames damaged more than others and now he can see the codes in black in the upper right corners: P–17, P–17; P–18, P–18 and so on in sequence top to bottom, pairs of numbers scratched into the negatives with a stylus it looks like, a correction on the first set with the P–17 on the left replacing something scratched out. He stands up and looks down at the top pair of photographs, holding the book flat, shifting around to face the window. There's a way to do it, he remembers, by defocusing the eyes, relaxing the muscles a certain way to bring the images together although it's not easy and some can't manage without a viewer. He rotates the book slightly–both images flat and evenly lit the way he recalls from the astronomy text that had pages of them, stereo pairs of lunar features modeled in plaster and photographed as they might appear from the surface, dreamlike vistas, the mountains of the moon as seen from a window which is how you were instructed to envision the effect, gazing past the pages into an imagined distance until the little reference marks converged and you had it as if by faith, entirely three-dimensional though dramatically more jagged and vertical than lunar peaks were known to be even in the fifties, the stars less than accurate as well, he suspected, artfully scattered and shimmering out of register. He bends a little closer then straightens again withdrawing a handful of change from his pocket and placing a penny below each picture in the top set, positioning them carefully and studying this arrangement for a moment before going to the sink to turn on the water, adjusting it to run down the side without splashing then returning to stand over the pictures. He reaches into his pocket again and replaces one of the pennies which is tarnished with a shiny one to match the other, turning each one so the portrait of Lincoln is right side up. Now he places both hands on the table, leaning over the book listening to the water and closing his eyes for a second then opening them without focusing, waiting for the pennies to come together, imagining the distance, the view across Sinus Iridium which was so difficult and spectacular without features, you might think, whereby depth could be gauged yet by far the most impressive, the most unexpected and comprehendable expanse across nothing it seemed for thousands of miles. He has to concentrate to be sure the water's still running, to distinguish it from silence as the portraits of Lincoln slip together so easily and suddenly he almost doesn't trust it but there's no way to check without sacrificing the achievement which would make no sense anyway; simply lift the eyes without jarring the state of grace. Again there's a dark area, in the middle ground a hazy puff of something more conspicuous by its sudden appearance than the sensation of depth which is actually rather slight. Lunar outgassing comes to mind and dreamily recommends itself as he extends this notion to the diesel smoke beyond the highway: the release to the surface of volcanic gasses suspected but never confirmed as the cause of strange glows reported on the moon periodically by amateur observers. It seems to float a little above the clearing, off to the left above the bare dirt at the edge of the grass and obscuring slightly the trees in the background like heat distortion or something on the lens. He wants to break away to check the pictures individually but it'll be too hard to regain the effect. Nor, he feels, should he even twitch his eyes to see if it's him–something in the eye itself, that little blind spot at the back of the retina. Lunar outgassing is what it sounds like (the hiss of the water is louder now) as if crossing one's eyes like this–defocusing, whatever–were like crossing one's fingers, defining a moment wherein distortion is permissible and so, for a moment, a few seconds at most until the doorbell rings, he permits this one for its consolation and its emptiness and the reasonable expectation that lunar gasses might in fact smell like roses.

It's Mike at the door, handing him the prints in an envelope and hurrying unescorted straight back through the den and into the yard, talking rapidly over his shoulder as if in continuation of some undertaking only briefly interrupted and still operating under the original grant of hospitality unaffected by Mr. Delabano's stiffness and reluctance to follow except to require a sort of shout from the garden where Mike's standing now by himself like a newsman reporting from some hazardous location his opinion that agaves shouldn't normally test positive for alkaloids and producing, at this point, a small white box and asking if Mr. Delabano would like to come watch.

Mr. Delabano can hardly move. He's feeling dizzy, leaning against the door frame, his mouth and face and hands terribly dry, a sensation of dusty dryness all around him, a glare to everything; he thinks he might faint.

"I bet I screw this up," yells Mike, kneeling by one of the plants now with the box open on the ground and a pair of scissors in his hand. "I just sell this stuff," he laughs and glances over at Mr. Delabano who's having trouble with his sense of distance, interpreting the interval between himself and the goings-on outside in terms of extremes one way or the other with Mike's head at the center of the perceptual conflict, approaching and receding simultaneously and possessing a very uncertain relation to the voice which seems to issue from some middle distance, detached from these ambiguities and calling him once again to come observe the proceedings.

"Just a second," says Mr. Delabano, making his way to the sink and turning off the water, turning it on again briefly to moisten a paper towel which he applies to his face and then to the back of his neck, holding it there as he walks out to the garden.

"Or it could be a palm," says Mike. He's assumed a contemplative attitude, facing the plant with both hands on his knees, the white box in front of him closed with the scissors on top. To Mr. Delabano he looks Japanese like that–as if about to perform some terrible ritual. "You get some strange ones," he says, "and alkaloids sometimes." He looks up at Mr. Delabano, "Janie's got the scribbles again." Mr. Delabano has to think for a second. "Not houses though, and no sky; none of that stuff. Just the scribbly part. Really getting down to business; just big old black scribbles all over the page." He continues to look at Mr. Delabano without saying anything, smiling slightly as if he'd made a joke, then turning once more to his preparations, taking up the scissors and opening the box.

"What are you going to do?" asks Mr. Delabano.

"Find a cure for cancer I bet," says Mike.

Mr. Delabano looks across the tops of the fences to the west but there's nothing; the sun descending, brightening that part of the sky. "Really," he says. "What are you going to do?"

Mike has another instrument that looks like a garlic press. Now he's got the scissors in one hand and this instrument in the other, opening and closing them both like castanets, looking up at Mr. Delabano and smiling again. There's a slapping sound from Mike's house and a second, softer one as Mr. Delabano turns to look, the screen door closing and rebounding.

"Don't laugh," says Mike. He takes from his pocket something like a gardening mask and hangs it around his neck. "Mask," he says, "nuisance odor, disposable." He smiles and places it over his nose and mouth. Mr. Delabano takes a couple of steps back, holding his moist paper towel to his face, looking around at Mike's back door then over at the sisters' house. "Had any gopher trouble lately?" asks Mike, his voice slightly muffled, examining one of the thick fuzzy leaves. Mr. Delabano shakes his head; there's a clatter somewhere like chains on a swing set and a child crying, really howling but quite far off, screaming like an injured monkey, some jungle tragedy. "None at all," says Mr. Delabano taking another half step back, "absolutely none."

"Shortness of breath?" asks Mike, bending closer and holding the leaf by the tip, tapping it lightly with the scissors then snipping off a small portion and dropping it into the garlic press.

Mr. Delabano wishes someone would attend to the child; it just keeps going like the cries in a hospital you don't expect to stop because they're attended already, to the point of anguish sometimes, to the limit, on and on, a kind of white noise where anything can happen, where it can't be helped.

"You want to come watch?" asks Mike. A milky fluid is beading and starting to run at the cut. Mike's waiting for him to approach, holding something with a pair of tweezers as Mr. Delabano advances a little, just enough so operations can resume. It's a thin white disc of something like felt or paper, like a sacramental wafer he's holding now under the garlic press, squeezing a couple of milky drops onto it then laying the little press aside and just kneeling there with the wafer for a moment, adjusting his mask, looking at Mr. Delabano and holding up one finger in a gesture Mr. Delabano is unable to interpret. He can hear Mike breathing, the sides of the mask popping in and out slightly. Someone has evidently taken care of the child; at least the crying has stopped, replaced by the squeaking of a swing set; or more than one nearly synchronized, now together, now apart. "Here we go," says Mike. He takes a little plastic squeeze-bottle out of the box, holding and unscrewing it with the same hand, turning to Mr. Delabano. "Dusseldorf reagent," he says, or something like that, pausing as if to let the information sink in, as if to establish consent, allowing a moment for second thoughts before some very risky business. The squeaking swings have been joined by another from a different quarter, a different note. They're like birdcalls. Whippoorwills, he thinks. Mike's holding the squeeze-bottle just above the sacramental wafer, his left hand–the one with the bottle–starting to shake a little as he squeezes harder to detach the drop of clear liquid jiggling at the tip. He gives it a little flick and instantly there's a bright red spot in the center of the disc and, for Mr. Delabano, an incomprehensible sense of injury and loss as if having had loss announced to him, some test having been performed to reduce all sorts of manageable apprehensions to a fact. The kiss of death, he thinks; no sense to it at all, no particular meaning he can attach; just the spot like a symbol, a red hand, a biopsy result. How terrifying Mike looks now with the mask and the name tag, putting his things away. Mr. Delabano places the nearly dry towel on the back of his neck again, retreating to the chair at the edge of the patio. After a minute Mike comes over to join him, dragging a chair across the pebbly concrete, his mask still on, holding the white box.

"We're going to have a barbecue Friday," he says, "we'd like you to come; might try to have some people from the neighborhood." Mr. Delabano nods; Mike looks both frightening and ridiculous–he's taking off his ID badge and putting it in his pocket, folding his hands over the white box in his lap, leaning back and extending his legs but leaving the mask in place. "There's a fossil that looks kind of like that," he says, "maybe an agave relative or an ancestor but it's tiny. It's got a flower like that, almost microscopic–these things are really rare apparently. I saw a photomicrograph." Mr. Delabano imagines the swings sound like redbirds now, closes his eyes and tries to imagine it; it's nearly the right time of day, the sun gold-red from the west, glowing through his eyelids. He wonders if Mike knows he still has the mask on; he must hear his own breathing, the little popping sound. Mr. Delabano opens his eyes and there he is still leaning back wearing the mask, perfectly at ease, looking at the garden. "There's something called a carrion plant," he says quietly, his voice behind the mask thin and breathy as if produced by a radio, "it blooms in the desert and smells like rotting meat. Imagine that. Lying out there waiting for vultures. Pollination at any price I guess." He looks over at Mr. Delabano, smiling possibly, the mask absurd as a party hat. "What we do for love," he says, regarding Mr. Delabano now with theatrical intensity and removing the mask like the Phantom of the Opera, smiling and standing and putting it back in his pocket. "I'm not sure what time yet. I'll let you know." And then he's off. Mr. Delabano hears him pause just inside the house–"Gee whiz," he says, "looks like Christmas."

After a while Mr. Delabano goes back in, stands for a minute by the fireplace looking over at the fancy packaging and the toy periscopes, then he bends to open the damper, bringing his ear down to it with the side of his head against the brick. There's just the soft rush of air. He ducks in under a little closer–a faint suggestion of something else like a telephone off the hook, something obscurely overhead in the background like machinery, a sort of booming, very low and steady as if it were coming from far away.

17

"Vultures," Mr. Delabano thinks, awake again in the middle of the night his skin so dry he hesitates to move. Vultures on the roof. The notion takes a while to dissipate even though he's alert now–vultures skittering across the shingles like sparrows; it makes sense as long as he's still, lies there desiccated, good as dead and listening to the wind. It must be the antenna again. Or the bag dog at last, vulturelike, sparrowlike in its movements, diffuse like a flock of sparrows, red eyes like stars. He can imagine it like this if he doesn't move, staring up into the dark. Is he crossing his eyes? There's no way to tell where his eyes are focused, at what point his suspicions converge. Is there crying? Just above the breeze and the scraping of the abelia bush? Another injury? Or more than one like cries down a corridor, coming and going, together and apart. The back of his neck feels hot against the pillow, sweaty in spite of the dryness, the dry sound of branches and the wind hissing through them in little gusts. There's a swing set again or he's imagining it. Between gusts he can hear it–no crying, just squeaking: a long interval and too regular to be caused by the wind; there's a governing weight, squeaking a rusty metallic squeak with a little snap at the end, right next door it sounds like, the practiced careless swinging of someone who knows exactly how high before the chains go slack, who's used to that limit. Do her parents know, he wonders? It's hard not to breathe in time with it, fall into phase, making it seem like he's gasping a little, producing that sound, a little wheeze with each breath like someone attached to a life support mechanism. He holds his breath for a second, then keeps his mouth open to make as little sound as possible. If he turned he might see her. In her nightclothes he imagines, dangling out there in the middle of the night having lost all fear apparently, having given herself up. What if she has on some sort of white nightgown flapping about her; how strange that would be. What if she were smiling? He lowers his eyes toward the foot of the bed; there's a yellow strip of light across the wall and the overstuffed chair where his pants are folded–Mike's outside light shining through the uncurtained window, the hooded bulb above the garage door. She might be silhouetted if he looked. For a second he stiffens, waiting for her shadow to cross but there's nothing, then the squeaking stops and the chains go loose, clattering against the frame. How can it be this subtle, he thinks. How can death and horror be so faint and indirect. The yellow light goes out. The wind has died down a bit. It's completely dark again and his eyes are unfocused, featureless he imagines, black dots like the eyes of Janie's toy figure. He thinks of the Oriental faces so horrified and gentle at the same time, featureless in a way, identical in their horror. How was it for them, he wonders. How would it be if all the subtle little noises, the wind and the branches, were seriously misinterpreted and in the morning he stepped out under a low pall of smoke to confront a scene of devastation, whole neighborhoods wiped out, here and there people standing around in robes and pajamas lost in their front yards looking for the paper and gazing at the sky? What can one grasp of such a thing, such a monstrosity? How could they have known what hit them, the residents of Tokyo or wherever, lanterns swaying, paper houses shivering in the wind; and those near the ocean especially, he thinks, awake for no reason and listening to the waves, pale smooth faces all awake in the dark like this. He withdraws his hands from under the covers and places them on his chest, folded to keep them still against the blanket that feels so bristly and unpleasant with static electricity. It's like a gunshot, he thinks, the subtlety of it, the way the real thing differs from what you'd expect from watching movies–more like a firecracker, a little pop, pop in the distance carrying no more sense of threat than someone hammering a nail or a backfire from the highway unless you think about it, analyze it for a second, separate the possibilities. And with something like this, who knows–an immense deviation from what you'd expect. He inclines his head slightly to look at his hands slowly moving his left across the blanket, tensing his jaw and forcing himself, leaving a path of delicate blue sparks. How can the Japanese ever sleep, he wonders. All that history, thousands of years and yet so pale and vulnerable–not really of course, he remembers the war, but as he can't help thinking of them–translucent houses and objects made of paper, everything, flowers and gardens, just so, right up to the edge like that, right to the water's edge as if it might last forever. There's a scraping on the roof again, like a knife against sandpaper, the thin edge of an aluminum rod across the composition shingles; gusts of wind like waves hissing up the beach.

How pale and translucent his neighbor looked. On her porch yelling in that way, gasping in that loud whisper like the sound the TV was making, her face flashing white and featureless in the light like an X ray of herself, features coming and going as if she were paper, light shining through her. A prolonged dragging sound now progressing some distance across the roof. It's broken loose, he thinks; popped the bottom strap and about to come tumbling down into the yard any minute. What a racket that will make; he's unnerved simply thinking about it, anticipating it–an antenna, all those appendages–rolling off the roof, dragging its lines and catching as it falls, jerking back against the side of the house, through a window possibly. He can picture it, like a great claw through the glass. There's a gentle ebb and flow to the wind now, rising and falling. To people near the highway it must seem like the ocean; almost unbearable, he imagines, to those near the playground confronting that gulf, the vacant expanse between the houses and the interstate so much worse than unobstructed prairie which might allow one's thoughts and apprehensions simply to escape, drift away into the dark. As it is, wakeful notions must be captured in that space; they must echo off the highway, bounce back across the weeds and grass. He wouldn't live there; he could never inhabit one of those bedrooms with windows on the highway side, salmon-colored sodium lights–like being kept alive artificially, what a thought; kept from fading into the dark. He thinks of people silhouetted, sitting up in bed, heads turned to the windows, unable for a moment to forget their predicament as if they were hospitalized and had no choice in the matter. Why would anyone live there otherwise? Unless it were a kind of illness. His arms are asleep. It's poor circulation and not wanting to move them, holding them too long across his chest like this, keeping himself still against the feeling of everything dry as dust. The sounds outside have the quality of dust, every little noise like the touch of the blanket. He's become sensitized. It's like lying in the grass–dry grass and weeds with insects buzzing around, gnats like dust. He opens his eyes but the feeling persists–discomfort from the threat of discomfort, almost worse for its absence like a limb gone to sleep, a sort of apprehension in the skin itself anticipating pain, significant information. Nothing sounds like anything exactly; the wind is more like static as if meanings were spread out, governed by some upper limit and, so, spread out to compensate. Like the notion that mortal wounds are painless, he thinks (presumably because the use for pain has passed or because the senses are overloaded; he feels wounded–he thinks of Mike's activities in the garden as having established that somehow, the round white patch with the red stain in the center like a bandage, a handkerchief pressed to the site of an injury, that same kind of shock as you hold it away). The noises are like that, and the feel of the sheets–a sort of whiteness like a bandage; and a conspicuous absence of pain as if any information were inadequate at this point, as if it could do you no good to know about events so terrible; they just sound like static, overload your ability to understand and fall upon you before you know it: the collision of worlds; the great extinctions; certain firestorms perhaps like the one in Dresden–what could that have been like? Little popping sounds for bombs and then a breeze, not at all what you'd expect. Just enough to keep you awake, make you sit up and turn your head to the window. He rolls over slowly. There's a darkness within the darkness, more specific, more defined the longer he looks: the gray darkness of the side of Mike's house and within that something black at the center, floating right in front of his face like a speck in his eye or the residual blindness after looking away from something too bright. His arms are tingling now; he rearranges himself, pulls his pillow up under his head and the sheets up around him, lying on his side with his face near the window, moving his eyes to capture the thin darker shapes of the ivy and the abelia at the edges of his vision, separating these from the problem and studying it for a while as a sort of omission, a gap in the grayness, in his perception of it and the breeze as well–a vacancy there too, a further blotting out of his senses in this area as if the breeze were excluded from this small region, no air but his breath (isn't the periphery supposed to go first–when you die or black out, not the center? How pathetic if he were to die now, painlessly, gazing into the gray space between houses darkening to black as if no great transition were involved after all; if that's what it is; the bad dog finally, such a small thing like a change in the weather). He reaches up with his left arm–no longer tingling but numb–to touch the pane of glass nearest his hand. It's cool. Not frosty but just cool enough that his fingers might leave little rings of condensation. Then he brings his hand in front of his face and touches the window where the darkness seems to center. It feels warm and instantly the vacancy collapses, replaced by a presence as if something had rushed to the window or popped up from below–such an impact he receives from this subtle reinterpretation that he imagines himself in shock like a squirrel in the road, the image occurs to him, his thoughts racing this way and that as he lies there with his head on the pillow, motionless except for his eyes, scanning for features now, fastening on the symmetry, a slight movement–all this in an instant before he throws himself off the opposite side of the bed rolled up in the bedclothes and practically immobilized as he hits the floor, scooting like a caterpillar to the nightstand, knocking it against the wall as he props himself against it with one arm across the bed. He flips on the light. It's Janie with her face pressed to the window. Her lips and nose and forehead are so pale against the glass, so white and bloodless she's like something medical in a jar, something in alcohol squinting at him and inflating her cheeks like a blowfish in and out, mouth open and sealed to the glass as if dying for lack of oxygen, amused now it appears as she intensifies her performance, puffing her face up and crossing her eyes, twisting her head a little side to side. He turns the light off and slips back down to the floor, lying on his back; here it comes, he thinks–there's a noise from the roof like a transformer humming, then a snap and an attenuated sort of crashing sound, the gradual coming apart of some complex structure; a reduction, he would tell his students (speaking above them, watching their faces) to a lower state of energy. He thinks of the grackles. In the dark he imagines them, miles of blackbirds as the antenna goes tumbling off the front of the house, catching at the end of its wire, swinging back and crashing through the picture window.

18

"You hold this part," says Mr. Delabano, handing Janie a brand new roll of silver duct tape, showing her how to grasp it tightly as he peels some off the top, drawing her toward him like a tug of war, several times having to do this tugging gently and quickly to get enough tape, Janie giggling, not wanting to stop and making it difficult to use the scissors.

"Now put that down," he says, holding up one of the periscopes. He presses the button to make it beep, letting her take it as the tape goes rolling across the patio caught by the wind, bouncing into the yard and disappearing around the back of the house. Janie's got the periscope to her face doing pirouettes, beeping and spinning, about to fall.

"Look," he says, guiding her with one hand and holding the other away with the tape stuck to it, "stand over here"; he positions her facing the brick, extending the periscope to the side past the corner of the house, "you can see through walls." She's trying to tilt her head sideways. "Just one eye," says Mr. Delabano, "hold it straight out." He goes to retrieve the roll of tape. Carol's at the fence.

"Hi," she says. "Is it going to be okay?"

"Oh, sure," says Mr. Delabano. Carol's looking at the duct tape flapping at the end of his finger. "We're working on a science project," says Mr. Delabano.

"Ah," says Carol, "well good luck," she laughs. "I'll just be an hour or so." Janie's at the fence now holding the periscope upside down, beeping continuously. "Oh my, that does look scientific," says Carol kneeling, telling Janie to be good, glancing at the garden, the stiff dry stalks swaying slightly in the wind, then smiling up at Mr. Delabano. "You can come over here if you want; if she gets to be a problem, the back door's unlocked."

"All right, thanks," says Mr. Delabano.

"I want some gum," says Janie.

"If you're good," says Carol. She stands up. "Maybe an hour and a half; I've never been to one of these." She smooths the front of her skirt and stands there for a minute longer looking out of place dressed up, high heels a little unstable on the grass. Then a car pulls up and she has to go, exiting through the side gate, turning and waving.

"We'll need another piece of tape," says Mr. Delabano. He picks up the roll and places it under his arm, struggling to detach the now stuck-to-itself unusable wad from the end of his finger, rolling it into a ball and returning to the patio to wait for Janie who's circumnavigating the yard with the inverted periscope, progressing by means of rapid little steps as if to simulate the movements as well as the viewpoint of some small animal, making her way along the back fence now and disappearing behind the garage. He can hear her parka scraping the chain-link, the beeper wearing out, reduced to an intermittent rattle by the time she returns, sounding like an insect in the mechanism as she stands there pleased with herself, amused by the noise.

"Do you like tunafish sandwiches?" asks Mr. Delabano.

"Yes," says Janie.

"Would you like one now?" he asks.

"Yes," she says, handing him the periscope, "if you don't cut it straight."

He looks at her for a minute, puts the periscope down on the aluminum table.

"I'll show you," she says, leading him into the kitchen, offering suggestions at several points, setting out spoons and forks as they sit down in the chill with their jackets still on to cold milk and diagonally cut tuna sandwiches like campers listening to the wind and the plastic sheeting over the picture window torn loose at one corner and snapping like a tent on some bleak plateau.

"Is there a monster?" she asks with her mouth full, her face so pale above the sandwich and the milk.

"What kind?" he says, eating his corners first, noticing in the air a kind of oscillation, a rapid sort of compression and decompression caused, no doubt, by the flapping of the plastic over the window, a reed effect like the buzzing of the weather stripping but much lower in frequency, felt rather than heard.

"You know," she says, smiling at him, arranging her right-angle crusts on the plate like ghost sandwiches, drawing with one finger a bead of milk across the table. "A real one," she says, making squiggly wet lines with the milk now, swirling them around and making zigzags until it's just a big wet spot.

"One you can see?"

"Yes."

"Hmm," says Mr. Delabano, taking her plate, gathering the spoons and forks and returning these to the drawer then standing by the window, looking at the Band-Aids on his left hand–the palm and the little finger. Janie's fiddling with the zipper on her jacket.

"Like a dog?" he asks. She's going rapidly up and down with the zipper, interested in the noise.

"I don't know," she says.

He watches her for a minute, then slides open the door and she follows him out.

"My goodness!" says Carol, stepping out on the patio, Janie tugging her finger. "My goodness," she says again.

"I did the tape," says Janie letting go of Carol's hand to examine the contents of her purse.

"Wait a minute," says Carol, "here; that's for Julie." She helps Janie unwrap the package of gum then turns to the construction in the center of the patio, hands on her hips, appraising it as Janie strips the foil from all five pieces, placing them in her mouth one after the other.

"You did the decoration, too," says Carol.

"It's a time machine," says Janie.

"Oh, Janie," says Carol, "pick up the wrappers."

"It's a time machine," says Janie more clearly having removed the wad of gum for a moment, holding it in her hand and chasing the bits of foil and paper across the patio.

"Well, gosh," says Carol, looking around for Mr. Delabano who's still in the doorway uncertain of the situation, how to hold himself toward the project, the apparent silliness of it, having it here presented before he could say anything or make a joke, finding himself now standing in all seriousness before this woman in high heels, unable to imagine the kind of gesture he needs to place himself in proper relation to such a bursting forth of whimsy, such painstaking childishness: hand tools scattered around, sections of two-by-four and pieces of antenna, a fine powder of sawdust still blowing across the concrete.

"I shouldn't have worried," she laughs.

Mr. Delabano shrugs, looks down at the orange extension cord passing between his feet.

"It was a bunch of chatter." She turns back to the construction. "It just went on and on. I'm sorry." She stands there holding her purse with both hands as if protecting it, looking over at Janie then back at the project, the oddly reconstructed TV antenna rising from a sort of Christmas tree stand of old white-painted lumber: a chest-high tripod of metal tubing with a big cardboard box on top (once white, now covered with black crayon scribbles) from which opposed, horizontal periscopes emerge and a bristly array of small antenna parts all patched together with silvery duct tape and now, as Janie comes over to give it a nudge, slowly rotating in the wind.

Mr. Delabano walks out to stand beside Carol, watching it with her, encouraged by the effect of it spinning by itself, the soft rattle of the old roller bearings–loose ball bearings, actually, on a Lazy Susan race. "That was unintended," he says. "It just started spinning like that, like a pinwheel except it'll go either direction."

Janie has taken a seat nearby, curled up and chewing away, watching the demonstration like a movie. There's a movielike quality to it, each face of the box presenting a different scribble, the sequence suggesting movement, a sort of undulation, a smoky shifting and curling of the scribbly shape which, like the continuously rising stripes on a barber pole, seems progressive rather than repetitive, a contradictory illusion like Mr. Delabano's sinking spell the other night, a conflict of information, although in that case (as with the barber pole, for that matter) you readjust periodically, lose faith and try again.

"Does it keep going?" asks Carol.

"If there's wind," says Mr. Delabano. The wind is swirling now, lifting plumes of sawdust and lifting her hair a little. She's still holding her purse with both hands against her chest in that way, breathing audibly, almost sighing it seems. Somehow the periscopes don't destroy the effect–emerging from the centers of opposite scribbles, they should break the continuity, reassert the mechanism, but they don't. It's as if they were independent, spinning at a different rate and rotating through, penetrating the illusion without disturbing it.

Janie's back on her feet now, jaws at rest, standing very stiffly, Mr. Delabano thinks, staring at the rotating scribbles with her arms at her side. He looks for the chewing gum but it's not in her hand. He glances at the chair and along the pavement to where she's standing. It seems important that it be located.

"Janie," he says, "show your mother how it works."

The wind's whipping around, really blowing now, causing Janie to compensate, stagger a little, her parka like a sail.

"Show her the periscopes," says Mr. Delabano.

Her mouth is open and her eyes look like they're rolling back.

"She's choking," says Mr. Delabano too softly, but instantly Carol has her doubled over, slapping her on the back like fluffing a pillow, stripping off the jacket and trying again, lifting her into a Heimlich maneuver, three or four times squeezing hard like that producing a little crying noise–a reedy little sound like a squeezed doll makes–then laying her flat and reaching down her throat.

He's terrifically conscious of the wind, the sound it makes whistling through the chain-link fence, the shaking of the rose trellis; how, at one point standing at the phone by the back door having completed the call but unwilling to take his hand from the receiver (as if to do so might isolate unbearably this moment from the possibility of rescue as if some curve on a chart might thus be rendered a broken line, unsustainable, provisional and indefinite–the ambulance in a time exposure, lights flashing an interrupted streak to signify a false course or an uncertain one), how just at this point the wind seems to beat through the house like blood through the heart and even through all the commotion that follows how the house pulses with wind and every sound from outside–now the doors of the ambulance, then the siren receding–is like noise from outside the stillness of the body.

He sits at the kitchen table for a while with his eyes closed, then goes to retrieve Janie's coat from the patio, hanging it in the hall closet and standing there listening to the air moving through the house, the hollowness of the rooms, looking at the pictures, the pair of framed prints not there to be looked at but to sense in passing, to have been sensed in the hallway for as long as he can remember like something subconscious: the toucan or whatever it is and the monkey ("A. seniculus") gaping in alarm it seems, leaning straight out with its fringed head bristling. It reminds him of the terrified ornamental kitten on the redbud tree–the chilliness of it, the surprising ordinariness. He takes them off the wall leaving staggered rectangles of brighter paint, then removes another, a reproduction of something famous, from above the TV, placing these on the living room couch then taking down the bluebonnets. After that he's methodical, room to room, pictures first all stacked on the couch, then the knick-knacks, thoughtless ornaments from everywhere assembled on the coffee table and boxed quickly lest, gathered like that to a critical mass, they might form an idea, a revelation of some kind.

By four o'clock the wind has died down. The air in the living room is cold but nearly still, the plastic barely fluttering. He can hear traffic faintly–a generalized murmur from which, now and then, components detach, approach and recede. It's become more like a Japanese house, he thinks, evacuated of ornament, making him more conspicuous, more exposed although, from outside, invisible, the plastic sheeting translucent like rice paper transmitting only shadows so each time there's a car he leans forward on the couch listening for someone to drive up next door.

At some point this requires too much effort, too much investment in each shadowy possibility, and he moves to the patio, leaving the sliding door open to hear the phone, standing and watching for a moment how the science project, softly rattling, seems to register the slightest breeze. He scoots it over into the corner, takes a seat and arranges his coat around him, leaning back and closing his eyes, recognizing after a while the slapping of the sisters' screen door, irregular and very gentle. He turns to see if the TV is still there, catching his trousers on something. He reaches behind him. It's Janie's gum, strings of it now draped along the side of his coat as he holds it up and looks at it for a while, studying the mystery of it and listening to the screen door tapping softly with a little springy noise. He stands and picks what he can off his clothes then wraps the wad of gum in some Kleenex and puts it in his pocket. The traffic sounds like ocean or like wind, like a shell, any hollow thing, any emptiness held to the ear as if that were a residual or default condition, the sound of things diminished.

He has to jerk on the door to the toolshed then kick with his heel to get it to open. The ground is so dry it's shifted the frame. He can see where it's pulled away–a thin crack of daylight where the roof joins the garage. He gets the hoe and the big flat file and sits on the concrete at the end of the patio with the blade in his lap, holding it by the socket and stroking the file at an angle across the outside face, toward the back of the blade as he would sharpen a knife. When there's no reflection from the edge as he holds it up, no light along the edge itself, only sharpness as he tilts it side to side to be sure like reading a glass thermometer, he gets up and removes his coat, shakes off the filings then folds it and places it on the concrete with his wristwatch on top. For a moment he stands listening to a car passing down the street. Then he picks up the hoe and makes a little experimental chop, letting the blade more or less fall to the grass, just a couple of feet but it goes right in, half the width of the blade, as if it were nothing.

Around the rose beds the cedar edging is mostly rotten; it's like balsa wood breaking away in small fragments, disappearing into the pine bark as he works his way along, everything coming out without effort, falling to bits, roses and everything, a fine light dust rising and coloring his shoes and the bottoms of his pants. There's nothing to it. The brittleness is like that of something frozen; like bad dreams of one's hair simply falling away. His shoes are pink. And now the rosiness, the fragrance with something developing under it like a fossil being cleaned, held under the tap, the whisper of traffic like running water. The black flowers shatter and make a popping sound as they're cut; as he chops through the little rings of corrugated aluminum and into the stems, they produce that noise like stepping on a cockroach. Then the roots come up and the grass along with them (in those dreams it's always simply combing his hair, raking it away like dead grass). There's chalk and some sand now as he strikes bottom, the caliche, the original surface as he thinks of it, and his left hand is bleeding, the glass cuts have opened. He stops, holding still and looking at his hand, sensing the air, the dust, the rosiness grading into something nearly opposite. Whatever that might be. An old wet dog. Blood seeps under the Band-Aid, follows the creases in his palm out to the edge. There's a sweet animal smell like a dog but with no friendliness attached, no sympathy. Something under the roses, a different sweetness which, if not sweet exactly, becomes so by default as an overload of sound becomes ocean or wind (all circuits thrown open, there's too much to differentiate; one looks for the root, the more primitive expression: sweetness, in this case, for its uncertainty, its ambivalence between fruition and decay, for the constriction high in the throat like fear). He imagines a chart like the ones in biology textbooks to show evolutionary relationships–a capillary structure like a tree or a river system–then tracing the branches back along toward the trunk along the radiating lines of blood in his hand to the center where the bandage has soaked through. He stands there leaning on the hoe for a while; the reddening sunlight in his face goes to shadow; the sound of traffic seems to fade and unravel, disperse and resolve into particular sounds of cars passing by, more frequently now, then gradually tailing off. When the phone rings it's like a whisper or a memory; it takes him a minute to react and he has to run to get to it.

"She's okay; she wasn't choking," says Carol sounding breathless and a little giddy. They're at a toy store somewhere. He can hear Mike in the background, a child's voice and now Carol speaking away from the phone: "Oh, not that one," she laughs and there's a giggle, "Not the monster; oh, please," finally covering the mouthpiece, muted giggling, then she's back, "They called it a hypertensive crisis which sounds awful but apparently it's not,"–more giggling–"Janie, stop it," then Carol laughing, calling for Mike. "Sorry," she says, "we're getting ready for Halloween. Janie wants to say hi." There's a growling sound produced by a child, something bumps the receiver, then nothing for a moment–ambient voices–finally breathing, shallow and congested, gradually working itself into a terrible growl, drawn out and quite convincing over the phone, losing all connection with the child as it fades to a raspy sort of wail like the poorly recorded anguish of some wilderness creature.

From his bedroom he can see her like a shadow, all in black except for the horns or ears which must be silver the way they catch the last light, glinting and flapping as she darts across the yard, her features indistinct, dark and shiny, a suggestion of tusks as she runs by the fence and dashes over to crouch by the trash cans, motionless in the sudden twilight as the red glow leaves the top of the garage. He watches for a while as she seems gradually to develop a sort of stalking behavior, making furtive advances along the side of the house, disappearing into the bushes and becoming difficult to follow by the time her dad comes out to turn on the garage light and call her in. Mike stands in the drive silhouetted and looking around, calling again. There's movement behind him, then something scampering down the alley. Mr. Delabano steps back against the opposite wall, away from the light. Mike's out in the yard now, standing in the dark with his hands in his pockets, head down as if listening. After a minute he turns and walks toward the rear of the garage, pausing by the fence, looking up and down the alley, then behind the garage, calling once again, more softly, barely audible. Mr. Delabano has moved to the doorway, edging into the hall but still watching as Mike steps out of view bending forward slightly into the space between the garage and the fence, peering into the shadows. There's a commotion of some kind, something hitting the fence it sounds like, rattling the chain-link, then a sort of scream like that of an animal but very thin and distant as transmitted through the glass like something on TV, not entirely plausible. Mr. Delabano goes to turn out the lights in the den and the kitchen; now the whole house is dark. He's standing in the den away from the glass door, near the hallway where he feels he can monitor all quarters. Mike's garage light is reflected very faintly down the hall. He waits for it to fluctuate, listens for Mike's back door to close. He's very conscious of how exposed he is, how his house gapes open to the dark like a vacant house. He'll have to sleep on the couch, he's certain. The bedroom is out of the question; the uncurtained window. Now and then he can hear the plastic sheeting luffing gently, the loose corner retaped and still holding apparently. It's not quite so cold. He's watching the light, the slight glow in the hall which someone, at least a grown-up, he imagines, passing back across the yard would cause to dim; followed by the back door closing; and then a sense of emptiness if not release; of darkness without content. He takes a couple of steps into the hall. His eyes have adjusted. He can see the pale rectangles on the wall. The animals have fled. He's moving slowly as if waist-deep in water. What if turning into his bedroom she were there at the window with that mask with the ears and the tusks? Or worse than that. What could be worse. He looks at the floor, walks sideways into the room without glancing at the window, turns away from the light while reaching behind him for the bedspread and the blanket, pulling them both off the bed and at once over his shoulders with a great crackle of electricity. His hair is standing on end. He finds his pick handle in the corner and slowly makes his way out and down the hall to the living room, arranging himself on the couch with a slow release of breath, closing his eyes and listening to the rippling of the plastic over the picture window. It would be more like the Japanese if he placed the cushions on the floor and slept like that; or, unable to sleep, simply listened to the waves and the shivering of the house.

Sometime after midnight there's a siren not too far away, and after a while another, then a third, all heading in the same direction as if to a fire.

After that the wind dies away completely, not a flutter from the plastic, dead calm, a feeling of being adrift somehow and then a noise from the den like tapping on the glass door, fingernails clicking or the claws of an animal–like a dog's paw, blunt and habitual, pawing to be let in. This continues intermittently until just before dawn, increasing in frequency with the first gray light then stopping altogether.

At breakfast, as it brightens, he can see dirty streaks on the glass. They're fairly high on the door and smeared all over, not vertical and close to the ground as he would have expected, the way pet animals usually do, the way wooden doors look that have been scratched at for years–all the scratches up and down in the same spot until they run together like ruts in a road.

He takes his dishes to the sink and goes over to the door, kneeling and removing his glasses, bringing his face up close. Something on its hind legs probably, its nose against the glass which would account for the moisture, the thin muddy sleek. It should be possible to discover what it was, he thinks; a detective could do it. The little streaks within the smears would be nails or claws. A close examination might tell which, insofar as a dog's claw, like a stylus, might leave a thin, uniform trail through the smear where a fingernail, like one of those calligraphic flat-nibbed pens, should make a variable mark: broad up and down, and thin if drawn sideways. He stands and puts his glasses back on, looking into the yard at the devastation, looking at his left hand which is so sore he can't close it and flexing the other with the blister along the thumb. He gets a wet paper towel and steps outside to wipe the glass. There's a racket next door–an exclamation, something banging down the steps. Mr. Delabano gives the glass a couple of swipes and hurries to the bedroom. There's Mike out in the yard gathering garbage back into an overturned container–a big square plastic one with little wheels on one side, tipping it up then tying off the plastic liner before continuing to the alley. He pauses on the way back to survey the ruins of Mr. Delabano's garden, standing and just looking for a couple of minutes without expression.

It takes about an hour for the morning to settle down completely, for Mike to depart and then Julie with her car pool–for the general rush to subside into the trough of daily events even deeper than the predawn stillness, the diastolic moment about nine o'clock which seems, at times, too deep to be temporary, too long between breaths for life to recover.

Mr. Delabano has his coat on, standing in the dining room, glancing out the window, watching the cicada in the cut glass compote, how it responds to the air currents, the shallow bowl like a compass dial and the cicada like an instrument, glassy wings extended and so delicately balanced it rocks with the movement of the air, side to side, one wingtip then the other, motionless for a while then oscillating rapidly like a clock escapement.

He walks out to the patio and stands for a minute, looking past the old rose at the sisters' house, the screen door now blown all the way open, the TV on its trolley still out on the porch. He makes his way around the wrecked garden to the alley, walking past Mike's house, behind his garage, looking but not pausing, not wanting to be seen to pause and, so, continuing on for a second then slowing and stopping as if searching for something, turning back, walking very slowly now, close to the fence to get a better look behind Mike's garage at the stuff in the grass like pieces of fur, parts of a rabbit or some other small animal. He stops although not intending to. There's quite a lot of it–spilled garbage possibly, bits of that gray fluff that padded mailing envelopes are stuffed with; stained red with something that makes it look terrible. The garbage truck is coming. It turns into the alley at the east end of the block, inappropriately brilliant and glossy red-orange, heaving into its routine with the whining and crushing but very faint at that distance, in the emptiness of the moment like one of those plaintive marine noises, the communication of whales.

He kneels by the fence, studying the scatter of fur or whatever it is, putting out his left hand to hold onto the chain-link, supporting himself, keeping himself from going backwards but hurting his hand–the cut on the palm but also the fingers; there are spurs on the galvanized wire like thorns. He alters his balance, leans forward on his heels, his face right against the fence now three or four feet from the evidence. He can't tell what it is. If he could put his hand through and pick some up he might make a determination; flick the bits of yellow grass out of the way and nod to himself. Or might it remain ambivalent even then; even under the microscope at progressively higher powers refuse to develop beyond this initial understanding, a glance behind the garage, essentially vague, a single filament stained and mounted under the oil-immersion lens shimmering at the edges, in its cellular structure still teetering between possibilities. The hydraulic whine is much closer now, tending to fall in pitch, lugging and stalling at the end of its cycle. He gets up and looks at his hand. He turns. He can see the driver, close enough to require Mr. Delabano to wave or nod or something, too close now to walk away. It might lurch forward right behind him, pursuing him in effect, making him feel ridiculous. He edges along the fence a few steps away from Mike's garbage cans as the truck comes past, a single rider on the back with such a broad, plump face he looks infantile in a sort of woodsman's hat with earflaps, grinning at Mr. Delabano, pulling himself to attention and saluting as the truck comes to a stop and the crusher blade slides open as if, like a child, to display its mastications, holding open for a minute letting the contents uncompress a bit, sag out and separate, whatever it is, something awful among the plastic bags like parts of animals or possibly clothing stained and wadded like that as the whole mass starts to slump and certain portions, rearranging themselves, suggest things one might recoil from identifying as when witnessing for the first time a terrible injury, getting to glimpse the inner body, the mortal content of what should be contentless and imaginary–what it was like, he imagines, after Dresden or Hiroshima, collecting the refuse, the workers reduced to such idiotic behavior, grinning like idiots at the appalling necessity.

19

Very gradually it seems, one by one, without appearing to arrive, without slamming of doors or the visible release of occupants, cars have accumulated along the street, materialized as if by accident like something hatched out of season–out of nowhere, he thinks, such a large and mechanized gathering assembled like moths to a light. From his bedroom window he can see a few individuals starting to trickle out the back into the yard where Mike has the grill propped open, ready to go, brilliant red in the late afternoon, right out in the center of the yard–there's no patio as such, only dry yellow grass with long shadows now of people standing about, beginning to form into groups. There's a muted whump and a flash–all the shadows seem to pale, all motion seems to freeze as in one of those TV portrayals of laughing picnickers or whatever suddenly irradiated in the glare that precedes the atomic blast–then Mike jumping back from the cooker with his head down furiously running his hands over his hair, standing still for a second and looking himself over, looking around and starting to laugh, so much heat now rising from the grill he seems to distort with amusement. Mr. Delabano watches as the metal heats up and the flames beach away to the color of the grass, the distortion expanding, extending in a plume to one side or the other as the wind shifts around causing everything beyond to dissolve into ripples–the garage and the swing set and now the faces of the people making fun of the pyrotechnics, pretending it's a bonfire and warming their hands.

He has Janie's red parka laid out on the bed. Now he folds it carefully, the sleeves tucked inside, then left to right and top to bottom as if packing for a trip, placing it under his arm, standing and watching for a while longer the goings-on next door, thinking she might make an appearance, in some new configuration perhaps. But they're starting to drift back inside now–first the ones less warmly dressed, then the others leaving Mike by himself in his apron and his mitts trying to adjust something on the cooker which is catching the sunlight at such a low and direct angle it seems to glow with the heat.

"Oh wonderful, oh good," beams Carol, ethnographically got up in huge dangly earrings and a sort of floor-length sarong with colorful zigzags all over, gathering him inside, turning and smiling again with her hand on his arm and an inclination of her head as if regarding him anew from some compassionate perspective made possible by this exoticism. "Oh, good," she says again bringing her head upright as if having resolved in this estimation, reaching to give him a hug which is partially blocked as, misinterpreting her gesture, he extends Janie's parka which becomes sandwiched between them, his hand against her breasts. He's overwhelmed by the fragrance, such a dense jungly scent, and simultaneously, in the instant before he's released, the sound of voices all around him, indistinct, coming and going, cadenced and modulated like natural sounds, the tinkling of ice cubes like chimes or little finger-cymbals–all, for an instant, entrained by the fragrance and conveying a sensation of strangeness interposed, interjected into the ordinary progression of events like a slip of the tongue, a lapse of some kind. Outside there's another fiery display, then a secondary eruption–great billows of flame lifting clear of the grill and curling into the air as Mike steps into view and turns to acknowledge those watching from the kitchen, grinning and holding up a squirt can of combustible fluid.

"Here," says Carol, still touching his arm, now steering him toward the hall, "come look." She precedes him to Janie's room, waiting at the door as he pauses to look back at the sound of applause and the whole living room lighting up with a warm peachy glow. "Behold," says Carol with a gesture of presentation. He approaches and looks in–it's back to normal. She flicks on the light. All the furniture is back: a little white-painted dresser with floral stencils and a mirror and brushes and combs set out, all the toys put away, blocks stacked in the corner, the mural receding to the quality of wallpaper behind the bed with its dust ruffles and stuffed animals arranged on top against the wall in seated positions. He can feel the heat rising from the floor vent–it's been altered; someone's lifted out the damper, the adjustable vanes, leaving only the cover plate. He looks at Carol. She smiles, a warm light flickering across her face. He turns to the window and there it is again–reflecting off the beige brick of his house like sunrise, this time accompanied by an audible thump and, from the kitchen, a murmur of appreciation or alarm.

"What's he doing?" says Mr. Delabano.

"Who?" says Carol.

"I think he's using gasoline," says Mr. Delabano at the window now. There's a brief, soft flicker across the grass and the brick then a sound like an explosion, like a shotgun going off, followed by shouts from the kitchen, the screen door slamming and then slamming again.

Mike's laid out on the grass spread-eagle, his chest jerking up and down, convulsing it looks like, his face obscured by someone kneeling. Carol pushes around past the others to take his hand and help him sit up. He's laughing. "You're crazy," someone says. Mike looks around–"Did you see it?" he's still laughing, "did you see where it went?" Carol's trying to find out what happened but Mike's distracted, holding her hand but paying no attention, calling out to someone walking in from the alley–a man in a blue blazer with an ID tag like Mike's shaking his head and holding out his hands then stopping to pick up something off the ground.

Carol's jerking Mike's arm.

"Sorry," says Mike, no longer laughing but looking wild, standing now and raising his arms. "I have become Death," he says, "destroyer of worlds."

"Here's the booster stage," says the man from the alley, handing him a little white plastic disc. "It's the squirt nozzle," he says. "The can's in orbit."

"God," says Mike.

Carol's looking back and forth. "Was that gasoline?" she asks.

"It went clear over the garage didn't it?" says Mike, studying the nozzle.

"Still climbing at burnout," says the man in the blazer.

"Was that gasoline?" asks Carol again, stepping between them.

"High test," says Mike holding up the nozzle, smiling calmly now, looking serene.

Everyone seems invigorated. There's a card table now, with plastic dishes and silverware, folding lawn chairs set about. Mike's back at the grill laying on more charcoal, opening a bottle of beer as Carol examines the side of his head, forcing him to look sideways at the man in the blazer who's standing slightly away, making spiraling, ascending motions with his hand.

How quiet it is, Mr. Delabano thinks, except here. He looks past the fences along the series of backyards, across the alley and then the other way, beyond the sisters' house to the west. There's no one else apparently. He imagines the fuel can shooting away with a thin flame trailing out, arcing into the gray sky over the neighborhood like a flare.

"How about an eggnog," there's a mitt on his shoulder; Mike's handing him a beer. "Janie, here's a friend of yours." She seems to disengage from the background like the other night at the window–right in front of him, becoming visible as he makes a slight psychological adjustment. She's still a monster; entirely black except the ears (they seem to be ears) which are a kind of silver lame, unraveling at the tips. He holds out her jacket, still folded, which she takes without a word, gazing at him for a moment then darting away, leaving him embarrassed as if having committed some thoughtlessness, presenting her with something unusable, no longer appropriate in her present condition.

Another card table has unfolded to support a big translucent plastic container of something and a Coleman lantern already going, hissing quietly with its strange greenish light. He wonders who these people are, everyone now in coats and windbreakers, apparently resigned, settling in like an expedition. Mike has a great pile of steaks by the grill, stacked up on the little bracketed shelf attached to one side of the cooker, so conspicuous above the lawn, the meat and the dry grass, as if contingent somehow, slabs of game–some grazing animal quite recently brought to violence. There's a slap of the screen door and then again a couple of times like little rifle shots, then just the tinkling of ice as the sun beams out from between the houses catching the whole yard in a red glow accelerated, as it were, rendered nearly combustible by the smell of gasoline, Mike suddenly quite still (one can see in the raking light where his hair has been singed) looking above the cooker toward the west, like that time in the fireplace, obscurely attentive, as if there were something uncommunicable approaching from that direction. He lifts his beer and drains it as the heat ripples up, causing him to dissolve slightly like a figure portrayed as entering a dream or one viewed at a great distance through a telephoto lens. He's shaking the beer now, whatever's left, holding it upside down over the fire and releasing his thumb, producing a volcanic rush of steam and ash that rises above him pink in the light like clouds at sunset.

"Oh shit," someone says as Mike turns with his arms raised in benediction over everyone gathered in an arc, more or less, on that side of the grill, seated or standing, some cross-legged on the grass. Now a couple of giggles.

"Any synthetic chemists?" asks Mike.

"Me," yells a frilly-looking woman at the back.

"And I," says Mike's friend in the name-tagged blazer, standing up like Spartacus; everyone laughs.

"Then I must ask you to leave." He lowers one arm, extending the other toward the street with a bow. "Before us are matters of organic simplicity," he reaches into the ice for more beer, shakes his hand at the fire for another cloud of steam then twists off the cap with a foam-slinging flourish: "God's domain," he continues (there's Carol behind the others, looking unhappy now, unexotic), "here is meat, and here is smoke, a free radical or two," he glances at Mr. Delabano, "and sustained upon the vapors of the earth, dare I say it–Frank, I need you to step forward," Mr. Delabano doesn't move, "the gentle fragrance of the alkaloids."

Carol's going to take care of it; here she comes across the grass. "Telephone," she calls to Mike; there's no ring, it's a joke; he's got both arms up, looking heavenward to dramatize the interruption as Carol pops off the top of the big plastic tub–potato salad it looks like–and the moment deflates, attention collapses, people circulating now, reforming smaller groups as Mike, provided with a chair (received into shadow, the red glow climbing the side of the garage and the hiss of the lantern extending its influence), holds forth unconstrained. "Hey Frank, what did you do?" Mr. Delabano, caught in the open, has to commit, takes a seat at the edge of the group as the breeze whips heat from the grill into his face. "What happened to our specimens?" There's Janie by the fence, he thinks–a shadow under the bushes–but it's not; just some paper captured for a second, now flapping loose and blowing down the alley. "What have we got now?" Mike looks around at his friends who are smiling, "No, I'm serious," he's smiling, too, grinning now at Mr. Delabano. "I mean who's going to believe us?" He turns to the man in the blazer sitting next to him, grasping him by the shoulder, "You believe, don't you Harland?" he implores in a silly accent, Karloff possibly; now releasing his friend, leaning back and speaking normally: "I know I showed you the fingerprint on that stuff." He finishes his beer, raises his eyebrows at Mr. Delabano and reaches once more into the ice chest.

"Three or four zones," says the man in the blazer, glancing over at the steaks.

Mike puts his beer down quickly so he can lift his arms in astonishment–"Five," he says, "solid five, like a battle ribbon; all over the place," he picks up the bottle. "That's no prescription." Harland shrugs. "That's the end of life as we know it," he's doing Karloff again. "Listen," he says, "there's no one but us." And, in fact, beyond the compound it's silent at the moment. Beyond the immediate screen of voices, the creaking of chairs, there's no sense of activity, no traffic on the highway.

"You used a chemistry set," says Mike's friend Harland, leaning back, looking up. The stars are coming out.

"Damned right," says Mike. "Toy chloroform, toy benzene."

Someone's fiddling with the lantern now, turning up the hiss until it starts to cast shadows.

"I'll tell you what though," says Mike, looking around at everyone, shaking his spatula, making a little fluttery noise, "if the spirit's moving–and I do believe it is–we could have a real good round of clinical trials right here; yes indeed," he's raising his voice now like an evangelist at the others reassembling toward the glow of the lantern or the possibility of food, "I mean right here tonight," he jerks his right arm across like one of those televisions preachers; Carol's next to him now, on the grass sitting quietly, leaning on his chair. "You all know about the Beast," he turns to look at Mr. Delabano who feels things are about to get out of control. "Frank, what did you do?" If he sits perfectly still someone else may distract him. "You sly old ethnobotanist, I believe it's too late; them gophers ain't comin' back." He cocks his head and puts one cook's-mittened hand behind his ear, "You hear that?" Not a sound. No one's speaking, no swing sets or traffic, no clinking of ice: "That's an absence of gophers." Carol's hand is on his arm but he's into it now, "That's the Pleistocene, oh beloved; an absence, I dare say, of all comfort and compassion, that old empty backyard where the dragon creeps,"–here he's quiet for a moment as if considering this obscurity before rising beatific like the Buddha, mitts out in a gesture for attention: "Behold, the Golden Path," Mr. Delabano is transfixed, "of his breath upon the night." He begins scraping the grill with a great flurry of sparks, blows three or four times quite powerfully into the vents, his face aglow, creating discrete clouds of little sparks curling up one after another, spreading out above everyone in the dusk, sustained there at a certain altitude by convection presumably, at last floating away without descending, like fireflies, disappearing among the stars, as if everything before had prepared for this effect, as if Mike, by application to the barbecue grill, had become a sort of master pyrotechnician, proceeding by necessary degrees toward this moment. Everyone's still looking up as the last sparks wink out, some lying on the grass stretched out like it was summer, like the Fourth of July as the red glow finally leaves the top of Mike's garage and the steaks plop down sizzling quietly, no one speaking, some remaining on their backs as they seem to pass into a new regime.

At the grill Mike's working with a fresh beer in his hand, shuffling the steaks, rearranging them like cards, "Remember the coelacanth?" he says without raising his eyes as if talking to himself.

"Pronounced *seelacanth,*" says Harland quietly like someone whispering to someone in a dormitory at night.

"Seelacanth," repeats Mike, flipping steaks and taking a swig, the soft hissing from the grill and the lantern sound like static out of which, now and then like an imperfect signal, other sounds seem to develop as if propagated over some distance across the yards and the fences, like Channel 17 filtering through, like wind through tall grass–natural sounds, little cries and barks coming and going like children or animals in distress. "Imagine that," says Mike. "Imagine hauling that in; all those Japanese fishermen–was it Japanese?–standing around looking at it. You think they would have done that, Harland? Just stood there for a while with all the smelts or whatever flopping around maybe, all around their feet, slipping over the deck back into the water. Hey, they start thinking maybe this thing's edible," he laughs, "God, can you imagine?" He's turning and rearranging the steaks with great precision, automatically like solitaire, keeping his eyes down, smiling at his joke and watching the steaks. No one's listening surely. His voice is practically lost in the regular scrape and slap of the spatula, the hiss of the lantern. The other noises have a wildness to them now, like a dog pack in pursuit, more disturbing at such a distance, such frenzy so far removed as if concentrated to a point.

"Cookin' up a mess of coelacanth," he's still amused, "wouldn't that be something, better than chromatography I bet–taxonomies based on fragrance and whatnot. Free association. I have not been sleeping well, Harland." He's smiling a compressed sort of smile, falling silent, working the steaks as all the sizzle cooks away and all the whispery, peripheral conversation seems to disperse–just the rush of gas, now, and the sound of the spatula. A faint chorus of howls from somewhere to the south. "How about you, Vijay; did you get a whiff of that stuff?" A dark-complected man beyond the lantern raises his eyes. "Boy," says Mike, "you went right ahead and popped the top didn't you." The steaks should be done; they no longer sound quite the same as he shuffles them around. "You might have noticed your old buddies did a trick with bamboo; did you see that Vijay?–your friends at NCL?" The dark-complected man is leaning back in his chair, letting his gaze drift up. There are quite a number of stars now although it's not yet dark–clear blue at the horizon, perfectly clear without haze. "Got that sucker to bloom on command, didn't they," says Mike, "found the trigger and bingo." He's permitting himself a little performance at the grill like a croupier, like a shell game, a little choreography with the spatula flipping steaks like flapjacks. "Bingo," says Mike silently, pronouncing the word with an exaggerated movement of his lips, flipping each steak two or three times, catching it on the spatula with a leathery thunk before moving to the next. "Now, your monocarpic flowering," says Mike, pausing to fish another beer out of the ice, having trouble with the screw cap, gripping it with his apron, "Your monocarpic flowering," he starts again as the top pops off–"can you say that, boys and girls?"–standing back from the grill and holding it away as it spews, "in bamboo is intriguing," wiping the bottle on his apron, "because," taking a long swig now and looking at the bottle–the steaks are going to be cinders–"it may occur only once every one hundred and twenty years; think of that, Frank," he looks around, his face lit from beneath in the gathering dark like a child's with a flashlight held under for effect. "And when it does, boy watch out. May I quote?" He reaches for his billfold and extracts a slip of paper, producing as well a pair of little half-round reading glasses, unfolding the paper and holding it above the fire, reading through the translucency of it apparently like a secret message revealed; he looks appallingly Faustlike in the glow, in the little spectacles and the apron like a lab smock, his hair singed and all around, now, a sort of call and response–west to east more or less–like whippoorwills in concert, or even swing sets possibly, the chorus taken up by some and left off by others as it seems to rotate about the compass one way then the other, penetrated now and then by individual barks and yelps more like children's imitations than real animals and more unpleasant for it as the confusion at night of cat and human voices can be chilling, the ambiguity, as in this case maintained too long, creating a sort of blankness, a sort of window through which may be glimpsed whatever frights one cares to assemble. Mr. Delabano looks around; no one's moved very much; it's too dark to see faces except near the lantern but no one seems to be looking at Mike at the moment; attention is scattered, diffuse like the noises, directed here and there–a couple of those who were on their backs are sitting up now as if awakened, stiff and gazing off across the fences to the east or the west. Beyond the houses across the alley the street lights have come on and, behind them, a few night lights–probably left on all day, bare bulbs, some hooded, above garage doors and screen doors illuminating little untrespassable portions of property as if to represent the whole, or as if presented for analysis, or as a kind of piety like a creche: this spot where the driveway runs up against the house; where the concrete steps down from the kitchen door to the walk beside the flower bed–all these, especially, to be distinguished from darkness, to be held and kept secure. Some more paper, it looks like, goes flapping down the alley. Mike's clearing his throat.

"David Hanke at Cambridge (Hank? Hanky?)," he experiments, "a real botanist in any case says, 'The aftermath is truly apocalyptic as rotting culms collapse in heaps, fires rage and hordes of rats gorge on seed that lies up to fifteen centimeters thick on the ground. Spasmodic mayhem,' says Professor Hanke, 'is the ultimate outcome,'" he closes the note in his fist like a Bible, replaces it in his pocket and gazes down at the grill, looking solemn in his spectacles, examining the charred meat like a necromancer or a carbon-dating technician, as if taking a reading, sufficient processing of the samples having apparently taken place. "That's not how we usually think of flowers is it?" His face is close to the grill, his glasses reflecting little incandescent half moons, "That's not how we think." He's stopped using the spatula it seems, content now to observe, interpret or whatever–something slaps into the fence, catches briefly and blows away overhead, a tumbling irregular shape like a rag, barely visible against the sky. Mike's looking over his glasses. From the direction of the highway there's a prolonged high-pitched squeal with a series of hisses like the application of air brakes. It seems to go on and on like the mad sister screaming on her back porch the other morning, an unthinkable attenuation of some catastrophe whose impact must already have happened, after all; like the light from a star, there's an interval required for the sound from the highway to travel the distance–some huge trailer truck, maybe a tandem, sliding jackknifed and helpless, fully loaded no doubt with God knows what. Before the squeal dies away there's a flash at the horizon and a small, blossoming cloud of smoke and flame rising and cooling from yellow to red and finally black, lit from below and spreading over the site which is itself invisible. Mr. Delabano waits for the sound but there isn't one, not even a pop, just the smoke spreading out like an overcast above the highway, reflecting the sodium lights so one can see it expanding. Two or three who stood up for a minute sit back down now as if conscious of exposure to danger, as if imagining the blast on its way tossing houses into dust like a rug being shaken, grainy black-and-white pine forests bending like grass. A woman next to Mr. Delabano sits quietly with her hands in her lap, having lost her plastic plate which, overburdened on one side with potato salad, has slipped from her knee. Mike's making noise behind them, fishing around in the ice chest again–mostly water now by the sound–walking over to the fence, extending his arms over as he twists off the top partway, letting it spew for a second into Mr. Delabano's yard. "Truly I have not been sleeping well; God look at that." He takes off the reading glasses and puts them away under his apron, leaning on the top rail now, holding his beer in both hands. The other sounds–the jungle noises, the children or whatever–have stopped. There's just the lantern hissing away and the whispering of someone who's unhappy and wants to go home, can't find her purse. Someone else now, too–standing on the steps having opened the screen door as if to go back inside but just standing there looking to the west through the screen, holding it open as if to provide a sort of shielding.

"I keep thinking about this big old wet dog," Mike sighs and takes a drink. "How about you, Vijay; wasn't that it? Just like a wet dog?" He looks behind him, squinting at the lantern which seems to have brightened by itself, hissing louder as if it were running out, less back pressure in the line possibly. "What could be more basic?" he turns back, gesturing into Mr. Delabano's yard. "You've got wet dogs in India; wet dogs in Spain." He pulls himself upright, holding on to the rail and looking above Mr. Delabano's garage. It's like a front coming in. "My God," he says, finishing the bottle, letting it drop on Mr. Delabano's side of the fence. Something electrical is happening–a powerline severed or one of the sodium lights throwing sparks like an old movie flashing and dimming, fading in and out, archival footage of some historical disaster.

"The age of the dinosaurs," says Mike, after a minute turning again, squinting into the pale green light, "Can you smell it?" looking excited now, "Vijay?" He smiles toward the lantern for a moment, lifts his gaze to survey the whole muted, shadowy gathering–the lady who's missing her purse seems inconsolable, weeps softly in the background. Mike lifts his arms. "You are there," he announces in a Cronkitish voice, making his way now to the beer. "You are there," he says again into the ice chest, fishing around for a while before returning to the fence, standing and looking to the west, holding the rail and craning back to note the obscuration of stars to an elevation of maybe forty degrees. "You all know about those peat bogs in Ireland or Scotland." He must be able to see a little better standing up, a little nearer the horizon–the light is flashing like lightning into his face now and then. "Scandinavia too I think–you know those things that get preserved, thousand-year-old bodies and stuff, clothes and everything, tanned like leather; somebody found a cheese–this was on the radio–somebody dug up an eight-hundred-year-old cheese, a great big ball of cheese a couple of feet in diameter and they took a sample and decided it was still good inside." More unhappiness; it sounds like someone at a funeral, sorrowful as if there were nothing to be done. "Can you imagine that?" says Mike. There should be sirens by now, Mr. Delabano thinks. "Can you imagine that?" Mike's holding on with one hand and leaning back, looking up–if he lets go, he'll fall. "Eight hundred years old; somebody lost his cheese," he laughs, "Hey Og, where's the cheese," now gaining his balance to open his beer, spewing again, laughing, "Hell I don't know–must have dropped it in the swamp. Jeez, look at that." He sloshes beer in an arc, looking up and then catching himself as he staggers a little. "The light of the Pleistocene, ladies and gentlemen," a bluish flicker across his face, "Godzilla looming above the bay." He's got hold of the rail now but lets go, jerking back as something strikes the fence close to the alley it sounds like, making a clatter and setting up a sort of wailing behind Mr. Delabano–the purseless woman; no one's attending her. Such a long and desolate descending note. Mike turns, eyes wide, addressing the lantern, "There!" he says, unconcerned about the woman, "how about now; smell that? Isn't that it?" He takes a deep breath and exhales, looks over his shoulder to the west, back to the lantern breathing rapidly. There's no sound except the woman and the lantern starting to sputter. Mike's quiet for a moment, finishing his beer, watching the lantern, now hurrying over to the grill which casts a dull red glow but no sparks as he blows directly down from the top and then into the vents as if this were a matter of some urgency. "Did you know they had wet dogs in the Pleistocene?" he says breathlessly, trying again from the top–if he faints Mr. Delabano hopes he falls away from the fire–"Did you know that Vijay?" now back to the vents, long slow breaths, the glow responding faintly. Vijay appears to be unconscious, leaning back in his chair, eyes closed, mouth open. "'Tis but a dream in any case, right?" says Mike standing back now, quite unsteadily reaching down into the ice chest as the lantern wheezes out, "A tale told by alkaloids." The woman is quiet now in the darkness. Mike seems to be standing above the ice chest with his beer, letting it drip into the water, pit pat like water off leaves into a pool, just the left side of his face showing in the light from the coals. "It's like ergot poisoning probably–all these alkaloids; you remember that little book, Harland." He's going to hold it like that until it stops dripping apparently–very slowly now like leaves after a rain. "All those people in France, that whole town that went crazy from eating bread contaminated with ergot which contains, of course, about a hundred alkaloids including lysergic acid which, as some of us may recall"–he seems to be smiling, turning to look beside the lawn chair for Carol who's no longer there; turning back now, opening the bottle–"is LSD," the prolonged escape of pressure sounds ominous in the dark; he must be down to one or two, opening it more carefully to conserve the contents. "How about you, Frank?" The bright star, Vega–nearly overhead–is slipping under, fading out. "Do you need a fresh one?" Now it's gone. "Last call," says Mike. No response; no sounds whatever. The intermittent flashing at the horizon prepares one for thunder which, never arriving, makes it seem more quiet–only the wind now, the sound of it whistling softly through the fences as if they were designed to do that, make that sound like wind chimes–all the way out to the horizon like antennas receiving it, producing that sound like a signal, a faint, vaguely directional signal like that picked up by the first radio telescopes which looked rather like fences or something to hang laundry on. That's the hissing he hears now–from all the chain-link fences like a radio telescope. It's what's left over. Everything else filtered out, suppressing all the nonessentials, there's this signal like the interstellar background radiation, the frequency at which galvanized fencing will oscillate in an extended array laid out at these intervals east to west in such a way that it hums in the wind with faint and threatening information like that received by radio telescopes, like what you hear through the walls of a motel room at night (neon flashing outside–"Oh my God what is that," one thinks; "is that here?")–one of those little motels at the very edge of everything.

Mr. Delabano can hear Mike coming up behind him, taking a drink, clearing his throat very quietly and speaking so softly right behind him it's like an inflection of the wind–the way one can form words voicelessly into a directed stream of air, the way a mouthharp makes sound or someone who's had a laryngectomy.

"Suppose the mammals died out but not the plants," whispers Mike. Rattling chain-link again but further off, a couple of yards down. "Would there not be something to remember us by? If we assume," he takes a drink, "that, of the various types of carrion plants, some continued to function, attracting flies or whatever or even without flies or anything just relying on the wind for pollination–nothing left of the animals; just plants, say, insects and birds, maybe not even birds–but no furry animals: how long do you think, Frank, before the smell went away? Thousands of years maybe." His left hand appears in a sweeping gesture toward Mr. Delabano's backyard. "Thousands of years later–maybe only every now and then if the conditions are right–you'll still get these flowers and a perfect recording of recently dead animals. Can you imagine that?" He's kneeling down now; Mr. Delabano can feel the weight of his hand on the chair. He takes a swig. The back of the chair bends slightly. "Don't you know any flies left around would sit up and take notice, little brain stems starting to spark. Hell, love never dies does it Frank." He places his hand on Mr. Delabano's shoulder. Even through his coat he imagines it cool and damp from the ice chest. He can smell burnt hair and gasoline now as if this also were communicated by touch. There's more paper or something being blown down the alley and a sort of weeping, a different person right behind him and also off to the left someone coughing–that's a man, and now again but this time muffled as if his hand were to his face.

"There, smell that," says Mike, squeezing Mr. Delabano's shoulder, "that's it," whispering right in his ear, turning away for a minute and breathing deeply a couple of times. Someone's walking away down the drive to the front. "God almighty," says Mike. He takes another deep breath like someone afflicted with hiccups. "I'm not going to make it." He drains the bottle, rises and tosses it as hard as he can over Mr. Delabano's head clear into the sisters' yard–there's no sound of impact, a little whistling sound as it goes. "Now, here's the deal," he's back in a crouch as if they were, together, confronting some sort of dangerous game across a field of tall grass; as if it were tall grass through which the wind was blowing and making that noise. "That particular smell, that smell right now, is not the way something smells if it's dead, right?" A rhetorical pause. A friendly pat on the shoulder. "No, it's not. What we have here is altogether different and more interesting I think." Mike stands up again, inhales, holds his breath. Mr. Delabano feels himself floating in his lawn chair, drops his half-full bottle of beer in the grass. He's being lifted slightly, reoriented more toward the west a few degrees–now facing the fence between Mike's yard and his own maybe ten feet away. "You can smell that, can't you? You're not immune?" Mike assumes his station again, "You realize there's a whole new paleontology here; I mean who needs experts," he pauses for a second, still catching his breath, "we want connoisseurs, right; like those African Bushmen stick their finger right in that elephant turd and tell you all about it; I mean . . . oh shit," he turns away again; Mr. Delabano can feel him release the chair, he seems to be sitting cross-legged now. "Getting used to it, though, might be a problem–I mean your elephant turd ain't nothing; this is really old shit," he's laughing at that, scooting up next to Mr.

Delabano, "I mean really old shit"; something's moving by the fence along the bottom on the other side. "Imagine there was an animal that really smelled like that once upon a time–maybe a million years ago, some godawful extinct thing's lady-love probably, in heat don't you figure?" It's like a kitten, Mr. Delabano thinks, pawing at the fence–about the size of a kitten. "Don't you figure that makes sense?" Mr. Delabano leans forward slightly. "Sounds like a procreative strategy to me; if you can't screw it eat it–eat everything maybe–this monster eats the flowers and the seeds get scattered, fertilized and everything. Heck of a deal." Mike's facing the fence so he must be able to see what's climbing up, just discernible when it moves–a darker shape against the shadows. Now he's quiet like a fisherman with his line twitching, staring at the spot, whispering again, "Do you sleep okay?" He's leaning forward on his hands; "I used to sleep like a baby but not now–goodness no. I just lie awake–God, don't you suppose it must have been something awful to still give you bad dreams, do that to you like a memory, keeping you awake after all this time, after thousands of years trying to think if you left the water running or did something bad or forgot to lock the door, forgot to lock the cave, screwed up and let the fire go out or something. Those gophers didn't waste any time did they? That's what those things were for, right? Getting rid of gophers?" He's craning forward on his hands and knees, peering at the fence, "It's like we're blind isn't it?" crawling forward a little, tilting his head and studying it with a sort of detachment, "I believe that's it," he whispers very quietly, barely audible above the wind, "screwed up and let the fire go out–rule number one in the Pleistocene." He's within two or three feet of the fence, reaching into his pocket, "I've got a match."

"Don't," says Mr. Delabano.

Mike sort of slumps and looks back. Mr. Delabano glances around; everyone's gone it appears, and so are all the stars horizon to horizon.

"Don't do that," says Mr. Delabano. Mike's got it in his hand–a book of matches, a little flicking sound as he opens it with his thumb.

"It's nothing," whispers Mike. Mr. Delabano can see his face now faintly in the gray light of the overcast–eyebrows lifted, smiling gently. "That's really nothing," he says, "just residue, I expect," he turns to the shadow on the fence–halfway up and now motionless, hard to make out; it could be paper or anything, just a small dark shape, either a vacancy or a presence, like something unfamiliar glimpsed at night across one's room about to resolve itself, become known. "Something left over," he says. Mr. Delabano stands and steps back against the lawn chair, causing it to fold and collapse, stepping over it now and backing away across the lawn past the card tables and the grill, black and cooling, no sensation of heat as he nearly brushes it, stumbling over the ice chest which produces a regular slow sloshing sound for a while like waves as he makes his way to the driveway and stands by the corner of the house. There's a spark and a glow showing Mike's outline for a second on his knees hunched over, protecting the flame as it burns back to the paper, lifting it up to the fence and holding it there a long time it seems for a paper match in the wind without burning his fingers. Then the light seems to drop, reappearing after a minute at his knees, whipping around him as the grass starts to catch, lighting him from behind–the perfect bow of his apron, the gray soles of his shoes–shooting out along the taller grass by the fence and sweeping back with the wind toward the garage in little arcs, a great crackle of green flames from Mr. Delabano's lawn chair, the plastic webbing going up as smaller fires fan into each other making a single front coming across the yard like peeling it away–like a cloth, one edge catching the wind then the whole thing ripping up–spreading out now from the alley into the yard behind, leaping ahead catching an entire row of big rounded bushes which ignite along the fence like old Christmas trees in sequence, each flaring and dazzling then instantly going dark, one after the other within a few seconds as if almost nothing were there to begin with as if it were all like dust in a silo suspended and just waiting to go up, the less substantial the more combustible, a sort of miracle for everything to have lasted so long.